Freeze Frame

Ilona Joy Saari

ISBN: 1-4663-9215-0
ISBN-13: 9781466392151

ADVANCED PRAISE

ACKNOWLEDGEMENTS

Most authors thank their researchers, editors and agents. Since I didn't have any of those, my acknowledgements will be short—but heartfelt.

For all your support...for all your reading and red-lining and those dreaded notes...thank you to Michael Miller, Craig Anderson, Kyle Crowner and Susan Lehman.

A special shout-out to the ATF for answering all my email questions about guns, and for not putting me on the no-fly list for asking.

And last, but never least, thank you to my husband, Richard Camp, who read and edited this book too many times to count. You are my patience, my supporter (literally and figuratively), my rock and my love...and now that it's published you can stop asking for a co-writing credit!

Dedication

To my Mom, Vi Fiske. Thank you for reading to me when I was a child.

PROLOGUE

HELL'S CANYON, IDAHO—LATE AUGUST

The early morning light was just beginning to shine over the canyon. Jefferson Leeds sat in a weathered wooden chair on the front porch of an isolated fishing cabin near the shore of the Snake River, his sandy brown hair flopping over eyes barely open. Even unshaven and not quite awake, Jefferson was a handsome man with his olive complexion and intense brown eyes…traits that his parents attributed to his great-great-great grandmother, a Cherokee Indian. He still looked more like the Yale Law School student he used to be than the thirty-four year old man he was today.

Robert Stainbrook, Jefferson's friend and colleague, stepped onto the porch carrying two mugs of steaming coffee. He took a deep breath, the cool air filling his lungs, and watched as the sunlight moved over the pines and danced on the river. WASP-y blond and blue-eyed, muscular and dressed to fish, he was a walking advertisement for Idaho rural living, even though he was a Los Angeles native.

He handed one of the mugs to Jefferson as a bird chirped in a tree. Robert loved watching birds. He reached for his binoculars, but they weren't in their usual place on the hook by the front door. Seeing Jefferson's rifle leaning against the cabin wall, he grabbed it and looked through its telescopic sight. Damn, the bird was gone! He put the rifle down and leaned against the porch railing, not noticing the rattlesnake that slowly slithered out from under nearby bushes.

"Erskine, Newcombe, Labine," he said.

"Brooklyn pitchers," Jefferson answered as he curled his fingers around the mug and blew at the steam rising in the air. His eyes focused on the coffee as if he were trying to make up his mind to drink it.

"Shit! Thought I had you," Robert grumbled.

Jefferson looked up and smiled as he spoke: "John, George, Ringo."

Robert placed his mug down on the floor and took another deep breath.

"Three fourths of the Beatles," he bluffed.

"No, but nice try. Why don't you give up now and save your overworked brain cells?" Jefferson asked.

"You wish. Gotta get up early to stump me."

Jefferson laughed. "We *are* up early. It's 6:30 in the fucking morning."

"That's when fish eat."

The rattlesnake slinked toward the porch.

"Come on, man—- John, George, Ringo."

Stalling, Robert picked up his coffee cup and sipped slowly.

Jefferson smiled. He could smell victory. "I'll give you a hint. John, George, Ringo and Crockett."

"Three Beatles and an Alamo defender," Robert answered with a straight face.

Jefferson hummed the theme from "Jeopardy" as he leaned back in his chair, bumping against the cabin wall. The vibration spooked the snake, which quickly coiled, ready to strike.

Robert sensed the movement, turned and saw the snake. His eyes widened.

"Jeff—-"

"So, three Beatles and Davy Crockett? Is that your final answer?" Jeff continued, still laughing then noticed the strange look on Robert's face.

The snake began to rattle its tail. Robert didn't move.

"I hope that's not what I think it is," Jefferson said as he followed Robert's stare. Not three feet from where he sat the snake's tongue darted at him. He froze.

"I forgot," he asked, stretching for the humor in the situation, "you supposed to stare this thing down or scream at it?"

The rattle intensified.

"You think it just wants some coffee?" he continued, as the snake stared straight into his eyes then stretched its body forward as if to kiss him.

"I think it wants *you*, ol' boy," Robert deadpanned.

Lightning fast, Jefferson slipped a fishing knife from his belt, leapt up and sliced through the air, lopping off the snake's head. He then grabbed the chair and pushed the snake's body away from the cabin and back into the bushes. He kicked the head away.

"I really hate snakes," he shivered.

Another shiver ran through him as he picked up the rifle, then his duffel bag clumped by the front door. He slung the bag over his shoulder. "Well, that was fun. You put together that file for me yet?"

Robert went into the house as Jefferson made his way to a Land Rover parked in the dirt driveway. He threw the duffel bag in the back of the SUV, along with a tackle box and fishing rod, just as Robert walked up with a legal-size manila folder. He handed it to Jefferson.

"Here's everything we talked about. Nothing but grunts out here. The 'generals' are back east and it looks like the esteemed Senator from New York is a four star specimen."

Jefferson read the file label: "Senator Harold Lauder." He placed the folder under his arm, shut the back of the Land Rover and walked to the driver's side.

"You e-mail a copy to Fowler?" Jeff asked.

"Nope. It's just bits and pieces I've dug up by living here this past year. But I've been filling him in."

Robert slapped Jefferson on the back. "Hey, just one more day of fine fishing then it's farewell to flannel shirts, mountain living and rattlesnakes. I'm heading home to put all those pieces together into one big incriminating mosaic."

Ilona Joy Saari

As they shook hands, Jefferson pulled Robert into a quick bear hug.

"See you back home," Robert said as they separated and Jefferson opened the door to his SUV.

Before he could get in, Robert grabbed him by the arm. "Not so fast, buddy, who the hell are John, George, Ringo and Crockett?"

"John Wayne movie characters," Jefferson answered then laughed. "What kinda 'merican are you?"

Robert groaned, pulled a ten out of his jeans' pocket and gave it to Jefferson with a flourish. "You win."

"Has it ever occurred to you that we've got way too much useless knowledge percolating in our brains?"

Robert smiled. "Yes."

Jefferson embraced his friend again then carefully placed his rifle on the floor within easy reach next to the driver's seat. He climbed into the Land Rover, put the file on the passenger seat and started the car.

Robert hit the driver's door with the heel of his palm, gave him a "thumbs up" then walked down to the river.

As Jefferson drove away, Robert unmoored a rowboat with an outboard, cranked up the motor and headed into Hell's Canyon for a day of fishing.

Jefferson drove up the winding mountain road. At the top of the rise, he pulled over and walked a short distance through the woods until he came to a cliff. The view of Hell's Canyon reminded him of a nightmare he had had as a child. The jagged, barren cliffs gave him a chill as he remembered plummeting into a dark crevice, falling and falling, until he woke up screaming and his mother ran into his room and held him, stroking his hair and rocking him until he calmed down.

He looked at the Snake River far below and saw Robert, alone on the water, silently heading upriver.

4

***

Robert sat in the boat, his face lifted toward the mid-morning sun. He unbuttoned the top buttons of his flannel shirt and pulled it off over his head. The sun felt hot on his bare shoulders. Alone, deep in the river with the high rocks of the canyon on either side, he listened to the quiet. He reeled in his line and cast it out again.

Suddenly, a loud noise reverberated off the canyon walls. He knew it was a rifle shot, but that was all his mind was able to compute. No time to think——- was it for him? No time to react——- only a split second of awareness before a dark hole appeared in the middle of his forehead. His eyes flickered with confusion as he slumped forward to the boat bottom, the fishing rod falling into the river. He felt no pain. Somewhere in the distance a hawk screamed, then silence.

NEW YORK CITY—MORNING

Every year Manhattan had six perfect days when the air smelled like freshly laundered cotton sheets and the buildings sparkled like towers of Baccarat crystal. Three of those perfect days were in the spring and three were in the fall, voiding any reason for New Yorkers to live anywhere else. This wasn't one of those days. But Lorna Raven didn't care. Despite the city's blistering heat wave, today was going to be the seventh perfect day. She had done the responsible thing. She'd gotten into the office at seven and had spent a couple of hours editing a wedding video that she and her brother had been hired to shoot. Now it was off to Barney's to buy something outrageously expensive, funky and fun. At twenty-six she was about to hit the big time and she wanted a treat…she'd think about their mountain of bills tomorrow. Today was a day for optimism. Tomorrow was their big break. Raven's Video had been hired to be the 'news' pool camera for Senator Harold Lauder's fancy-schmancy re-election fundraiser and she was determined that nothing was going to keep her from basking in this high-profile opportunity. And for Lorna, basking began with shopping.

It was ten A.M. and rush hour was still in full swing. Why they called it rush *hour* she never understood. Not a single empty cab was in sight as she hurried along Central Park West. She grabbed her cell out of the large canvas bag hanging off her shoulder and called her brother. Even though the fundraiser was just a little over twenty-four hours away, she was still worried about the nuts and bolts of the business *and* the bill collectors knocking at their door.

"Hey, Poe, what's happening?" She listened to his usual litany as to why he wasn't in the office, but was in too good a mood to get angry. It was *his* contacts, after all, that got them the Lauder gig. "OK, OK,

Ilona Joy Saari

just finish Ted's commercial today. Pretty please. I know he's a big fat jerk, but we still need his big fat check."

She was about to go into her oft-recited "the bills are piling up" soliloquy when she saw a bus approaching. She said a hasty goodbye and shoved her phone into her canvas bag then fished around for her wallet at the bottom of the bag. The bus pulled into its stop. Lorna ran toward it, still scrounging around for her wallet, causing the bag to slip off her shoulder and fall into the gutter. The snappy "Raven's Video" logo stamped on the bag's flap seemed to have lost its snappy pride lying in the street. She flashed on how excited she had been when she had ordered the bags from L.L. Bean for their new company…how proud she was when she had had their logo stenciled on them. She let out a huge sigh as the bus pulled back into traffic and headed downtown. Well, the good news was, she found her wallet. The bad news was, it had fallen out of the bag and was nestled in curb grime a few inches away. She reached down and rescued her fallen belongings, then wiped off the wallet with a large, wrinkled, white bandana she kept in case she ever needed a makeshift tourniquet. "Hey, I was a girl scout. I'm prepared," she had explained to a friend who questioned her reasoning.

Lorna looked down the street. Not another bus in sight. Since the 72nd Street entrance to Central Park was only a couple of blocks away she decided to hoof it to the east side. Why not? The temperature was still a moderate 85 degrees and the humidity hadn't yet choked the air.

Traffic was crawling, but the sun felt wonderful as it beat down on her long mass of unruly auburn curls. The blue sky, dotted with puffy white clouds over Central Park, reminded her of the Dutch landscapes she liked so much at the Met. I don't care how hot it gets, she thought, nothing was going to ruin this day.

Without the slightest twinge of guilt she leisurely entered the park, walking east toward Fifth Avenue. After Barney's, maybe she'd splurge and treat herself to lunch at the outside cafe in Rockefeller Center. She left the walkway and climbed a small knoll a short distance away from where some kids were playing soccer. She decided to watch for a couple of minutes. As she began to descend the little hill, the white rubber tip of one of her worn, black Converse All-Stars got caught under a tree root, causing Lorna to lose her balance and tumble down the knoll. She wondered how long she could lie there before anyone came to help her. "Forever" immediately sprang to mind.

She looked at her once white tee, now covered in grass stains and her brand new, ruined, khaki cargo pants. She pulled out her trusty white bandana and started brushing dirt off her arms. So much for her perfect day and it wasn't even noon yet.

NEW YORK CITY—EVENING

Barefoot, in worn jeans and a black pocket tee, Alan "My friends call me Poe" Raven sat alone in a dark editing room, surrounded by tall, steel, erector-set bookcases overloaded with canisters of film, tapes, CDs and DVDs. At thirty-one he had a quirky charm that began as far back as the sixth grade when his classmates dubbed him "Poe" after his overly dramatic reading of Edgar Allan Poe's "The Raven." His girlfriend Carol described him once as a man whose ambitions were always on some Poe-like plane yet to be approached by his reality.

The only light in the room emanated from one of several monitors on the editing console wall. About two dozen wind-up toys decorated the side of the console where he was working. Bored and cranky, he fiddled with the levers and knobs in front of him, distorting the screen's image of Ted, a twenty/thirty-something, slick-looking salesman, who stood in front of super-sized rolls of carpeting holding a sign that read, "Casta Carpets." Poe rewound the tape then hit "play" again. Ted's once sharp image was now as bloated as a Macy's Thanksgiving parade float as he began his spiel in a thick Queens, New York accent, which, of course, added all the "r's" that floated south when Bostonians dropped them into the Atlantic.

"Hey, I'm Ted Caster of Caster Carpets, and I want ya to take a ride to Astoria and I'll cover your floor for ya. Caster carpets are a hundred percent all natural dextro-fibro-dacron with our exclusive plush guard, for a long lasting and finer fiber. So walk on by, for a carpet you can walk on, a carpet you can buy."

As Ted droned on, Poe absentmindedly wound up a toy dragon and set it loose on the console. The dragon spit tiny sparks at the monitor as it scurried along, then crashed into the NY Post. As he grabbed the toy before it fell to the floor, his eye caught the headline, "Happy Fundraiser For Hap?" What grown man goes by the name of "Hap?" he thought. But, then again, Lauder's wife *is* "Kipper." Shit! Carpet commercials and pissant fundraisers...

"How did I end up here?" he uttered to the empty room. But, he knew how. His remarkable inability to put a zipper on his smartass mouth.

Poe fiddled again making ol' "Ted Caster of Caster Carpets" thin, then fat again, then thin—- a funhouse mirror of grotesque "Ted heads" as Ted continued to babble.

"Yeh, take a walk yourself, Teddy boy," Poe muttered then glanced at his watch. Five o'clock.

He turned to face an empty chair a few feet down the editing bay console, "Sorry sweet sis, they're gonna have to put us in debtors' prison...I just can't do this anymore today."

The monitor went black, as Poe quickly shut it off. He blindly slipped his feet into his favorite beat-up brown loafers, ran his fingers through his shaggy brown hair in a useless effort to get it out of his eyes, then grabbed a crumpled tan linen blazer and dashed out of the editing room.

WASHINGTON, D. C.—EVENING

Jefferson Leeds carried a garment bag slung over his shoulder as he walked up the steps to a nondescript Federal building in the middle of Chinatown, unfazed by the historical backdrop of the nation's capital. He missed the thrill he used to get every time he came to Washington and tried to remember the last time he actually smelled the cherry blossoms or marveled at the Washington Monument.

Upon entering the building, he immediately went to the electronic security check. He put his garment bag on the conveyor belt to be x-rayed. "Hey, Charlie," he said to the security guard monitoring the machine. "How was maternity leave?"

Charlie looked up and smiled as Jefferson flashed his ID, handed him his gun, then walked through the metal detector. Charlie returned the gun, which Jefferson immediately holstered at the small of his back. Charlie then handed Jefferson a cigar, thought about it, then handed him two more. Jefferson looked at the cigars. "Triplets?!?"

Charlie laughed, "That's what *I* said."

"Think positive. Two more, you got a basketball team."

Jefferson grabbed his garment bag and walked across the lobby into an elevator.

When he arrived at his floor he went through another security check before heading for a heavy wooden door marked, "George Fowler—Deputy Director" in thick brass lettering. Centered above the name was the seal of the Bureau of Alcohol, Tobacco & Firearms. He walked in and flashed a brilliant smile at a smartly dressed woman in her 40's sitting sentinel over Fowler's inner office. "Vi, you look great in red."

It's scarlet, hon," she answered, her voice as liquid as molasses.

Her eyes lingered on his face a moment then slowly moved downward, giving him an appreciative once-over. "And, to paraphrase my priggish father, may he rest in peace, 'Many a harlot worked in scarlet.'"

Jefferson leaned over her desk, barely an inch away from her face, looked straight into her hazel eyes and flashed that smile again. "Is that some kind of hint?"

"Subtle, ain't it," Vi answered, returning his smile. She held his gaze. "Got an appointment?"

He laughed as he straightened up, threw his garment bag on a chair and walked into Fowler's office. "Do I ever?" He closed the door behind him.

Inside the office, Jefferson's immaculately dressed and manicured boss sat behind his government-issued desk. Fowler had been given a decorating budget when he was first promoted, but hadn't felt the need to "tart up the place" as he once told Jefferson.

Fowler growled. "Where you been all week?

"Idaho," Jefferson answered. "I like the fishing."

Fowler shook his head. At age fifty-eight he was beginning to acknowledge his mortality and that he was in a high-risk business. It didn't matter that he was now behind a desk—- he felt the odds had turned against him.

"Find anything new from Robert?"

"No," Jefferson lied, failing to mention Robert's file on Senator Lauder. "All I know is, he's so tight with the militia they wanted to make him one of their grand pooh bahs."

Vi walked into the office, visibly shaken.

"What?!" Fowler asked, annoyed with the interruption.

"It's Robert."

"What? He runnin' for Boise mayor?" growled Fowler.

Not able to talk, she walked over to her boss's computer and brought up the agency's internal webpage, then rushed out of the office in tears. A bulletin appeared on the screen coldly announcing Robert's death that morning. Fowler opened an e-mail addressed to him from the Idaho ATF office. As Fowler read the email, Jefferson leaned over the Deputy Director's shoulder and read the details of Robert's murder. The e-mail also reported that all of Robert's possessions, including his computer, guns and IDs were missing from his cabin.

"Didn't you just tell me he was all buddy, buddy with those assholes?" Fowler yelled at Jefferson.

"He was," Jefferson answered coldly, his face showing no emotion.

"Then why'd they blow his fuckin' brains out in the middle of a river?"

"How the hell do I know?"

"For Chrissakes, you just left him a few hours ago. He must have told you something."

"Nothing."

"Look, Jeff," Fowler said, frustrated with the conversation and frustrated with Jefferson. "I know Robert was your friend, but he must've blown his cover."

Jefferson just stared into Fowler's eyes. Neither man said anything for at least thirty seconds then Jefferson turned and walked out of the office. He ignored Vi sitting at her desk crying, grabbed his garment bag off the chair and left without a word.

By the time Jefferson got home to his Georgetown row house, the sun had set. He hadn't been there in months and it felt good to be surrounded by his own things, even if they were relics of his family's history. In the small foyer the antique pewter tray on the console was overflowing with mail placed there by his housekeeper. Since his bills went directly to his accountant for payment he ignored the pile and headed up the narrow center hall staircase to his bedroom. He threw his garment bag on the bed then pulled a suitcase out of his walk-in closet. He immediately started packing—- jeans, khakis, a few polo shirts and tees, a couple of dress shirts, cuff links, ties, a pair of tan linen trousers, a navy blazer, brown loafers, underwear and socks. He went into his bathroom and jumped into the shower.

Refreshed and dressed in jeans and a black linen, long-sleeved shirt, he went downstairs. Without turning on the lights, he walked into his small study filled with books and comfortable leather club chairs. He reached for the crystal decanter atop the butler's tray and poured himself a stiff drink. He stared a moment at his desk drawer and thought about rolling a joint from his private stash, but decided against it. He downed his drink and poured another. Tonight the scotch would have to be enough to calm his inner demons. He picked up the phone receiver on the desk and called a cab then sank down into a chair.

The lights from the street lamps shined into the room, high-lighting his possessions...his French antique desk, the antique lamps and framed architectural renderings. Seeing them filled him with self-loathing. In the past, his agency friends had wondered how he could afford such pricey living quarters on an ATF agent's salary. His flip answer was always the same: "Privileged DNA." His parents had insisted on buying this house for him so he could live in a "proper" neighborhood even if he was *only* a government employee. It wasn't that they were snobs—- they just didn't have a clue how people in the real world really lived. They weren't uneducated or uninformed. They were just very rich. Not newly rich, but "generationally" rich—- tobacco rich. And even beyond North Carolina where they raised him, that was rich. The struggles of mankind were something they understood intellectually, but could not relate to emotionally.

The more Jefferson saw of life through a cop's eye and the more he witnessed people's inhumanity the more jaded his views became. He no longer believed that people were innately good. He certainly didn't believe that governments were good. The world was a place for the privileged, and he was one of the privileged. Living dangerously in a life and death game made him forget his distaste for his family's exalted status, his unearned privilege and his inability to reject that privilege.

As he waited for his cab, he sipped his scotch...another sign of rebellion. With his heritage, he really should have been a bourbon man.

14

***

As always, Dulles airport was crowded. Jefferson thought about going to the VIP lounge but decided against it. He didn't want to run into anyone he knew and that was more likely to happen in the lounge where you couldn't remain anonymous. Just in case he did run into someone, however, he waited at the gate for Los Angeles.

An avid Red Sox fan since his days as a Harvard undergrad, he had been following the American League division race between Boston and the New York Yankees and was lost in the pages of the Washington Post sports section when he heard his name called. He looked up and saw Diana Brown, a fellow ATF agent and former lover. He was trapped. She sat down next to him.

"Thought that was you, darlin,'" she said, emphasizing her lilting Savannah accent.

"You coming or going?" Jefferson asked as he pecked her cheek and wondered if she had heard about Robert.

"Comin.' It seems George has missed my effervescent presence in the office," she volunteered. "Where you headed?"

Nope, she hadn't heard, he decided, and he wasn't going to tell her. The three of them had too much history and he didn't want to get into it. To answer her question, he indicated the flight information behind the check-in desk. "As the board says, warm, humidity-free, Los Angeles."

"You hate L. A."

"Maybe. But, I don't hate the weather. Besides, I'm going down to San Diego for a little deep sea fishing."

"Ah, darlin,' when you gonna stop killing those defenseless little things?" she asked teasingly as she absentmindedly ran her fingers through her short brown hair.

"Defenseless—- hardly. Little—- never. It's all how you play the sport, *darlin',*" he teased back. Playing along, he ran his fingers seductively down her bare arm.

"I do remember, you were very good at game playin'," she smiled as she leaned in closer to him and gave him a knowing smile.

"I learned from the master," he replied as he returned her smile and gently brushed her lips. She took his face into her hands and kissed him passionately. He returned the kiss, feeling the warmth of her tongue move inside his mouth. She definitely had a way of triggering a young man's fancy, he thought. Thankfully, he was no longer a young man who had fancies. She finally pulled away as the loudspeaker announced that the flight to L. A. was now boarding.

"Saved by the bell," Diana said as she stroked his face tenderly.

"Who? Me or you?" he asked.

"Why me, of course, sugar. You better get goin' or we're gonna have to look for a utility closet or somethin' to finish this conversation."

Jefferson grabbed his bag, kissed her again, this time less sensually, but before he could leave, Diana took his hand.

"I miss us, Jeff," she stated matter-of-factly. No accent.

"*Us* was a long time ago," he whispered then turned and joined the boarding passengers. Standing at the end of the line, he watched her leave her seat. As she walked toward the terminal exit she smiled and blew him a kiss then disappeared in the mass of airport humanity. The passengers to L.A. were slowly moving onto the plane when a loudspeaker announced the last call to board the flight to JFK. Jefferson left the line for Los Angeles and quickly walked to the next gate, gave the airline attendant his boarding pass and entered the cabin of the plane for New York.

In the air, Jefferson tried to focus on what he needed to do about Senator Lauder, but memories of Diana flooded his thoughts. It was almost five years ago that he had been invited to a huge Christmas party given by the social climbing, society wife of one of the ATF "higher-ups." He had no desire to go, but agency politics proved too strong. Ignoring the invitation would have been tantamount to a slap in the man's face, so he put on his best WASP attire—- a Brooks Brothers navy worsted suit, a favorite blue dress shirt with white collar and cuffs and red club tie—- gritted his teeth and made his way to the hotel banquet room where the party was being held.

When he arrived at the overly-decorated, cavernous room filled with D.C. society, he saw her for the first time, sipping a glass of champagne, flirting with a half dozen men by the bar. Tall, lithe, with rich, chestnut brown hair, no strand more than two inches long, wearing a strapless black velvet cocktail dress, adorned only with a single strand of pearls and pearl earrings, she was breathtaking. He never took his eyes off her as he made his way to the bar, meeting and greeting along the way. She spotted him looking at her and smiled, then said something to the bartender. By the time he disentangled himself from the crowd, she had freed herself from her admirers and was holding a scotch rocks. She handed it to him, then picked up her champagne and clinked his glass. They each sipped their drinks.

"Ralph Lauren would just love you," she said, staring straight at him with large, almond-shaped eyes the color of milk chocolate.

Normally quick on the uptake, Jefferson just looked at her quizzically.

"You're the real thing, darlin.' Even ol' Ralph would have to bow to your breedin.' You just can't manufacture that on Seventh Avenue."

Jefferson smiled. "And I try so hard to hide it."

She ran a finger down his tie. "Well, your cover's blown."

Jefferson gave himself the once over and shrugged his shoulders.

"First, it's the shoes, darlin.' Shined, but worn brown tassel loafers with a navy suit," she said with a hint of laughter. "Then the shirt... an old favorite I'm sure. Collar and cuffs got frayed, so your own personal haberdasher saved it by puttin' on the new white ones. Of course, Ralph copies the look for a princely amount that only the nouveau riche will pay. But you can always tell when the collar and cuffs weren't part of the original shirt. Frugality of old money——- I love it. You are from old money, aren't you?"

"Even older than my shirt."

"Thank god! I'm so weary of listening to men talk about how they're going to make it. It *is* only paper, after all." She held out her hand. "Hi. I'm Diana Brown. You do like single malt, right?"

He shook her hand then took another sip of scotch. "If I didn't, I'd be barred from the polo field and have to join the rest of mankind in the pursuit of money. Then where would we be?"

Jefferson smiled to himself as he remembered how they snuck out of the party during dinner, got a suite at the hotel and made love until morning.

"Would you like a drink?" the flight attendant asked him shaking him out of his reverie.

"Scotch rocks."

chapter

ONE

NEW YORK CITY—THE NEXT NIGHT

Excited about the night's shoot, Lorna left her office early so she'd get to the boat where the fundraiser was being held before the guests arrived. She couldn't believe her luck. She got a cab in less than five minutes and headed downtown. But her luck ran out a few blocks before she reached the pier. She was trapped in a cab with no air conditioning going nowhere.

Lorna was normally a person who loved the invasive commotion of the city, but the oppressive heat, honking horns, and shouting people were not helping her frayed nerves. Not only was she *not early*, she was going to be *very late*. Poe was going to be furious. She tried to regain her optimism about tonight's gig. If all went well, they wouldn't have to rely on weddings and bar mitzvahs to pay the rent. That is, if she ever got there in all this traffic. The cab hadn't moved an inch for three minutes. She knew this because she was staring at her watch, begging time to stand still just until she got to the pier.

She noticed that her paper-thin, black linen trousers were beyond wrinkled. She tried to smooth them out and realized they were damp with perspiration. I *never* sweat, she thought to herself. I hate this! The temperature was still hovering at one hundred and the air was wetter than her bathroom after a steamy shower. The weather and the brownouts made everyone in the city just a bit edgier and Lorna was no exception. Frustrated, she shoved her fare into the money chute and got out of the cab, slinging a video camera and her large canvas bag over her shoulder. The pier was still five blocks away, but she'd get there quicker on foot, she reasoned.

As she ran down the street, struggling with the camera, "Raven's Video" on her canvas bag bouncing off her backside, the cabbie couldn't help but admire her long, slender legs outlined by her clinging, damp pants. Even now, post college, Lorna was still unaware that her beauty and figure made men's hearts stop. Not to mention the effect it had on their other organs.

Finally reaching the pier, she pushed her way through a throng of people toward a dock. At the end was a Circle Line sightseeing boat, crowded with passengers dressed in black-tie, sipping champagne and eating hors d'oeuvres under a banner that read "Be Prouder, Vote Lauder." A security guard stopped her. "Credentials," he barked.

Lorna pleaded with him while she searched her pockets and canvas bag. "Please, I just had them. I'm shooting the party. I know I'm late, but there was a two-bus accident in the middle of Seventh Avenue. How often do you see that?"

The guard wouldn't budge.

"Look, I'm not a terrorist. Would I be so disorganized if I were a terrorist? I know this looks weird, but my partner and I were hired last minute," she vamped. "Somebody else was supposed to do this, but she broke her leg on a nautilus machine at the health club. Can you believe that?"

The guard just stared at her. As she held his stare, she noticed that the collar of his uniform was soaked with sweat and realized this guy was probably more miserable than she was. He wasn't going to give her an inch.

"You don't believe that. You don't really care, do you?" She saw someone on the boat and waved frantically. No one waved back. "Poe! See! There! My partner. He's already on the boat, and he's not gonna be happy cause I'm late, so trust me, this is not something I'm looking forward to, it just happens to be my job." She knew it was pointless to keep talking, but she couldn't help herself as she watched two crew members begin to unfasten the ties connecting the boat to the dock.

"I'd be perfectly happy turning around and going home to my air-conditioned apartment...Ah!" Finally, she found her credential on a chain, deep in the recesses of her canvas bag. She held it up in front of the guard, trying to stay calm as the boat began to inch away from the dock. "There. Credentials. Something I could've forged in ten minutes, but hey." She put the chain around her neck.

The guard looked at her. "Get out of my face."

"Wow. Never heard that line before," she quipped as she ran down the dock, her equipment once again banging against her ass. She reached the moving boat, now about four feet from the dock heading out into the Hudson River. Oh, hell, she thought, why not. She leapt over the water gap, video camera and canvas bag along for the "flight" and crashed onto the deck. For a moment she sat stunned—- this was definitely a new personal "best."

Sprawled on the deck of the boat, Lorna smiled. No one was looking at her. No one asked if she was all right. No one offered to help. Ah, I love New York, she thought, everyone minds their own business. She looked at her black Converse sneakers and said a silent prayer that she hadn't worn her cute Manolo Blahnik black sandals or had on her three inch heels. She checked her camera. Nothing broken.

Poe walked up. "That was quite an entrance."

"Oh, shut up and help me up."

He grabbed her arm and pulled her to her feet.

The stars shimmered above the city as the Circle Line boat slowly glided up the East River. The United Nations building and the east side skyline glittered in the background. A band played on the top deck while some couples danced under the Prouder-Lauder banner hanging from a wire across the dance floor. Others ate, drank and mingled while Lorna and Poe videotaped the party. Poe turned off his video cam.

"OK, enough with the B-roll. I'll stay up here. Why don't you get some of the people on the lower deck?"

"What? Coming out of the bathrooms? Gimme a break." She stopped taping.

Before Poe could snipe back, Perry Reiner, a columnist in a pure white suit, white shirt and white silk tie approached them. His New York Post press credential hung from a chain around his neck. Reiner always gave Lorna the creeps and tonight the creep-o-meter was on red alert. Or white. As he leered at her, she felt his eyes were seeing more than her white cotton blouse as they scanned her body. He smiled lasciviously then zeroed in on Poe.

"Well. News bug bites, you scratch forever," Reiner said.

"Only a hack like you would think a campaign fund raiser is news."

"Correct me if I'm wrong," he said to Lorna, "isn't that the arrogance that got your brother fired from the network?"

"You wouldn't know real news if it pissed all over your nice white suit," Lorna spit out. "*That's* the kind of arrogance that got my brother fired from the network." She picked up her camera. "I'm going below for some fresh air. Have a nice day."

As she headed for the stairs, Poe turned to Reiner. "You heard the lady. Have a nice day."

Harold "Hap" Lauder, a tall, elegant man in his 60's, leaned against the deck railing sipping a scotch as he talked to his wife, Kipper, twenty pounds overweight and twenty years past her prime. Thirty-odd years of marriage, the past twenty as the wife of a United States

Senator, with a beautiful brownstone in Washington and a mansion in New York suburbia had not changed Kipper from the over-indulged, petulant child that Hap had thought so adorable when they had first met at a dance at Penn. She had been a senior and he a dirt-poor scholarship student from a less than stellar family in his second year of law school.

Two years later, he couldn't believe his good fortune when she agreed to marry him. He stopped feeling that way shortly after their first child was born and she checked into a spa in Southern California to be pampered and waited on, leaving their two-week-old daughter with the newly hired nanny. He thought of divorcing her then, but he was a nervous new father with designs on a political career. He could never forget that "Kipper" was the former Elizabeth Kipp Browning of the "Philadelphia" Brownings, a prominent banking family. Having them as in-laws practically guaranteed his dream. If he had left her, it would appear that he had abandoned her and the baby—- the press would have shredded him faster than CEOs shred documents and his political career would have been over before it started.

"You're spending far too much time with me, Hap. People will think we're happily married," she said as she finished another glass of champagne.

"No one is that naïve," he snapped.

"Only your little harem of Congressional aides who still believe that *you* believe in anything," she snapped back, far too loudly. Angry and slightly drunk, she turned on her heels and pushed her way toward a white-jacketed waiter who looked vaguely middle-eastern as he carried a tray of champagne. She switched her empty glass for a full one and continued on. As always, Hap ignored his wife and turned to see Perry Reiner coming up behind him.

"Perry. In pure, virginal white."

"An image you've long discarded, Senator," he bantered.

"What twisted, distorted little tale are you planning to print tomorrow?" Hap asked, slightly amused.

"Don't know. You've yet to pontificate tonight." Perry paused, then looked straight at Hap, something he usually avoided doing with people unless they looked like Lorna Raven. "As a matter of fact, I want to do a column about your work on the arms committee—something that could resemble the truth if you didn't stare at it too long."

"My dear man, you and the truth parted ways years ago.'"

Poe continued to shoot the party. Through the lens he saw the middle-eastern waiter approach the Senator standing near the back of the boat where a chain spanned a five foot gap in the railing. He was surprised when the waiter handed off his tray of champagne to a startled guest. Poe zoomed in closer. In an instant, the waiter pulled out a small semi-automatic hidden in his jacket and fired point blank into Hap Lauder's chest. Blood soaked the front of the Senator's tuxedo and spread onto Perry's white suit as the powerful force of the bullet smacked him into the columnist.

For a brief second they seemed to be dancing then Hap fell backward over the sloping chain and into the water below. Perry, about to plunge in after him, frantically tried to regain his balance. He grabbed the chain and pulled himself to safety. On his knees and in shock, he hugged the ship's railing and stared blankly as people screamed and ran for cover. Others hit the deck. Poe quickly looked at Kipper and turned his video cam on her as she ran to the spot where her husband had been standing. She looked down just in time to see him disappear into the black river.

"Oh my god, Hap!" she screamed.

A crew member turned a large beam of light onto the water, but the Senator was not visible beneath the murky river. He threw a life preserver overboard then jumped in after it as someone screamed, "Stop the boat!"

Lou Edwards, one of a detail of uniformed policemen providing security on the boat, chased the assassin as passengers scrambled to get out of the way. Poe followed them with his video cam.

"Freeze! Police!" Lou yelled as he pulled out his gun.

The waiter stopped and turned, his hands slightly raised, the gun still in his right hand. Lou fired. An anguished look crossed the waiter's face as his life seeped out of him. He slumped to the deck, his weapon banging against the floor as it fell out of his hand. Poe continued to shoot for a moment longer then turned off his video cam.

The boat engines off and the danger apparently over, several horrified passengers rushed to the railing to see what was happening in the water. Kipper watched in a daze as the crew member, a balding man in his forties gave up his search and struggled to climb back on board. No one moved to help him until a woman in a revealing red matte-jersey gown pulled the dinner jacket off a man standing next to her, leaving him bewildered, as she rushed to give the crew member a helping hand. She stood anxiously as he finally heaved himself back on board, then she put the jacket around his shoulders and led him to the interior of the boat. Kipper watched them walk away, at first not comprehending. Then it hit—- her husband was shot and sinking into the East River.

"No! You can't give up!" she cried before she collapsed to the floor.

A few guests rushed to her side. They helped her up and tried to lead her away from the railing, but she wouldn't budge. They spoke softly to her, assuring her that everything would be done to find her husband, though no one seemed to be doing anything.

Lorna, who had hurried back up to the top deck when she heard the screams, found Poe just as he started to strip off his jacket and kick off his loafers. "Poe, what are you doing?" she yelled as she ran toward him, pushing past Perry who was still in shock and trying to rub the blood off his jacket.

"I have no idea," he yelled to her as he dove over the chain and jumped into the river.

"Poe!" she screamed as she reached the railing and watched anxiously for her brother to surface. She sighed with relief when his head popped out of the water. He disappeared a moment later as he submerged himself again to look for the body.

Lorna stared at the forbidding water as Poe continued to bob up and down, frantically searching for Lauder, each time coming up empty-handed.

As passengers scrambled to help each other, and part of the police detail protected the crime scene surrounding the waiter's body, a man dressed in a perfectly tailored Armani tuxedo, leaned against the railing. He watched dispassionately as he sipped his scotch rocks. It was Jefferson Leeds.

The press had already arrived when the boat reached the dock. News trucks were parked everywhere and reporters swarmed like flies, cornering passengers after they were questioned by the police and allowed to leave the boat.

Poe, wrapped in a wool blanket, sat shivering on a pile of rope on the dock. His and Lorna's video cameras and their logo-stamped canvas bags were next to him. How bizarre he thought, shivering in the dog days of August.

"I hope you didn't swallow any of that water," Lorna said as she rubbed his arms, trying to stop the shakes. "You don't know where it's been."

Near them, a reporter was doing a stand-up in front of her camera: "The police have confirmed that Senator Harold "Hap" Lauder has been shot. His body plunged into the East River and has not been recovered. No identification was found on the gunman, but he's been tentatively identified as possibly Afghani or Pakistani, fueling speculation that Al Qaeda was responsible for the assassination."

As the reporter was about to wrap up, she noticed Lorna and Poe's canvas bags and recognized the Raven name. Still holding her microphone, she moved toward them. "You jumped into the water to find the Senator," she said shoving the mike into Poe's face.

"You think?" Lorna answered, annoyed by the intrusion.

"Anything you can tell us about the gunman?" the reporter continued, ignoring Lorna.

"Yeh," Poe said. "He had a gun."

A few people helped an obviously distraught Kipper through the crowd to her waiting limo. The reporter looked at Poe. Realizing she wasn't going to get anything from him, she hurried after Kipper. "Kipper Lauder, wife of the murdered Senator…Mrs. Lauder, do you know anyone who might have a reason to kill your husband?" She shoved the microphone in front of Kipper's face.

"This is America. Since when does anyone need a reason?" Kipper shot back, then got into her limousine. The reporter looked around for another interview victim as a second reporter hurried up to Poe, who still sat on the pile of rope. "I'm with Metro Cable News. I understand you have a video of the actual shooting."

Poe looked up at him. "Well, I don't know. The actual shooting?" he said sarcastically. "Maybe I actually have a video of the virtual shooting. Or it could be the actual shooting. Is English you second language?"

"My station is willing to pay handsomely for the video," the reporter continued, undeterred.

"Handsomely? Forget it. I like getting paid ugly."

"Fifty thousand dollars."

"Fifty thousand dollars! Jesus, Zapruder only got one twenty five, and he got a President. What's the matter with you people?"

"Hey, you're no different from…"

Poe leaped up, forcing the reporter to jump backward in fear. Lorna grabbed her brother's arm. "Come on, Poe."

He pulled away from her and moved closer to the reporter. "Yes, I'm very different from you. You're a gnawing rat with a checkbook. You should be embarrassed!"

Lorna dragged him away. "Poe, come on. We're outta here."

They grabbed their bags and video cams and were about to leave when the reporter handed Poe his card. "Think about it and call me. Any time."

Poe looked at the card then dropped it to the ground as he and Lorna walked away. They passed a recovered Perry Reiner pacing on the sidewalk dictating into a cell phone.

Ilona Joy Saari

"He was admiring my suit when he was shot. No, no. Uh...with his last breath he admired my suit and in a flash, the pure white linen was covered with bright, red blood." He listened a moment, then continued. "I don't give a rat's ass what color you think my prose is that's my lead! Now, paragraph two: Tonight, a political career that began in upstate New York has come to an abrupt end..."

"And you tell me you actually miss that?" Lorna said to Poe as they moved through the crowd, Reiner's voice fading into the ether.

Poe looked at his watch. "Forty bucks and the damn thing isn't waterproof. What time is it?"

"One A.M., why?"

"Oh, shit! Carol!"

From a short distance, Jefferson watched Poe run into the street and hail a cab.

chapter

TWO

LARCHMONT, NEW YORK

A taxi drove through a throng of reporters, news crews and paparazzi and up to the iron gates leading to the Lauder waterfront estate. The cabbie opened his window and pushed the buzzer. No one answered.

"Buzz it again," his fare commanded from the back seat.

He hit it again. Still no answer.

"Oh, hell," she said. "Keep buzzing it til you wake the dead."

Good lord, that was a poor choice of words, she thought, as the cabbie leaned on the buzzer. A security guard finally came to the gate.

"Get lost," he yelled at the cabbie.

The passenger, an imperious, icily beautiful woman of a certain age, stuck her head out of the passenger window. "Tell Mrs. Lauder that Pauline Lawson is here and I'm not leaving until I see her." She closed her window and watched him relay the message into a walkie-talkie. A moment later he opened the gate. As the cab drove through, reporters tried to follow but the security guard pulled out his gun, stopping them in their tracks. No one else made it through as the gate slowly closed.

The taxi reached the circular driveway then stopped in front of the large Tudor mansion. Before paying the driver, she pulled a tiny silver flask from her purse and took a sip. She realized that this had become a habit in recent weeks, but she didn't care. The vodka felt warm and soothing as it slid down her throat. She looked out the window at the huge house. All the lights were out but for a small glow from a lamp in the library.

As the cab drove around the circle and back down the long driveway through the estate gates, she made no move toward the front door. How many times have I been in this house in the last twenty years, she wondered? A hundred? Two hundred? How many beautiful summer night parties have I been to on the back lawn leading to the water's edge? She sighed as she remembered fondly the night Congressman Miller had playfully thrown her into the Long Island Sound fully clothed.

She looked at her watch. Three in the morning. She considered going back to Manhattan, but couldn't now that her taxi was gone. I could call another one on my cell, she reasoned, then quickly quashed the impulse. How could she leave now that she had probably aroused Kipper from what would most likely be a drugged sleep? She pulled her shoulders back as if she were in a military review. This is ridiculous, she scolded herself. I'm forty-seven years old…I can do this. She took another little sip from the flask, put it back into her purse, walked up to the front door and rang the bell.

She stood erect, taking deep breaths as she waited for the door to be answered. The night air was much less humid here in Larchmont than in the city and she could smell the roses planted along the edge of the circular driveway. She rang the bell again. She shifted her weight to one foot as she waited and fidgeted with the buttons of her linen blouse. Finally, a foyer light went on. She braced herself as the door opened and she looked down on Kipper who, at five-four, was four inches shorter.

Kipper was dressed in a flowing black silk nightgown and matching robe, a half-empty wine bottle in her hand.

Pauline briefly took her into her arms then moved into the house. "Where is everybody? Who's with you?"

"I sent them all home. Why aren't you in Washington?" Kipper asked, confused and surprised to see her friend.

"I was in town for some last minute shopping. I'm leaving for Europe later today," Pauline answered. "I couldn't leave without seeing you."

Kipper could only stare at her as Pauline led them back to the library.

Bewildered, Kipper looked around the room as if she had no idea where she was. She sat down in a brightly colored floral print easy chair, still clutching the wine bottle. The only light in the large mahogany-paneled room came from an antique floor lamp alongside the chair, making the flowers on the fabric seem grotesque in the mostly dark and somber atmosphere. The visual contrast was stunning, Pauline thought, then debated with herself about turning on another lamp. She decided against it.

"I was in my hotel room when I saw the news on television," she said, barely above a whisper. "I felt awful. Then I realized how devastated you must be."

Kipper was totally unresponsive. Almost catatonic. She looked at Pauline——- so tall, so thin, so beautiful, so very sophisticated——- and wondered what she was talking about.

"Kipper?" Pauline moved a bit closer to her.

"Pauline." She stared at her a moment, then suddenly the night's events crashed around her and she began to sob.

Pauline knelt down beside her, took the wine bottle out of her hand and placed it on the floor, then took Kipper's hands in hers. They were cold and dry. "I know. I know," she said, trying to comfort her.

Kipper controlled herself and wiped her eyes. They had been friends for almost twenty years and had never discussed anything more serious than a designer's spring collection or what new gimmick they

Ilona Joy Saari

would come up with for their next charity event. She had never confided in Pauline about her marriage and Pauline had never really confided in her. If Kipper thought about it, she really knew nothing substantial about Pauline. What she knew, everyone in their social circle knew. How Pauline had gone to D. C. to seek her fortune. How she had married well and was widowed early giving her the financial freedom to live life on her own terms. But Kipper really knew nothing else. Yet, here Pauline was trying to be of comfort to her on the worse night of her life.

She looked at Pauline. "Thirty-four years of marriage. I never thought it would end like this."

"I know."

"I always thought *I'd* end up shooting him. The son of a bitch!" She didn't realize how angry her voice had become. They were quiet a moment. "Didn't expect someone else would do it right in front of my eyes."

"Is there anything I can do?" Pauline asked.

"I haven't been able to talk to Peter and Nancy. They've been calling, but I just didn't have the strength. Maybe now that you're here..."

"Let me get them for you." Pauline stood up and walked over to the telephone on an antique desk.

"He never did any wrong in their eyes," Kipper said to no one in particular.

"Have you thought about funeral arrangements?"

"God, they haven't even found the body!" Kipper wailed, then pulled herself together again. "Not that they need to. He wasn't around for the last ten years of our marriage—- he might as well not be around for his funeral."

Pauline looked at her for a moment. "Let's call the children."

Kipper took a deep breath. "OK." She picked up the wine bottle and went over to a bar located in the library wall. Decanters of liquor, bottles of wine and an assortment of glasses stood among books, photos and other memorabilia. She poured herself a glass of wine as Pauline dialed the phone.

"I did love him once, Pauline. I never wished for this. Really."

"I know. People always say be careful what you wish for—but what you don't wish for still hurts."

"Yes it does," Kipper answered quietly.

They stood quietly for a moment.

"Nancy?" Pauline said into the receiver. "I'm sorry to be calling so late. This is Pauline Lawson…"

NEW YORK CITY—MORNING

By the time Poe had gotten home from the pier, showered and changed into his uniform of pocket tee, faded jeans and beat up loafers, the sun was rising. He rushed out of his apartment and hurried down the street. After a few blocks, he stopped and stood outside an old tenement walk-up, gentrified into a small but charming apartment building with a beautiful wood and beveled-glass door. He stood a moment, immobilized as he deliberated over pushing the buzzer. He had tried reaching Carol on Lorna's cell and again when he got home, but she didn't answer.

As he debated what to do next, he pictured her sitting at a table for two in the original P. J. Clarke's on 53rd and Lex, a popular old tavern, becoming more and more furious when he hadn't shown up for their midnight rendezvous. If he pushed her buzzer, she'd probably ignore it. Through the beveled glass he saw a junior exec type barrel down the hall staircase and enter the tiny vestibule. The exec stopped at a console table to pick up a newspaper as Poe pulled his own apartment keys out of his pocket and rushed up the front stoop. He pretended to put his key in lock just as the exec opened the front door. Poe held it open for him, then slipped into the building, grabbed hold of the wrought iron banister and hurried up the marble stairs to the second floor, his mind racing.

Why had he returned Carol's keys the last time they fought? They'd been together again for the past two months, yet he still hadn't asked for them back. Why? A year on a shrink's couch could probably answer that, but right now what was he going to do if she didn't let him in? Hell, doesn't she watch the news? She was gonna be sorry when she realized that he almost drowned trying to save a U.S. Senator.

He reached her apartment door, hesitated a moment, then knocked. No answer. He knew she'd be up. She always woke up early, so he put his ear to the door. Music was softly playing. "Aha!" he said to no one but himself.

Poe knocked again, but still no answer. He banged loudly.

"Carol! Let me in. What'd you want me to do? *Not* try to save a Senator's life? Just let him get shot and drown?! Hell, *I* almost drowned."

Still no answer.

"Do you hear me?" Poe practically screamed. "How could I call? There are no phones in the East River! No, I lie. *My* brand new iPhone is there somewhere on the bottom——- in sludge——- probably next to a dead senator."

The door across the hall opened and a large man stuck out his head. He was maybe six foot four, two fifty, wearing a U.S. Marine khaki tank top and matching boxer shorts. His head was shaved and his face needed one. Bottom line, he looked like he could beat the shit out of Poe and would enjoy doing it.

"Hey, keep it down or I'll break your head!" he threatened, then closed his door again.

"Break my head?!" Poe whispered to himself then hit his head softly against the door. "Carol?"

Poe heard the top lock turn and sighed in relief. Then the middle lock sounded and finally the twist of the dead bolt. The door opened and Carol stood framed by the doorway in a white mid-thigh NY Yankee tee. With her natural blonde hair pulled back in a ponytail and her face void of all make-up, she looked more gorgeous to him than Gwyneth Paltrow and Naomi Watts combined. He gazed into her huge blue eyes and totally forgot what he wanted to say.

His heart was racing. Why does it do that, he wondered, every time he looked at her? Why doesn't she get tongue-tied and behave like a fool the way I do each time I see her?

"I tried calling," he mumbled.

"I know."

"It wasn't my fault. Honest. I dove into the East River..."

Carol put her index finger over his mouth to quiet him. "I know. I saw the news. You looked quite dashing, soaked to the bone with a police blanket around you."

She put her arms around his neck and kissed him. Poe picked her up—- all five-three and a half, one hundred and four pounds. She felt light as a feather as she wrapped her legs around his waist and kept kissing him as he carried her into the apartment and kicked the door closed.

chapter

THREE

A taxi drove down a narrow tree-lined street past tasteful brick and stucco townhouses and understated apartment buildings. But there was no mistaking the simplicity of these buildings…they reeked of old WASP money, though the residents were no longer strictly WASP or *old* money.

Ever since Lorna had rented the Barbra Streisand/Robert Redford movie, "The Way We Were" a few years ago, Beekman Place had become one of her favorite streets in Manhattan. You could keep "An Affair to Remember." She liked it well enough, but when Deborah Kerr said at the end, "If you can paint, I can walk," or some such maudlin drivel, the movie was ruined for her.

To Lorna there was no comparison. "The Way We Were" was the ultimate Hollywood love story. Melodrama mixed with social commentary. It broke her heart when Streisand, in the last scene of the movie, reached up with her gloved hand to brush a wisp of Redford's hair off his forehead. Then when she said, "See ya, Hubbell," there was no way Lorna could close the floodgates. She had started crying when Streisand found out that Hubbell had cheated on her. Not with just anyone, but with one of his old girlfriends…someone from Beekman Place…a place Barbra had never fit into…a place she had never belonged. It was then Barbra realized how different they really were and that they wouldn't make it. By the time the movie was over, the front of Lorna's shirt was soaked with tears.

After that, she must have rented the movie twenty more times before she finally broke down and bought the DVD. So, when well-heeled Kathryn Worthington's insurance rep called to hire Raven's Video to videotape the interior of her Beekman Place home, Lorna insisted to Poe that she be the one to do the shoot. She was dying to see what one of those places looked like from the inside.

The taxi stopped and Lorna looked out the cab window at the Worthington's brick townhouse. The shutters and door were painted a shiny black enamel, and there was a tiny brass plate above an old-fashioned brass knocker. She was a WASP, born and raised, but Lorna knew how Streisand felt. She didn't belong here, either. This was way beyond her middle-class Bayside, Queens, Long Island, New York upbringing. But, there was something exciting about being on this street and knowing she was going into that house. Like the great plantations of the old south, "Beekman Place" was of a time and lifestyle that had long since vanished.

Lorna paid the cabbie, grabbed her video camera and canvas bag and got out of the clammy, air-conditioned cab. She breathed deeply and laughed to herself. The air definitely seemed cooler and cleaner then in Soho where she lived. Just then, a warm breeze off the East River softly caressed her face, momentarily convincing her that the air *was* different. This time she laughed out loud as she walked up three stairs to the front door. Discreetly engraved on the brass plate was the name "Worthington." While Lorna fished around in her canvas bag for a key she noticed a flame flickering in a little lantern to the right of the door. She couldn't believe it—- a *real*, old-fashion gaslight. She wondered how long it would burn before it went out. Finally her fingers felt the large plastic disk she had attached to the Worthington keys. She pulled them out of her bag and opened the front door.

Lorna entered the long foyer and immediately wished she had brought a sweater. A hundred and one outside with humidity to match, it seemed ten below in the townhouse. She reached for the alarm and was surprised to find it turned off. There was only one live-in servant, but the insurance company had told her that he, as well as the daytime maid, were given time off while the Worthingtons were out of town. No one was due back until after Labor Day. The last person to lock up the house must have forgotten to turn on the security system, she reasoned. She better remember to do so when she left. There's no way she wanted to be blamed if someone broke in and stole the family jewels.

Secure in her reasoning, she walked down the elegantly appointed foyer past an antique red lacquer Chinese side table displaying a small collection of celadon pottery. She picked up a delicate vase to admire more closely just as a cold blast from a nearby air-conditioning duct hit her bare arms. She immediately put the vase back on the table and thought she better hurry and get this job done before she froze to death.

The deeper she moved into the house, the colder she felt. Dressed in summer-weight blue denim overalls, a little white silk shell and flat Jimmy Choo sandals, Lorna looked for a shawl or a blanket that she could throw over her shoulders. She never even considered that the Worthingtons would leave their air-conditioner on while they were away. Or maybe the manservant or housekeeper, whatever he's called, forgot to turn it off when he forgot to turn on the alarm.

She scanned the walls for a thermostat but couldn't find one. Her toes felt like they were about to break off when she remembered the socks at the bottom of her canvas bag. Lorna always carried a pair of white ankle socks in the summer. She learned after her first month working as a production assistant on the soap opera "One Life To Live" that no matter how hot it was outside her feet were always cold in the air-conditioned studio. Five minutes in a movie theater, a TV studio or an editing room and her feet were freezing if she didn't have socks on. She was vain enough that she liked to show off her painted toenails in sandals, but not vain enough to suffer if they got cold. She cautiously sat on a delicate bamboo chair and put the soft cotton socks over her icy feet. She remained seated for a moment, reveling in the feeling of her toes warming.

To her right was the entrance to the living room. Her toes back to normal, she decided to start there. When she walked in, the beauty of the room took her breath away. Authentic antique Aubusson rugs. Pale yellow and rose floral fabrics covered the sofas and hung from the high encasement windows. The woods were rich ebony, and the artwork consisted of mostly Impressionist-style landscapes. With the sun streaming through the windows, Lorna felt she had just walked into a garden in the south of France and for some reason, she was a lot warmer. *This* is Beekman Place, she thought.

She let her canvas bag slip off her shoulder to the floor near the archway, then unbuckled one of the flaps, took out an inventory list and leafed through it. She found the page she was looking for, studied it, then readied her camera and began shooting. "Mr. and Mrs. Scott Worthington of Beekman Place," she said, slating the tape.

After she finished a general sweep of the room, Lorna focused on a single statue situated on a concrete pedestal. "Number one: a pre-Colombian statue of a very ugly man."

She moved to a four foot ancient urn that burst with an arrangement of dried flowers. "Number two: one really old urn. Pre-Colombian, pre-Christ, pre-Noah, maybe *the* original urn."

She chuckled to herself then pointed the video camera at a beautiful grand piano. "Number three: your basic Steinway Grand. No home should be without one. Number four: resting nonchalantly on the piano a letter, framed in antique silver, signed by..." She zoomed in closer.

"Leonard Bernstein!" She whistled. "Wow! I want to live here."

She moved her sights to a large painting hung above the sofa. "Number five on the menu: Chagall under glass." As Lorna pointed her camera straight at the painting a man walked in behind her. He quickly ducked out of the room before she saw him or his reflection in the glass covering the painting.

"Five feet wide and four feet high," she continued then checked the inventory list.

"Number six: 17th century—-"

Pauline Lawson walked into the room.

"What the hell are you doing?" she barked.

Startled, Lorna's body flinched at the sudden intrusion. "God, you scared me! You're not supposed to be here for two more weeks."

"Really," Pauline said imperiously, her eyebrows lifting ever so slightly.

"You're not the housekeeper, are you?" Lorna asked as she turned off her camera.

"Hardly. Now who are you and what are you doing here?"

"Back at ya."

"Pauline Lawson, a dear friend of Kathryn's, something I'm positive you are not," Pauline snapped as she started punching in numbers on her cell phone.

"Wait. I'm Lorna Raven of Raven's Video." Lorna bent down and pulled a card out of a side pocket of her canvas bag. She gave it to Pauline. "We hire out for weddings, birthday parties, anniversaries, reunions, you know, celebrations."

"None of which is going on here." Pauline turned and saw her own reflection clearly on the glass covering the Chagall. She looked at Lorna's video camera on the floor.

"We also freelance for insurance companies," Lorna explained.

Preoccupied with her reflection and the video camera, Pauline hadn't realized Lorna was still talking. "Excuse me?" she asked.

"We tape things so people have a record."

Pauline continued to stare at her own reflection.

"You know, so they can prove they're rich in case they're robbed." Lorna rattled on as she searched her bag and dragged out the Worthington keys. "See. Keys. Up and up."

Pauline's attention was, once again, focused on Lorna. "Kathryn told me nothing about you and, while I'm her house guest, I will not allow anyone else in her home."

"Fine. Call her and she'll explain everything."

"She and Scott are in Kenya on safari and can't be reached."

"Then call the insurance company," Lorna said persistently.

"Why don't I just call the police," Pauline snapped back.

"All right, I'm going." Frustrated, and not wanting the hassle, Lorna picked up her gear and hurried into the foyer. Pauline followed. Lorna opened the front door, but Pauline pushed it shut. "The keys?" she demanded.

Lorna looked her straight into her eyes, and dredged up all the bravado she could muster: "Girls from Queens don't give out their keys." She opened the door and walked out, slamming it behind her.

Standing on the sidewalk with no cabs in sight, Lorna dialed her cell phone. She stared at the front door of the townhouse until someone answered. "Vivian, let me speak to Joe." While she held on, she kept thinking about Pauline Lawson and who the hell she thought she was. Beekman Place didn't defeat Barbra and it was not going to defeat her. She started walking toward First Avenue.

"Joe, what the hell is going on? I told you guys we were going to do the Worthington job today. Who the hell is Pauline Lawson? She threw me outta there before I even got started."

As she was talking, Lorna realized that she was no longer cold. She began to calm down. "Look, Joe. The Worthingtons are your company's clients and I still have to bill them for this morning. Call me when you find out what's going on." She threw her cell back into her canvas bag then stopped walking, bent down and removed her little white socks, throwing them into the bag as well.

From a window, Pauline watched, furious with herself, as Lorna disappeared around a corner. What possessed me to give that silly girl my real name, she thought. I'm smarter than that! I don't care how annoying she was, I should have thought before opening my mouth. I've got to take care of this. She walked to the back of the house and into the sun room. She went to a window overlooking the East River and watched for a moment while the police and FBI boats dragged the river for Senator Lauder's body.

chapter

FOUR

Lorna walked out of the West 79th Street subway station and took a deep breath. It wasn't even noon and the temperature was already over a hundred, but for the moment it seemed cool. No matter how carefully she chose, if she had to take a subway on a hot summer day she always found herself in a car with no air-conditioning. The one consolation for this torture came when she left the oppressive heat and pungent smells of underground New York and stepped out onto the street. It was then that the city air seemed sweetest…fresh and cool like a spring day in the hills of Vermont. Of course, by the time she walked half a block her body temperature readjusted and the heat and humidity had returned.

Her long mass of uncontrollable curls was getting bigger by the minute as the smells of the street once again assaulted her. There was only one thing that could save this disastrous morning…a Pinky's double bacon cheeseburger with Swiss, crisp fries and an ice-cold diet coke. She fumbled in her bag for her cell phone and punched in the numbers she knew by heart.

"Hey, Anthony, it's me, Lorna. I need a fix to go," she said, pausing to take a deep, suffocating, hot and acrid breath. "See you in five."

Sweaty, frustrated and still just plain pissed off, she lugged her video camera and canvas bag down the block to her office in an old deco building two doors from the corner. The intoxicating smell emanating from the brown paper bag she was carrying prodded her to reach her destination with the promise of a sinful culinary experience. She didn't care if it was chock full of a million grams of fat.

Evidently, someone also didn't care if a terrorist or gang banger got into the building, because once again the lobby door was wide open. Did the culprit think a breeze would flush out the sweltering heat and musty smell caused by the original purple and gold velvet furniture—- furniture she doubted had been truly cleaned since the 50's? The building's maintenance crew, however, did vacuum the faded area rugs, mop the marble floors and polish the brass wall sconces, so she really shouldn't complain. Yeh, right.

She sighed with relief when she saw that the old gilt elevator was on the ground floor. The door creaked open when she pressed the "up" button. She got in and rested her video camera on the floor, pushed "six" and leaned against the back wall, breathing in the cheeseburger fumes as the car began its ascent. Though the shiny brass and the smoked glass mirrors gave the elevator a certain charm, Lorna was losing her patience as it stopped on the third floor to pick up a passenger, only to let him out again on the fourth floor. My food's gonna get cold, she thought, then laughed out loud. Nothing could get cold in this weather.

When the elevator door finally opened on "six," she hurried down the hall past numerous office doors boasting suite numbers and company names. She couldn't remember the last time she saw anyone go in or out of any of these offices, but didn't think any more about it since her head was pounding and she was still too upset with her day. Between her face-to-face with Pauline Lawson and the extreme temperatures she was beginning to understand why people picked up Uzis and fired into crowds. If one more clammy body had brushed up against her bare arm in that subway she would have gone berserk. In fact, if this heat wave didn't break soon, she was positive the whole city would go berserk.

At the far end of the hall, she stopped at a door with "Raven's Video Co." stenciled on the opaque glass. The door was locked. She struggled with her video camera as she fumbled in her canvas bag for her keys, wondering where the hell Poe was. He was supposed to finish Ted's carpet commercial today. She shook the canvas bag. "Damn it, I know you're in there."

She fumbled some more, than pulled out what looked like a metal crochet hook. She put it behind her ear, shook the canvas bag again and reached in. "This is ridiculous."

She dropped the canvas bag, put down the video camera holding tight to her brown paper bag, then took the metal hook from behind her ear and deftly picked the lock. A feeling of triumph came over her. "Thank you, Tony Natale," she said to herself then smiled as she remembered her high school friend turned second-story burglar. He had tried to impress her when he gave her one of his cherished lock picks. But she refused to have dinner with him until he taught her how to use it. She thought of that steak dinner at Peter Luger's as her brief walk on the wild side. And, the last she heard he was spending a few years at Ossining. A tinge of sadness washed over her at the thought of her old friend in jail. She gathered her things and entered the miniscule reception area.

She switched on the light. A very large, black-and-white photograph of people at a New York street fair hung on the "Swiss coffee" white painted wall behind a pine desk. She remembered the day she and Poe signed their lease. They had been hunting for office space for weeks, concentrating in Chelsea and lower Manhattan...closer to their homes. Nothing they found was in their budget so they were forced to look farther and farther uptown. When they found this space already equipped with an editing bay, they grabbed it. It didn't matter to them that the building was rundown or that the elevator often didn't work, it was in their price range, in a hip area and close to the subway. At least they weren't commuting from the suburbs.

She kicked the front door closed, then picked up the mail off the floor under the mail slot. Her canvas bag fell off her shoulder. She hoisted it up, but her video camera slipped off the other shoulder. As she tried to get it together, she dropped the mail. Feeling like she was in the middle of some kind of Jim Carrey slapstick riff, she managed to get it together. With her equipment and mail securely in her possession, she walked down a short hallway to her office.

Upon entering the large room she once described as "early-IKEA," Lorna let her bag and camera slip off her shoulder and tossed the mail onto her desk. More large, framed black-and-white photos hung on the white walls...photos of cabaret singers, street people, children playing in a rush of water from a fire hydrant, crowds of people shopping on the lower east side, a violinist playing on the steps of the Forty-Second Street library. The whir of an old window air-conditioner blocked out the street noise below.

Before she even sat down, Lorna tore open the brown paper bag, popped a few fries into her mouth as she unwrapped her juicy bacon cheeseburger and took a huge bite. Savoring the moment, she chewed slowly, swallowed then took another huge bite. Having reached food nirvana, she methodically went through the mail, muttering to herself as she chewed and tossed each bill onto her desk, "Your check is in the mail. Your check is in the mail. Your check is in cyberspace. Your check is in the mail."

She looked at her answering machine and saw that it had twenty-three messages. She knew from the slew of messages on the machine earlier that morning that most of these would be people wanting to see or buy the Lauder Circle Line boat party/murder tape. She let out an exasperated sigh then shoved some more fries into her mouth, wondering why anyone would eat cake under stress. To her nothing was better than a rare burger on a big bun—with or without cheese and a mountain of *pomme frites*.

Knowing she was in no mood to wade through her voice mail and e-mails for any real job offers, she snatched up the remains of her cholesterol festival, along with her camera and canvas bag and headed to the editing room across the hall. She opened the door and found Poe sitting in the dark, bare feet up on the editing bay console listening to music through his head phones and watching the Circle Line tape. Images of the party filled the monitor. Poe absentmindedly played with one of his wind-up toys as Lorna hit the lights, startling him. He pulled off his head phones.

"Jesus! You nearly gave me a heart attack," he said as he guiltily shut off the Circle Line tape.

"Damn it, Poe, that's not Ted's commercial!" she snapped. She tossed her food onto her side of the editing bay, spilling fries all over the console. "And the front door's locked! How's anyone gonna know we're open for business if you're here and the door's locked? Huh?" She put her camera down on the floor then dumped the contents of her canvas bag onto the gray metal worktable behind her, almost knocking the phone off. Poe watched his sister search through her debris looking for her keys.

"Ever think of de-cluttering?" Poe asked.

"Don't start with me, Poe. I've had a very bad day."

She finally found her keys, then meticulously divided the rest of her belongings into two piles, as she snuck another bite of her bacon cheeseburger and a few more fries, then swept one pile off the table into a wastepaper basket and put the other pile, including her keys and the Worthington keys back into her canvas bag.

"De-cluttered. Happy?" She plopped down in her chair and continued to devour her food as if it were her last meal. Poe stared in amazement. Suddenly, Lorna spun around and faced her brother.

"Aren't you at least going to have the decency to ask me what's wrong?" she asked accusingly, her mouth full of food.

Except for the rumbling of another ancient air-conditioner, the room was silent.

"What's wrong?" he asked dutifully.

"This day!"

Poe waited patiently for Lorna to continue, knowing that if he said one wrong word, life as he knew it would be over.

"I got tossed out of the townhouse!" she continued.

"The Worthington townhouse?"

"Was I shooting any other townhouse?"

"OK. What happened?

"Some house-sitting bitch said I had no right to be there, blah, blah, blah and I'm out on the street."

"So you got nothing?"

No, Poe, I didn't get "nothing." I got some really ugly artwork, a very expensive piano and a Chagall."

"Chagall? My favorite painter and I'm not looking at it right now?! Are you nuts?"

"No, just pissed."

"Very pissed?" Poe asked, as he wound up one of his toys.

"Yes."

"Outraged?"

"Yes."

"Burning?"

"Yes!"

"Hopping mad?"

"Yes."

Poe let loose the wind-up toy, a miniature hamburger with feet. Its tongue darted in and out as it "walked" along the edit bay.

"In a pucker?"

Lorna laughed. He always seemed to know just what to do to make her see how foolish things can be and she loved him for that. She rolled her chair over to him, leaned forward and hugged him.

"This is serious, Poe" she said as she took hold of his hands. "We need to pay the rent. Circle Line tape, no. Casta Carpets, yes."

"It's done! All I gotta do is sweeten and online it. Just show me the Chagall first."

Lorna rolled over to the work table and rummaged through her canvas bag. She pulled out a tape and popped it into an empty drive.

The interior of the Worthington house came up on the monitor. Lorna's voice filled the room, "Mr. and Mrs. Scott Worthington of Beekman Place. Number one: a pre-Colombian statue of a very ugly man."

Lorna devoured some more French fries as she turned down the Worthington audio and fast-forwarded the tape to the painting.

"By the way, kiddo, there's a skazillion messages from people who want to see the Lauder tape," Lorna said as she stopped the tape on the Chagall. "You better deal with them."

"To hell with 'em. The FBI and New York's finest have copies of the tape. If they wanna to see it, they can deal with *them*."

Lorna's voice again filled the room, "Number five on the menu: Chagall under glass."

"Beautiful. Beautiful," Poe gushed. He rolled his chair over to Lorna's area and froze the frame, just as a person's silhouette appeared on the painting. "Look at that, it's signed and everything."

Lorna looked.

"What the hell's that?"

"What?"

"That blur. What is that? I don't do blurs!"

Poe fiddled with the buttons. The silhouette became a bit more defined.

"It looks like somebody..." she continued.

"Yeh...somebody who ruined a perfectly good Chagall," Poe interrupted as he froze the image again.

"Probably that bitch who threw me out."

"'Bitch' would be female. This is no female."

"What?"

"That's a man, kiddo. Or one very large woman."

Lorna looked at the image more closely.

"You're right." Disgusted, she reached for the "eject" button, but Poe stopped her.

"No, no, no. Leave it up."

"Whatever."

Poe played with some knobs on the console, making the Chagall image sharper. He moved closer to the monitor. Something about the image bothered him.

"What are you doing?"

Poe ignored her question as he unfroze the image of the Circle Line party on the other monitor at his end of the edit bay. He fast-forwarded until he found what he was looking for. He froze the tape on a clear image of Senator Lauder, who stood with his head tilted in a similar stance as the person in the Chagall "blur." The images were eerily similar and he started to say something to Lorna, but stopped.

"What?" she asked.

"Nothing," he answered as he tried to sharpen the silhouette even more.

"Come on, Poe. What are you doing?"

"OK. Seem odd to you that this blur looks like that guy's shadow?" Poe said as he points to Senator Lauder and the Chagall blur.

"Some ink blots look like Abraham Lincoln. So what?"

"I'll tell you what!" For starters they haven't found Lauder's body yet."

"It's a big river," Lorna quipped.

"OK. Where do the Worthingtons live?"

"Beekman Place."

"Yeh. Right on the river! When Lauder took his dive the last thing he could have seen was that house on the distant shoreline."

"Right. And with a bullet in his chest, he swam to shore, climbed up to the house and moved in."

Poe ignored her.

"Ah, hell, Poe. Are you going to start this stuff again?"

"Come on. If this is Senator Lauder then he's risen from the dead. That's a miracle that should at least make the local news."

"Fine. Then let local news cover it," Lorna said, her anger rising. "It's not your job anymore."

"Damn it Lorna, we're better than this! We're better than shooting bar mitzvah brouhahas and piss-ass commercials."

"If this is so beneath you, then go back to the network…Oh right, the network doesn't want you anymore," she said icily as she stormed out of the editing room.

Poe was still playing with the blurred image when Lorna walked back into the editing room a few minutes later.

"I'm sorry, Poe. But, you promised to give this business a fighting chance," she said pleadingly as she held back her tears.

"I am," he answered. "Every chance I get, we fight."

Lorna shook her head as she picked up the phone. "I'm calling the insurance company back and tell them either that witch lets me finish my job or…"

Poe took the phone out of her hand and hung it up.

"Hold on. Hold on. Let me take a crack at her."

"And you can do better because…?"

"I have sex appeal?"

Lorna whacked him and the tension between them was broken. He laughed as he stole the last bite of her cheeseburger.

"You know how excited I was about that shoot, Poe. I wanted to see everything in that house. I wanted to see how people live on Beekman Place. I wanted…"

"I know. I'm sorry."

"All right. Go do your *charm* thing."

She searched through the remaining hundreds of things in her canvas bag looking for the Worthington keys.

"Never mind, I'll wing it," Poe said as he grabbed his equipment bag and left the office.

Jefferson Leeds was on a mission. He needed to see the footage taken of Lauder's assassination. He had to know if he was in any background shots on that tape. But if he went to the FBI or the local police handling the investigation, Fowler would know he was in New York

Ilona Joy Saari

snooping around the assassination. If he wasn't on the tape he wanted Fowler to remain ignorant of his whereabouts. However, if he *was* on that tape, he'd need to come up with a plausible reason for being on that boat before Fowler saw it. His only other source for the tape was Raven's Video. He had to be careful how he approached them. Lorna Raven was a neophyte and therefore, no threat. But he remembered her brother from television...Alan Raven was no neophyte. He was just about to enter the old deco building where they had their office when Poe rushed out, his equipment bag over his shoulder. He stopped and watched as Poe hurried past him. Jefferson thought a moment then followed him.

chapter

FIVE

Poe approached the Worthington townhouse and studied the building carefully before walking up to the front door. As Lorna had done, he noticed the discreet nameplate and used his thumb to wipe away a smudge. The heat didn't seem to bother him as he buzzed again and again and again. Across the street Jefferson stood in the shadows, watching. Certainly one way to win someone's affections, Jefferson thought...buzz them into submission.

"Hello? Ms. Lawson, are you in there?" Poe yelled out.

Pauline was furious that someone was yelling out her name at the front door drawing attention to the house. She had to shut him up before the neighbors became suspicious. She opened the door.

"May I help you?" she asked, her voice chilling the torrid air.

Poe's reporter's training kicked in as he memorized everything about her. Her platinum blonde hair was pulled back off her face and into a knot. She wore no earrings. Her beige linen trousers barely had a wrinkle and her sleeveless, white vest fitted snuggly over her braless breasts, accentuating her tanned chest and arms. She wore a man's gold Rolex on one bare wrist and a dozen wire-thin gold bangles on the other. No rings on her fingers. She was tall, slim and barefoot. Her dark blue eyes stared into his and he thought she was one of the most stunning women he had ever seen. Regal.

Not missing a beat, he handed her his business card.

"Alan Raven, ma'am," he said on his best Cary Grant behavior. "And may I say Lorna was right."

"I beg your pardon."

"My partner. She was here earlier? Said the woman of the house was movie star beautiful."

"Save it, Mr. Raven. And I would appreciate it if—-"

"I just need to shoot a few more things," Poe blurted out, cutting her off. He tried to wiggle past her, but she quickly blocked him.

"Just a quick spritz around the place...the insurance company'll be happy, I'll be happy and—-

"I'm not in the business of making people happy," Pauline interrupted.

"And what business *would* you—-"

Pauline closed the door in his face.

"...be in?"

Inside the townhouse, Pauline hurried to the back sunroom, banging into a chair as she reached for a pair of binoculars on a nearby occasional table. She rushed over to the wall of windows and looked past the townhouse's beautiful rose garden, down to the river and the FDR Drive that ran parallel to it. Traffic whizzed by, the drivers oblivious to the drama taking place nearby as FBI and NYPD boats dragged the river in search of Senator Lauder's body. A frogman pulled himself out of the water onto a floating boat. Men and women, some in NYPD uniforms, searched the shoreline. In the distance, on the Long Island City side of the river, more people were searching for any sign of the Senator.

After a few frustrating minutes of searching, Pauline spotted the little bastard. Yes, she almost yelled out! She knew it! That persistent son of a bitch with a door buzzer fetish is here for something more than a lousy insurance job! She watched Poe walk up to a uniformed cop on the shoreline and take out a narrow notepad. Anger and an overwhelming sense of foreboding enveloped her. She had recognized him the minute she had opened the door but just didn't know *where* she'd seen him before. But now she remembered. Alan Raven! It'd been awhile since she had seen him on television, but she knew he was a reporter. Now the question was...who was *Lorna* Raven? Were they really hired to videotape the Worthington possessions or were they here for a story?

Poe suddenly looked up at the townhouse and Pauline quickly moved away from the window. A few moments later, she snuck a look and saw him walk to the foot ramp that crossed over the FDR Drive. He climbed the stairs that headed back to Beekman Place and disappeared out of sight.

"Am I still dead?"

Startled, Pauline turned and faced Hap Lauder who sat in a large wing-backed chair holding a glass of melting ice cubes. He needed a shave. Funny, she thought, all the years she'd known him and even these past few years when their relationship crossed the line from friends to lovers, she didn't remember him ever needing a shave. Not even on those rare occasions when they woke up together.

"I think somebody's hoping to resurrect you," she answered.

Hap got up and went to the bar for a refill. Screw the ice cubes, he thought as he dumped the remains into the ice bucket. More room for the booze. His hand trembled slightly as he picked up the bottle of scotch as if it were a carton of eggs then carefully filled his glass to the rim. He stared into the liquid, the rich amber color somehow giving him comfort. He smiled...or was it the aged malt taste?

He took a sip and tried to remember what real comfort felt like—- the comfort of your own home or the comfort you felt in the company of someone you loved. He wondered if people confused comfort with safety. Had he ever felt safe? Was he ever comforted? He didn't think so. Maybe in his mother's womb, but even that was questionable when he remembered how cold and distant she was when he was *out* of the womb. He took a big sip. Well, if he ever did feel comforted or safe, he doubted he'd ever feel that way again. Oh, hell, he thought, the whole issue was moot anyway. He turned his attention back to Pauline who was again looking out the window through her binoculars.

"You know he's a reporter, don't you? I recognized him from the boat," he stated matter-of-factly.

"We'll be fine. Don't panic."

"I don't panic. I would just like to get out of the country before I have to watch my own funeral."

She put down her binoculars. "According to Kipper, you've been dead and buried for years now."

"Jesus, how could I have married someone named Kipper?" he remarked as he placed his untouched drink on the bar.

"Oh, come on now, look at the bright side——- watching your own funeral does have a certain cachet, doesn't it?"

"Don't try to humor a dead man."

Pauline rubbed his shoulders, trying to ease his tension.

"We can't stay here anymore, Pauline."

He was right to worry, she thought. We need to get out of here before Raven or someone else comes snooping around. She watched as Hap picked up his drink, lost in his thoughts and fears. Why, she asked herself, did she always get involved with weak men? Her mistake was in believing he was strong. He had been powerful…Christ, he was a United States Senator! Yet, he had never learned that being in control of your life was an illusion——- that you had to have an inner reserve to keep it together when things fractured.

"Was she very upset?" he asked, feeling a little guilty for the way he had treated his wife over the years. He may not have really loved her, but they *had* built a life together. No one could have asked for a better political wife. He had relied on her advice throughout his career, but when politics lost its adrenalin rush he had moved further away from her. He changed. He lusted for a new way to feel powerful and manipulate events. Then he had met Pauline's Russian "friends"…friends living on the edge, becoming filthy rich in the black market. The rush had returned when he surreptitiously started using his insider's access to government plans to help them smuggle in guns to home grown terrorists…enjoying the challenge of staying one step in front of the ATF then capping the "high" by anonymously informing on those terrorists. He smiled. A win-win situation as far as he was concerned. But his smile faded. It had been a year of secret phone calls, clandestine meetings and secret bank accounts that made his heart race with excitement. But, the thrill was gone the minute he had splashed into the sludge of the East River. The life he had taken for granted was over. That realization nearly paralyzed him in the water. The fear of living in some third world country with no extradition for the rest of his life was only rivaled by the fear of being exposed and going to jail.

"Of course she was upset. So was I." Pauline answered, not wanting to talk about this. She was afraid he was having second thoughts and, like most men when trapped, would do something stupid.

"I'm sorry, what?" he asked forgetting that he had asked her a question.

"Your wife. Of course she was upset."

He remembered now. "You didn't have to go see her, Pauline."

"Yes, I did. She was my friend long before you and I got involved."

"You were my friend, too, if I recall."

He stared into his glass as he swirled the liquid around, watching the empty part of the glass turn amber, then clear again as the scotch slid down its sides. He brought the glass to his mouth and drank until it there wasn't a drop left. Pauline smiled ruefully. If this stress continued much longer it wouldn't matter if Hap cracked, they'd both be dead from alcohol poisoning before they ever got out of this house.

"In any case," she continued, "she's upset but suspects nothing. We talked to your kids."

"How are they?" he asked as he put the glass down on the bar and joined her at the window.

"Devastated."

Now it was Hap's turn to massage *her* shoulders.

She tried to let his fingers release some of the tension that had been building since the night of the Circle Line fundraiser. But the stress of being forced to leave the townhouse and make new arrangements to get him out of the country caused the muscles in her shoulders to tighten up painfully.

Hap abruptly stopped the massage and went back to the bar for more scotch, trying to blot out the memory of being in that filthy river…his blood-soaked tuxedo weighing him down like a cement suit. Whose blood was *in* that blood-pack, he asked himself as he sipped his drink. Was it even human? But before he could follow up on that thought, his mind went back to the river. He had only been in the water for a few moments when he had felt his panic rising like bile in the back of his throat. The water had engulfed him like a slimy sarcophagus. He had to breathe. He had frantically begun to swim to the surface, when suddenly someone had grabbed his leg and pulled him down. Before he completely panicked a breathing apparatus had been forced into his mouth and he remembered the ex-Navy SEAL that they had hired to help him swim underwater to safety. He had taken a few deep breaths to calm down, then focused on taking off his shoes and jacket. The SEAL had helped him put on a small scuba tank as they swam toward the shore where someone else was waiting to get him out of the water and safely into the townhouse as the SEAL sank out of sight.

He shivered at the memory.

She instinctively walked over to him and kissed him.

He ran his hands down her back then up the front. He unbuttoned her vest, slipped it off her shoulders then cupped her breasts in his hands. He desperately needed to escape his inner terror and lose himself, if only for a moment. As his passion rose, Pauline's cell rang. She grabbed his hands and kissed them as she answered, then handed the phone to him. As Hap listened, she watched his passion turn to fury.

"Look, I handled my end. I kissed ass with that nicotine-stained Russian Mafioso and got you the information needed for you to peddle those guns to every wacko in the country."

Pauline stared at him, praying that he didn't have a heart attack, then praying that he did. She was losing her patience. She didn't know how much longer she could deal with his whining self-pity.

"Yes, and now we have a dead phony assassin in New York to add to a dead government agent in Idaho. And don't tell me he was getting close; I *know* he was getting close. Isn't that why we faked my assassination?" As he listened, Hap tried to reign in his fear and anger, but failed. "God damn it, this whole thing is out of control! No one was supposed to get killed! And now we have a reporter sniffing at our door."

He listened for a moment then calmly said, "Just get me the fuck outta here." Hap threw the phone onto the sofa.

"No one was supposed to get killed?! You were supplying guns to militias for God's sake!" Pauline exclaimed.

"Don't flatter them by calling those half-assed, half-cocked Saturday soldiers a fucking militia. And you know I don't let them *keep* those guns!"

"I don't know anything anymore. Smuggling guns, abandoning your children…"

"Oh, for Christ's sake, Pauline, don't start getting self-righteous. My children are adults."

"Adults don't have feelings?"

Whatever passion Hap had felt for her a few minutes earlier had left him. "I'd rather have them upset by my death than embarrassed because I'm in prison for treason."

Pauline picked up her vest and put it on.

"Look, you know how it worked," he explained. "After we're paid, the local police in New York, North Carolina, Idaho or wherever else these *militias* swarm get anonymous tips. The police are all over their asses before they get the guns out of the crates. Voila, the good guys get the guns and some of those assholes get arrested. When you think about it, I should get the medal of freedom!"

Ilona Joy Saari

***

Poe headed to the west side on foot. He didn't care if it was 200 degrees, he needed to calm down. The long hike across and up town back to the office would do just that. He had to think. He knew he was onto something. Something big. Something was going on in the Worthington townhouse. Instinctively he knew it had to do with the Senator. It wasn't Pauline Lawson's image on the Chagall. So whose was it? And it's just too coincidental that the townhouse overlooked the east river where the Senator took his swan dive. And why did the Worthingtons hire us to videotape their townhouse if their houseguests weren't going to let us do the job? And where was Lauder's body?

His head hurt as these thoughts and questions raced through his mind. He needed to do some digging.

He picked up his pace. A half a block behind, Jefferson did as well.

chapter

SIX

Some days just weren't worth the effort. Or at least, that was what Lorna was thinking as she navigated herself into her loft building. Because she had absolutely nothing in the house to eat or drink, not a can of tuna or a tea bag (well, she did have wine and coffee, but that didn't count), she had stopped at D'Agostino's to pick up some "Lorna" staples. Consequently, she was now lugging two large grocery bags, plus her large canvas bag. She thanked god she didn't have her video camera. But, it really wouldn't have mattered. She'd still have to put the bags down, find her keys, open the front door, then pick up the bags just to enter her building. No one ever said living in Manhattan was easy. She wondered if people in other cities experienced the weather as if it were a stalker in their lives. No matter where she went the last few days or what she wore, her body was continually damp from the sweltering humidity in the air. Humidity?! She had to laugh. Steam bath was more like it.

She walked across her little vestibule and was able to push the elevator button without putting the bags down again, but to get into her loft Lorna knew the "bags down, bags up" dance would have to be repeated. It was late and she was exhausted just thinking about it.

When she finally made it safely into her loft, she put the groceries on the kitchen area island, poured herself a glass of chilled chardonnay and immediately switched on her window air-conditioner. She stood a moment as the cooling air noisily blew on her damp skin. She took a long sip of wine. Actually "sip" was too polite a word. She gulped it. Feeling refreshed, she went back into the kitchen and started to put away her perishables. Of course, with so many preservatives, "perishables" was a stretch. Into the fridge went a package of Nathan's hot dogs, a brick of Velveeta cheese, a quart of milk, some bologna and packaged ham. Into the freezer…a half-dozen boxes of frozen Lean Cuisine dinners, a box of White Castle hamburgers and a few Wolfgang Puck pizzas (her concession to fine dining). She pulled open the crisper drawer and threw in a head of lettuce and a tomato (her concession to health food).

She opened the cabinet she used as a pantry, took another big sip of wine then finished emptying her grocery bags…two cans of tuna and some Hellmann's mayo, a jar of chunky Jiff, a few cans of deviled ham, and a box of Paul Newman micro-wave popcorn were soon sitting proudly on the shelves. Last, but not least, she pulled out a six pack of diet Coke, a bag of Ruffles, a package of hot dog rolls and a loaf of Wonder Bread and left them on the counter. She laughed…haute cuisine this was not. By the time the bags were empty her wine was gone. She poured herself another glass and collapsed onto a chaise that she had found on the street and slip-covered in a vintage pink-and-white striped fabric.

She kicked off her shoes, took a deep breath and this time really sipped her wine. She loved her loft and doubted she would ever live anywhere else where she'd feel more comfortable. When she had found this space two years ago it was a mess. The prior owners had done nothing but let it deteriorate. The windows had been filthy and the floors covered in grime, but Lorna thought the space was spectacular. Grecian style pillars from a past incarnation stood like ancient sentinels in the middle of the loft. One wall of eight-foot windows left over from its sweatshop days let in the sun by day and the lights of lower Manhattan by night.

The first thing she had done after the cleaning crew had finished was white-wash everything...the brick walls, the pipes and radiators, even the old scraped up, wooden plank floors. An ex-boyfriend built her a ceiling-to-floor library wall half the length of the loft, complete with a sliding ladder. She arranged her living room and office areas in front of this wall filled with her books, CDs, video tapes and DVDs. The couch, like the chaise, was covered in the same faded striped fabric. Her office desk, side tables and dining table were all old pine farm pieces she had found at a flea market on Long Island. And, the living spaces were delineated by very worn, faded, floral hooked rugs, 20x30-foot creations that she had bought at bargain basement prices at an auction. Hanging on the whitewashed walls were more large black-and-white photographs.

The downstairs doorbell rang. She looked at her kitchen clock. Six-thirty. She spoke into the building intercom.

"Who is it?"

"It's me, sweetheart."

Lorna recognized the voice of her Aunt Helen and buzzed her in.

As she waited for Helen, she took out another wine glass, tore open the bag of Ruffles and dumped the chips into a plastic bowl on the counter. She foraged in her pantry for the deviled ham. She mixed it with a bit of mayo and a little sweet relish.

"Voila!" she said proudly as she put her dip alongside the chips. Hors d'oeuvres in place, she opened the door before her aunt could knock.

Helen was a fifty-two year old elementary school principal...a "menopausally" plump whirling dervish with Lorna's high cheekbones and Poe's nervous energy. She gave her niece a quick peck on the cheek as she walked into the loft carrying a large grocery bag.

"Sweetheart, I only have a minute. I'm meeting Maryann at the theater," she said without taking a breath. "Another Albee revival she's dragging me to, but I just wanted to drop in and bring you a few groceries."

Lorna laughed. "You came all the way into town for the theater, yet you schlepped down to Soho to bring me groceries?

"Well, sweetheart, I know you forget to eat healthfully sometimes and it's not like I'm in Manhattan all that much to check up on you. Just consider this a "two birds with one stone stop," she explained. She nibbled on some chips, ignoring Lorna's dip as she unpacked the bag, putting fruit into a bowl and some boneless, skinless chicken breasts and veggies into the refrigerator. She was folding the now empty bag when she noticed the wine glass on the counter.

"Is this for me? Well, of course it is." She opened the fridge again, found the open wine and gave herself a hefty pour. She brought the glass to her nose, sniffed then drank it down.

"God, that tastes good. It's hotter than hell here and I thought Queens was bad with all the brown-outs. My house is an oven at four o'clock."

She looked at her beautiful niece. The worst and best day of her life was when her sister and brother-in-law were killed in an auto accident and she took their young children to raise as her own. To keep from uprooting their lives totally, she gave up her own apartment near her school in Forest Hills and moved into their home in Bayside.

She put the glass back down on the counter. "OK, I'm off! I expect you and your brother for dinner Sunday. Leg of lamb with mint jelly, Poe's favorite."

"I don't know, Aunt Helen."

"No excuses," she said sternly then kissed Lorna and gave her a big hug. "I love you. And please eat something green to go with your sodium nitrate."

Lorna laughed as Helen whisked herself out the door. "I love you, too."

After relocking the door, Lorna checked her computer for e-mails, but nothing seemed interesting or worth opening. She tried her answering machine.

"Hey, doll, Broderick—- I'm your business manager, not a juggler. Call me." Lorna shut off the machine, not wanting to hear any more bad news. Her eyes panned the loft, taking in all the things she loved. She had worked hard to get this home, working her way up from production assistant to a producer in daytime TV. She *really*, *dearly* wished that Poe would put his whole heart into their video business before it went bust.

It was time he got his act together, she thought for the hundredth time. So what if he'd been a hot-shot TV reporter covering the Beltway...hobnobbing it with the powers that be. He didn't have to have a hissy fit just because the network hired a "name" partisan pundit over him to cover the White House.

She knew she was being harsh, but Poe had a quick temper and often acted without thinking. Look what it cost him!

Back in New York he had landed a stint at local WNBC that tried capitalizing on his network credentials. But, a year later he was still there and going nowhere else. When Lorna suggested that they quit their jobs and start their own documentary film company, he was all for it.

She didn't care that he hated doing the weddings and commercials for local businesses that kept their company afloat. She hated them too. But, they were a means to an end. The Lauder party had been a great gig for them and should open a few more doors. Things *are* getting better, she said to herself.

Lorna looked at her empty wine glass and marveled at the speed of evaporation. She smiled. Must be the heat. She went back into the kitchen, poured herself another and decided she better have some food with the wine. Maybe she'd broil a chicken breast and steam some of Helen's fresh vegetables. Nah, too much work. She popped a Lean Cuisine into the microwave. The low calorie dinner, despite its high sodium content, would balance out her cheeseburger and fries frenzy. She laughed. OK, it wouldn't, but so what?

Almost immediately, she changed her mind. To hell with it. She stopped the timer and threw the dinner back into the freezer. The cheeseburger and wine were rewards for a lousy day, but she still needed another. She wanted something from her other favorite food group...red dye. She opened up the brand-new package of Nathan's Famous, dropped a hot dog into a pan of water and put it on the stove to boil. Hot dogs were best boiled if you wanted to savor the pop of the outer skin and let the dog's juices run into your mouth with each salacious bite. If she didn't have the hot dog bun, the calorie intake wouldn't be higher than the Lean Cuisine, she reasoned. But reason and food weren't compatible as far as Lorna was concerned. She pulled out a roll from the package, took out her new jar of relish and found a squeeze bottle of Dijonnaise mustard. She lined them all up on the butcher block island. Eat your heart out, Emeril.

While she waited for her hot dog to boil, she grabbed her wine and clicked on CNN.

She half-listened as she found a sweet onion that Helen had brought and started chopping. Tears were rolling down her face when she heard a report that a naked man had been found washed ashore in Long Island City, directly across the East River from the U.N.

She stopped chopping and hovered by the TV set. As the anchor continued, Lorna saw FBI and NYPD's finest milling around on screen. EMT workers lifted a covered body onto a stretcher and placed in an ambulance.

"Sources speculate that this is the body of Senator Harold Lauder, but neither the police nor FBI have confirmed these reports."

Naked?!? she thought. Why would Lauder's body be naked?

When the station broke for commercial Lorna hit the mute button and went back to her hot dog. It was boiled to the point of splitting. Just the way she liked it. She shoved the dog into a roll and smothered it with onions, mustard and relish. She held it under her nose and breathed in the fumes as if it were a snifter of aged cognac. Her

70

mouth opened, ready for that long-awaited first bite when she thought she heard the front doorknob rattle. She closed her mouth.

"Did you decide to pass on Albee, Aunt Helen?" she yelled out as she put the hot dog on a plate and walked to the door.

"Aunt Helen?" she called out again.

No answer.

She looked through the peep hole.

No one.

She considered opening the door and checking to see who was outside, but knew better. That's what stupid heroines did in horror movies, she thought. She double-checked all her locks and bolts and for good measure, pulled over a dining room chair and slid it under the doorknob. Maybe her ears were playing tricks on her, but even if they were, she thought it was infinitely better to err on the side of staying alive.

Back in the kitchen she looked forlornly at her hot dog. She pulled tin foil out of a drawer, wrapped up her culinary delight and put it in the refrigerator. She wasn't sure why, but she was no longer hungry. She grabbed her cell and called her brother.

"Hi, it's me. What are you doing?"

Poe could tell something was bothering her and called her on it.

"Nothing. Just thought I heard someone trying to get into my loft. Creeped me out."

She listened as he soothed her fears, talked a little business then told her he was about to leave the office and meet Carol for dinner at Joe Allen. "Why don't you join us. You love their lobster roll."

"Great," she said and meant it. She loved Carol and hoped her brother would marry her one of these days. "I'm too spooked to stay home right now."

She rang off and changed into a pair of old, very faded Levi's and a black pocket tee, smiling to herself when she realized that she had just put on Poe's "uniform." She slipped her "Jelly Apple" pedicured feet into a pair of black flip flops, adorned her arms with her stainless Cartier knock-off watch and a bunch of silver bangles, grabbed her wallet, keys and cell phone and threw them into her vintage, flea market Vuitton shoulder bag.

She carefully opened her front door and looked up and down the hallway. No one. She let out a sigh of relief, unaware she'd been holding her breath as she left the loft and walked to the elevator. Her appetite was back with a vengeance.

A taxi swerved in and out of traffic on West 46th then stopped short in front of Joe Allen. Typical New Yorkers, Poe and Carol got out of the cab, unfazed by the wild ride. As they entered the popular restaurant, a favorite hangout for New York theater actors and dancer gypsies, another taxi pulled up. Poe greeted the maitre'd who led them to a table against the brick wall that divided the restaurant into two rooms. Their table was by one of the large arched cut outs in the wall that allowed diners to view both rooms. Outside, Jefferson slid out of the second cab, casually strolled into the restaurant and took a seat at the long wooden bar.

The moment Poe and Carol sat down, a waiter came to take their drink order. Poe ordered a draft beer for himself and a "perky" pinot grigio for Carol. She smiled as she studied the menu. He admired her cool elegance as they sat in comfortable silence for a few minutes. Her honey blonde hair was off her face and tied in a knot, accentuating her high forehead. She rarely wore make-up, except for a little mascara and pale lip gloss, and tonight was no exception. He wondered for the millionth time how a sardonic "has-been" like him got so lucky as he watched her study her food options. He already knew what he was having, the rarer the better.

"Let me guess—- you're having the grilled fennel and shrimp salad," Carol said, still smiling.

"Yeh, right," he laughed as he saw Lorna walk into the restaurant. He waved.

She waved back as she walked over to the table and sat down just as the waiter brought Poe and Carol's drinks.

"Thanks so much for letting me crash your party, guys. Did Poe tell you?" she asked then laughed nervously. "I really gotta stop reading murder mysteries."

Lorna ordered a glass of chardonnay as Jefferson watched them in the long beveled mirror behind the bar. The bartender poured him a scotch.

Poe really didn't want to spook her any further, but he had to ask. "What exactly did you hear?"

"I don't know. Aunt Helen had left the loft and I was about to have something to eat when my doorknob rattled. At least I thought it was my doorknob. I went to see if she had come back, but when I looked through the peephole, no one was there. Probably just some rat scurrying in a wall."

"Rats don't jiggle doorknobs," Poe couldn't help saying.

Carol smacked his arm. "Poe!" She looked at Lorna. "Don't pay any attention to him. I'm sure it was just an old building doing one of its creaky noise things. My walls and floors talk to me all the time," Carol smiled, but Poe looked concerned.

The waiter returned with Lorna's wine.

"You know what you want?" Poe asked Carol changing the subject.

"Yes. The broiled flounder and new potatoes. Green salad. Dressing on the side, please."

The waiter wrote it down.

"And I'll have the New York strip, rare, mashed potatoes and whatever vegetable comes with it. Lorna? Lobster roll and fries?"

She smiled. "You're asking?"

He looked at the waiter. "And she'll have lobster roll and fries."

The waiter left.

Carol smiled. "Between the two of you, I'm going to get second-hand cholesterol."

The music from Norah Jones latest CD sounded through the loft as Lorna read in bed. The day's papers were spread around her. She thought she would go right to sleep when she got home from Joe Allen, but it just wasn't happening. She kept reliving the day…the Beekman townhouse fiasco; her argument with Poe over the tape; and the uneasy feeling she got when she thought someone was trying to break into her loft. Poe was right—rats don't jiggle.

Lorna glanced at her bedside clock. One-fifteen. She was tired. She searched her bed for the remote and finally found it under a pillow. She turned off the music. She'd will herself to sleep if she had to. She kicked some of the newspapers off the bed and turned off the lights. But it took less than a minute before she was again obsessing over Pauline Lawson. She switched the lights back on and dialed her cell.

"Hello. Can I have an overseas operator, please?" The papers were still strewn at the foot of her bed. She tossed them into a pile on the floor as she waited for the operator. "Yes, would you please connect me with the Mt. Kenya Safari Club?"

She listened as the operator asked where it was located. "Wild guess. It's in Africa," she said and wondered why she was being so snippy.

While she held, she went over her encounter with Pauline one more time. Why did the Worthingtons hire videographers and give them their key to videotape their home while they were gone if their house guest wasn't going to let them in? It made no sense. Finally a hotel operator came on the line. "Hello. Yes, may I speak to Mrs. Scott Worthington?"

When she learned that Mrs. Worthington and her husband were out on a safari and unable to be reached for a while, she decided to get her money's worth out of the call. In painstaking detail, she relayed the whole, sad, Pauline Lawson story to the hotel operator.

"And operator, please tell Mrs. Worthington to call Ms. Lawson and instruct her to let me continue videotaping the contents of her townhouse." That'll show her, she thought, as she rung off.

She picked up the latest Sue Grafton mystery. "OK, Kinsey what mess are you going to find yourself in this time?" Her voice echoed eerily in the loft.

***

Poe sat in front of the editing console working on Ted's carpet commercial, singing along with its inane jingle. He hated sending Carol home alone, but he had promised Lorna during dinner that he'd pull an all-nighter and get it online. He looked at his watch. One-thirty. It was tomorrow. A new day! He stopped the tape, rubbed his eyes and stretched in his seat. It was done. Finally! He snapped his fingers and shouted, "it's a wrap!"

Yup, Lorna's gonna be a happy girl when they get that big check from their old school friend. Hopefully, it will let them both breathe a little easier for the next couple of months.

He popped out the tape, swiveled in his chair and placed it on the worktable next to the Worthington tape. He stared at both tapes for a moment, then threw Ted's commercial into his canvas bag and got up to leave. I better catch some zzzz's, he thought, before the sun comes up. Then he stopped. Who was he kidding? He never met a temptation he couldn't yield to—- not when it came to a news story—- or even a *possible* news story. He felt a rush when he put the Worthington tape into the editing machine. He fast-forwarded to the Chagall and stared at it for a moment, his investigative nerve-endings tingling. He put a blank tape into another drive and made a dub. When it was finished, he took out the original, instinctively peeled off the Worthington label and stuck it to the dub. He laughed out loud. I could've been a spy, he thought, as he threw the original into his canvas bag where it joined Ted's cassette in L. L. Bean darkness. He put the dub into an FX monitor and the Circle Line tape into another drive, searching for the images he wanted to compare once again.

As Poe closely watched Lauder get shot and fall overboard, someone quietly entered the office and slowly moved down the hall to the editing bay.

On the FX monitor, the mystery man's image flashed onto the glass covering the Chagall. Poe froze the reflected image then used the special effects computer to enlarge the picture. A flash and the picture was bigger. Another flash and the picture was even bigger. After a third enlargement, Poe saw the grainy, but definite image of Senator Lauder.

Unseen, the intruder slipped into the editing bay just as Poe yelled out, "Yes!" and high-fived himself.

The intruder stepped out of the shadows and moved toward Poe. Suddenly a door banged open and laughter from the hallway filled the room. Poe immediately shut off the monitors.

"Yo, Poe!"

The intruder quickly retreated behind one of the steel racks which blocked his ability to see anything in the room. Broderick Wells, a chinos-and-topsider guy, walked into the editing room with his date, Becky. Pulling up the rear was Carol. All three were a little drunk.

Poe, still high from his discovery, didn't even question this late night visit from his old college buddy and business manager, his girl-friend, still in the tan linen trousers and tan cotton tank top she had worn to dinner, and an attractive, long-legged woman about twenty-five, dressed in a very short black skirt and cropped white tee.

Broderick knocked on the doorframe, then began to recite, "Once upon a midnight dreary, while he pondered weak and weary, a visitor, hell visitors," he laughed, then continued, "came tapping at his chamber door."

"And the Raven, never flitting, still is sitting, still is sitting," Carol added, giggling.

"As he watched his bank account hit the floor," Broderick improvised still laughing.

"I see you've started without me," Poe quipped, as Carol sat on his lap.

"Some things we couldn't start, my love..." she said, then gave Poe a passionate kiss.

"Didn't I just put you in a cab a couple of hours ago?"

"Yes, but it wasn't the same without you."

"Hi. I'm the cleaning lady," Becky joked.

"And a damn fine cleaning lady she is," Carol said as she jumped off Poe's lap.

"Hey, I'm sorry," Broderick interjected. "Becky Roberts, like you to meet my good friend and nearly bankrupt client, Alan Raven, here-after referred to only as Poe."

Poe smiled as he stood up to shake her hand, then looked at them a moment.

"You know, in case you hadn't noticed, it's past one-thirty in the *a.m.* What the hell are you all doing here anyway?"

"You didn't answer your home phone. I called Carol and you obviously weren't with her, since she's now with us, as it were," he laughed. "The evening was young…we were in the neighborhood and the rest is soon to be history."

Poe continued to look at his friend.

"What?!?" Broderick asked in mock surprise. "I was thirsty and these beautiful ladies felt like tagging along as I quenched that thirst. Now we want you to play with us. You got something better to do?"

"Duh…sleep?!"

Carol kissed Poe again. "This is New York, the city that never sleeps."

Poe smiled. "OK, just give me a second."

He took the Circle Line tape out of the editing machine and placed in on a shelf. He then took out the Worthington dub, pried off the safety record button from the cassette casing, threw it in the trash basket then tossed the dub into the worktable drawer and locked it, He grabbed his canvas bag and threw it over his shoulder.

"Come on," he said. "I can't wait around here all night."

As they left the editing room laughing and talking all at once, the building's real cleaning lady opened the office door and rolled her cart into the reception area.

"Ah, ha, Maria," Poe said to the world-weary, middle-aged wom-an then pointed at Becky. "You've been unmasked! In truth, you're a CIA spy sent to steal my video of the Makowsky retirement party."

Ilona Joy Saari

Maria looked at Poe as if he were an errant child as she made her way to the office and editing room.

The intruder waited until he heard the office front door bang shut. He peered out the editing bay door and saw Maria push her cart into the office across the hall. She switched on the lights. In the editing room darkness, he quietly began to search through the hundreds of tapes, but was frustrated in his attempt to find the tape he saw on the monitor.

Even with light seeping in from the hallway and office, it was too dark to read any of the labels and he hadn't seen where Poe had put it. It could be anywhere. Maybe he took it with him. Maria turned on a vacuum cleaner. As the machine whirred, the intruder gave up and left the editing bay. He quickly snuck down the hall and out of Lorna and Poe's office.

chapter

SEVEN

MORNING

Poe woke with a start when a stream of sunlight peeking through the bedroom blinds hit him squarely in the face. He glanced at Carol who was lying naked beside him, still sound asleep. He ran his hand lightly down her back as he thought about waking her so they could make love again. Then he remembered. He looked at the clock on the night table. Seven a.m. Shit! He wanted to be in Queens by eight. No way did he have time to go home first. He said a little thank you to the gods that he had left a clean tee and underwear in Carol's dresser. He started to jump out of bed but the sudden movement forced him to lie back down. It was then that he knew his head was about to explode from the sledgehammer pounding inside it. But, like the mailman, or was it the watchman?—- nothing was going to keep him from his appointed rounds, not even a world-class hangover and an hour's worth of sleep.

Lifting himself slowly off the bed, he made his way into the bathroom and turned on the shower. He adjusted the water temperature to cold then let it run while he swallowed a couple of aspirins. He stepped into the shower and let the icy water run over his throbbing head and body. If Carol hadn't been sleeping he would have screamed. God, how he hated cold water! And this was colder than the East River.

A half-hour later Poe was on a subway to Queens. When the train pulled into the Astoria station and he stepped out of the air-conditioned car, he was assaulted by the familiar sights and smells. Hanging out in front of a neighborhood candy story, a boy about ten defiantly smoked a cigarette. Seeing the kid gave Poe the willies. He tried in vain not to think of his misspent youth of smoking pot, indiscriminate teen sex, cutting classes, even stealing a car, all in a neighborhood just a few miles away. Lorna loved her Bayside memories—- dancing classes, singing in the church choir, being a high school cheerleader—- all that "normal" growing up stuff. But Poe was older and the memory of his parents' death in a late night car wreck on the Belt Parkway shattered his childhood beyond repair. His sister had only been four. But he'd been nine, old enough never to be able to recapture the innocence of his childhood. One minute longer in this place and he'd lose it.

He rushed into the Casta Carpet showroom and saw Ted, alone, sitting at a desk sipping coffee from an "I heart Queens" mug. Jelly from a donut seeped out of the corner of his mouth.

"Hey, buddy. Was just gonna call you," Ted garbled, his mouth filled with donut. "How's my commercial comin'?"

Poe put the tape on the desk in front of him. "Done. Personally delivered. Many mea culpas, man."

"No problem. How's it look?"

"Great. Just great," Poe lied. "Honest." He began to fidget. He really had to get out of there.

"You wouldn't lie to an old school yard friend, now, would ya?" Ted asked, fishing for a compliment.

"Nope. You're a natural."

"No shit!" Ted's mouth burst into a big grin as some jelly slid onto his chin. He grabbed a napkin and wiped it away, then pulled out a checkbook and started writing.

"Sit down, man," Ted instructed as he took another bite of donut. "Relax. The day's just dawning."

"Love to, but I gotta run," Poe lied again. He impatiently watched a drop of red jelly fall from the corner of Ted's mouth to the check. As soon as Ted ripped it out of the checkbook he grabbed it and headed for the door.

"Hope you sell a lot of rugs."

"Thanks. Hey!" Ted yelled. "Let's catch a Mets game next week."

"Sounds great. Call me," Poe yelled back as he wiped the jelly off the check onto his jeans then stuffed it into his tee shirt pocket and fled Casta Carpets.

Fearing the borough of Queens was going to swallow him and never spit him out, Poe practically ran back to the IRT station and a train to Manhattan.

It was still early and his car was still filled with morning commuters. No seats. He leaned against the door and watched through the window as the train sped past the dreary, dirty buildings in this run-down neighborhood, wishing he could change the past.

The train jerked. He glanced down as he shifted his feet to maintain his balance. A discarded Daily News headline caught his attention: "Naked Corpse Not Hap Lauder." He snatched it up from the floor. Now ain't that a coincidence, he thought as he read the story. A naked dead guy pops out of the same river a fully-dressed Senator plunged into and disappeared. All memories of Poe's childhood were now buried beneath his desire for a story. And this story was becoming a lot more than a man pretending to be dead. He decided on his next move.

Back in Manhattan, Poe went straight to his apartment and retrieved his old WNBC press pass. Too impatient to wait for a bus or waste minutes walking back to the subway station, he decided to hoof it. As he hurried down the street, his thoughts reeling with reporter's questions, he failed to notice a black Honda with Michigan plates pull out of its parking space and follow him.

Unlike Gracie Mansion, that grand old Federal-style home uptown that served as the residence for New York's mayors, the building downtown that housed the mayor's offices was architecturally boring. The last thing on Poe's mind, however, was the creative merits of the building.

Using the press badge, Poe managed to talk his way into the room where the mayor's special police detail was situated. It was empty except for a tall, lanky man a few years older than Poe who stood by the coffee machine dressed in an elegant navy designer suit, crisp white shirt and navy tie. A gold shield displayed like a silk handkerchief was clamped on the detective's jacket breast pocket. These pretty boys do dress the part, he thought, as he walked up to him and flashed his credential.

"Excuse me, Alan Raven, NBC," he lied.

"What's the problem now?" the detective asked as he poured himself a cup of coffee.

"Just following up on Lauder's assassination. Know where I can find the cop who shot that waiter?"

The detective ripped open four sugar packets at once and poured them all into his coffee. He turned and gave Poe the once-over as he stirred the sugar slowly in the liquid.

"No."

"What do you mean, no?" Poe asked rather defensively. He hated guys that duded themselves up with expensive outerwear then acted all superior and bored with the rest of the working class. The guy was probably from a walk-up in BedStuy.

"OK, let me ask this. What part of 'no' don't you understand?"

"Oh, yeh, I understand," Poe shot back. "What I don't understand is that you don't seem concerned or find it strange that a cop working out of this office…"

"You see, you're already in the box without a bat, my friend. We only had two uniforms on payroll that night. Neither one of them shot the waiter."

"And the third cop was?"

"Not a clue."

"And this doesn't leave you choked with self doubt, or at least, make you wonder?" Poe asked, incredulous.

"Look, do I look like information central for the foot patrol? The guy was some cop the Feds brought in, OK. Don't know his name. Don't know his number. So, why don't you go irritate the Feds? Or maybe the investigating precinct."

"OK, how about this one? Has the naked, dead John Doe been identified yet?

"Nope."

The detective sipped his coffee, reigning in his irritation. "Anything else I can help you with?"

"No. You've bent over backwards already."

Since leaving the mayor's office, every journalistic instinct Poe had was sending him signals. Why would the Feds bring in a uniform cop from some precinct when the mayor's detail had plenty of them? It made no sense, he thought, as he continued down the street. And, if the naked dead body wasn't Lauder, who was it? Was it connected to Lauder? Two dead bodies swimming in the East River was way too coincidental, especially since one dead body really didn't seem to be so dead.

A moment of paranoia stopped him in his tracks. He turned around. Half a block away he saw a black Honda slow to a stop, then accelerate and drive past him. He tried to see the driver, but had no luck as the car passed him and disappeared around the next corner. He did take note of the car's Michigan license plate. What's that old expression, he laughed to himself—- just because you're paranoid doesn't mean you're not being followed? How long had that car been following him? Was it following him? Poe shook his head as if to empty it. He'd better get to the bottom of this Lauder thing before he started imagining the Senator was an alien from outer space about to take over the world.

As Poe headed east toward an uptown subway, he got that ol' paranoid feeling again. He turned and saw nothing out of the ordinary. But, as he was about to continue on he noticed the same black Honda enter his street. He watched as the car made its way slowly toward him just as an uptown bus pulled up to the corner behind it. He waved at the bus and ran, trying to see inside the car as he passed it. No luck. All he could make out was white male. Hell, that narrowed it down to a kazillion suspects. He reached the bus just as it was pulling away from the curb. Poe pounded on the door. The driver stopped and let him on.

His face dripping with sweat, he watched the Honda turn and disappear again.

"Hey, man," the driver said. "This ride ain't free."

Poe took a deep breath as he fished in his pockets for his metro card. Running a block in 95-degree heat and humidity wasn't something he wanted to do again real soon. The fact that the bus's air-conditioner was working so well you could freeze meat didn't faze him. If he got pneumonia from the extreme temperature changes, so be it. Right now, the cold air felt great.

His metro card was nowhere to be found so he impatiently pulled out a fist full of change. He counted out the exact fare and dropped it into the coin container, then pushed his way through the crowded bus filled with late morning rush hour passengers. When he reached the back of the bus, he looked out the window to see if the black Honda had returned. It hadn't.

Suddenly, the bus jerked, nearly causing Poe to fall into the lap of a woman sitting below him reading the Wall Street Journal. Any other time he would have appreciated her striking good looks—- proper, but not prim in her black sleeveless dress—- he might have even flirted a little, but this morning he barely noticed her. Instead, he grabbed the handrail and hung on, worried about the Honda. Two stops later, Poe grabbed an open seat and stared out the window. Everything looked as it should—- people rushing along the sidewalk, taxis and cars weaving in and out of traffic, honking their horns as they barely missed the jaywalking pedestrians. New York, New York—- that toddling town. But no black Honda. He breathed a little easier as the bus drew closer to his office.

Lorna had an early shoot—- an advertising exec needing a speech taped for a marketing convention—- and didn't arrive at her office until almost noon. The place was dark. Poe must have overslept again. She prayed that at least he had finally finished Ted's miserable commercial and left it for her in the editing room. If she had to stall Ted one more time she would probably have to take him out to dinner—- something the company couldn't afford, not to mention the pain of having to sit through a meal with him wondering if his perfect hair was a rug. She started to giggle. Rug! Ted's business was rugs! Her giggling got worse. And then there was the probability of having to listen to another lecture from Broderick about their miserable financial situation.

She turned on all the lights, dropped her bag on her desk and fell into her chair, doubled over from laughter. This heat wave was really getting to her. Finally, she gained control of herself, ignored the light on the phone machine and walked into the editing room. She looked everywhere, but no note from Poe. No finished commercial. Well, that's one way to kill a laughing jag.

She went back into the office to make a strong pot of coffee. She looked in the little refrigerator. Damn, no milk. She grabbed her bag, locked up the office and hurried down the hall to the elevator.

Poe had been on the bus for a half hour when it finally reached his stop. As he got off, he looked quickly around. No black Honda. Then, like most New Yorkers, he didn't bother to walk to the corner to cross the street at the light, but stepped off the curb and into the traffic, dodging the cars so he could cut his distance to his office by a third.

85

Ilona Joy Saari

Suddenly the Honda swerved out of nowhere and drove right for him picking up speed. He took a Tiananmen Square stand.

"Hey! Hey! Stop!"

The car bore down on him just as Lorna came out of the corner deli carrying a carton of milk in a brown paper bag.

At the last second Poe dove out of the way and rolled onto the sidewalk. The car screeched away, drawing a symphony of blaring horns as it cut in and out of traffic.

Poe struggled to get up as Lorna ran to help him. The milk container crashed to the pavement spewing white liquid on their ankles as she threw her arms around him. "Oh, my god, oh my god!" she cried.

"Did you see that? Did you see that son of a bitch?" Poe spit out as he turned a color usually reserved for garish decorating swatches.

Lorna looked at him, checking for cuts and bruises, fussing like a mother hen. Two men, one in a Hawaiian shirt and shorts, the other in a twill suit, rushed to their side.

"Are you all right?" Hawaiian Shirt asked.

"Here's my card," Twill Suit said as he pressed a business card into Poe's hand. "If you find the guy and want to sue, call me. I'm an attorney."

Poe shook his head in acknowledgement and put the card in his jeans back pocket.

"Either of you get a look at the driver?"

In unison, the two men shook their heads and said "No. Sorry."

"Well, thanks anyway. Appreciate your concern."

"I'd give you my number, too, but I live in Nebraska," Hawaiian Shirt said apologetically.

"Don't worry about it."

"Well, OK then," Twill Suit said. "Call if you need me."

"Will do," Poe answered as the two men walked away.

Poe grimaced as he began to walk.

"Come on, let's go see Dr. Kimmel," Lorna said as she took Poe's arm.

"Forget it! Did you see that guy? He tried to kill me?"

86

"Don't be ridiculous, Poe. It was an accident."

"It was no accident! He was bearing down right at me!"

"I know you're freaked, but stop playing drama queen. He just didn't see you."

Poe pulled away from Lorna and looked directly at her.

"He saw me fine. He knew it was me. He's been following me for blocks."

"No one's out to get you." She grabbed his arm again, trying to placate him. "Come on, I'll buy you a wonderfully greasy corned beef sandwich."

"I don't need food—- greasy or otherwise. And stop fussing over me, I'm fine!"

Lorna let go of his arm. "Fine."

"You don't think it's the least bit suspicious that right after we try to tape the Worthington house…" Poe stopped himself, as Lorna looked at him, puzzled.

"What's the Worthington house have to do with this?"

"Nothing."

"Poe, what's going on?"

"You know, you're probably right. It was just a guy in a hurry."

"Poe?"

"Come on. I've changed my mind. A big, fatty sandwich is just what the doctor ordered." He half-heartedly laughed as he looked at his soaked feet. "Not to mention some more milk."

Trying to offset her food indulgences from the day before, Lorna picked at a meatless salad, dressing on the side, and a couple of dry Melba toasts. She was sitting across from Poe in a booth at Pinky's, all sympathy for his near-death experience buried in his corned beef and Swiss on rye, dripping with Russian dressing. She watched him eat—a jealous fox whose pal got to the hen house first. When he took the last bite of the sandwich that *she* should be eating, she imagined smashing his head with the ketchup bottle. Like a drunk in detox, she knew she was in the first stages of saturated fat withdrawal. By the time they returned to their editing room she couldn't look at his corned-beef-sated face. Her anger turned to the unfinished commercial.

"Poe, if you're trying to weasel your way out of finishing that commercial, forget it. We need that money," she snapped.

Poe looked at her with an amused expression. She turned and faced him, trying desperately to control her temper. More than anything at that moment she wanted to punch that smirk off his face. Twice, in less than fifteen minutes, Lorna visualized assaulting her brother because of two basic human needs—- food and money. If she weren't so pissed at him because he almost got killed, she would be ashamed of herself.

"Unless *you* want to go do the Juhola anniversary party," she said in her phoniest pleasant, business voice. "I'll finish the commercial," she continued. "It's six of one, half dozen of the other to me."

Poe pulled a folded piece of paper out of his hip pocket and ceremoniously handed it to Lorna. "Oh, did I forget to mention—- commercial done, commercial delivered at the crack of dawn. Check in hand. Solvency, mere minutes away," he said smugly as he plopped down in his chair by the console.

She unfolded the paper and saw that it really was a check. She felt the flush of embarrassment crawl up her neck and onto her face. "Ah, shit. I'm sorry. Why didn't you tell me?"

"Cause I love to see you eat crow."

"Please not a word about food. I'm starving."

"You just ate!"

"No *you* just ate. *I* grazed on some grass."

Poe laughed. "OK, the subject of food—- fini, finire, finito," he said as he rolled in his chair closer to her. "You and I are going to make headlines."

Lorna's brief moment of joy in her belief that everything would finally be all right ended with the word "headlines." The overwhelming urge to punch him returned.

Poe could actually see the anger flush her face.

"Don't tell me you're off on Senator Lauder's resurrection again," she demanded.

He smiled mischievously, "Don't worry, you're gonna love this. Trust me."

Lorna reached for something on the worktable to throw at him. Anything, she thought, as long as it was heavy. Her fingers landed on a cassette. She grabbed it and was winding up when a knock sounded at the office front door. She dropped her arm as footsteps clicked down the hall.

"Editing bay on the right!" Poe yelled, trying not to laugh.

Jefferson Leeds, dressed in faded jeans, polo shirt and carrying his navy blue linen blazer walked in and found Poe sitting with his legs up on the worktable, obviously amused about something. Lorna stood behind him, seething.

"Hey, sorry to barge in, but there's no receptionist at the desk."

Still smiling, Poe slapped his forehead. "*That's* who goes there. A receptionist!"

Ignoring Poe, Lorna shook Jefferson's hand. "Hello. I'm Lorna Raven."

Jefferson pulled out an NYPD detective's shield. "Jefferson Leeds, 17th Precinct."

"What? It's against the law to be without a receptionist?" Poe remarked glibly.

"Wouldn't know," Jefferson answered dryly. "I'm in homicide. Alan Raven, right?"

"Call me Poe."

"Poe?"

"As in Edgar Allan——- 'The Raven?' Nevermore?——- It's a stretch."

Poe looked at him suspiciously, as if he'd seen him before. "You drive a black Honda?"

"I buy American."

"What can we do for you, Detective Leeds?" Lorna interrupted.

"I'm investigating Senator Lauder's murder and I need a copy of the Circle Line tape."

"Well, sure, we…" Lorna began before Poe interrupted her.

"Sorry, no can do," Poe blurted out. "Gave it to the protectors and servers at your very own precinct. Were you one of the cops who questioned us the other night while I was soaked in sewage?"

Lorna couldn't take her eyes off Jefferson and he knew it.

"No. No, we've never met before. I'd remember," she said without thinking. "I mean I'm good that way. With faces. Good with faces." Lorna blushed as Jefferson smiled at her.

"Think you could make a quick copy for me?" Jefferson asked through his perfect white teeth.

"I don't see why not," Lorna practically purred.

"Well, I do. The machine's on the blink," Poe again interrupted.

Lorna gave him a quizzical look, which Jefferson caught.

"We could messenger one over to you as soon as the machine is *off* the blink," she offered.

"No, no, by that time I'll find the one at the precinct. Thanks for your time."

He shook their hands, giving Lorna a big smile which she returned, then headed out of the editing bay.

"You can take that silly grin off your face now, he's gone," quipped Poe.

Jefferson hurried down the office hall, through the reception area to the front door. He opened and closed it noisily, then quietly returned to the door of the editing bay where he stood just outside, listening to Lorna and Poe arguing.

"You didn't want to make him a copy because he irritated you?!" Lorna asked.

"Yeh, he irritated me. And so are you with all the questions. Can you please get the hell outta here? You've got a shoot in less than an hour."

"Lauder's dead, Poe. We saw him get shot and fall into the East River never to be seen again. He has NOT been resurrected. He is NOT living in the Worthington townhouse!"

"You're right. When you're right, you're right. Now go."

Jefferson quickly tiptoed down the hall and out the front door, this time closing it quietly behind him.

Lorna gathered her equipment and canvas bag and was about to leave, then dropped it all on the worktable. She stared at Poe, sitting in his chair with his back to her, then grabbed his arm and swiveled him around to face her.

"Poe, why are you doing this?"

Poe looked directly into her eyes. "Look, forget it. You're right, Lauder has left the building." He took Lorna's hand and grinned sheepishly. "I know you've been disappointed in me, kiddo, but I promise, I'm a new dog. No more chasing old tails."

"I know you're lying, Poe, but I don't have time to get into it with you. I'll be at the Juhola shoot." She grabbed her things and walked out.

Poe waited until he heard the front door close. His smile gone, he went into action. He jumped up, scrambled around for the Circle Line tape, and immediately put it up on a monitor. He hit fast-forward, the adrenalin rushing through him like a drug. He knew it was there, he knew it...There! Stop tape! Yes! There he is! At the back of the boat. Jefferson Leeds!

"Whoa!" He froze Jefferson's image and stared at it. "Some cop. Stand there with your finger up your ass," he said to the gods. "Guess you didn't vote for Lauder, either."

"Curiouser and curiouser," he continued as he shut off the computer and the monitor. He grabbed the phone and dialed.

"Hey, Elliot, it's me. Gotta huge favor." He listened for a minute.

"No, I don't just call when I need something. You gonna help me out or what?"

Again, he listened.

Ilona Joy Saari

"OK. Deal. Knicks tickets, center court. You pick the game. Look, I need your pal at the DMV to run a Michigan plate, number IJS 844."

"Great! Get back to me soon as you can." He hung up the phone, threw his digital camera into his canvas bag and headed out the front door.

chapter

EIGHT

WASHINGTON, D. C.

ATF Deputy Director George Fowler was lost in thought as he stared out his office window, sipping his five o'clock vodka. When he had been an undergrad at Bates in Lewiston, Maine, he had never heard of the Bureau of Alcohol, Tobacco and Firearms. The CIA, FBI and even the Treasury Department had all been immortalized on television—- from a myriad of secret agents, to Robert Stack's Elliot Ness to David Janssen's "O'Hara, U.S. Treasury." Those agencies were famous. But, the ATF remained in the shadows. George remembered how all that changed after the debacles of Ruby Ridge and the Branch Davidians in the 90's. Now everyone knew of the ATF and not in a good way. He laughed to himself. The agency definitely could use a few good Hollywood publicists even after all these years.

George had been a senior at Bates and hoping to go to Fordham Law School, but unless he scored high on the law boards and got a full scholarship, his dream would remain just a dream. But at that point he got the call from an ATF recruiter. The man had flown up to Lewiston and took him out for the best steak dinner in town at the very restaurant where George bussed tables for tuition money. He told George about the agency and offered to pay for law school if he gave the ATF "a shot." George wasn't told why they picked a struggling student from a rural "Podunk" New England town, but he didn't care…it was an offer he couldn't refuse.

Twenty years and three disastrous marriages later he was called to Washington to be Deputy Director, overseeing dozens of divisions around the country. Life was good and he treated himself well. He ate in the best restaurants, traveled first class, drank fine wine and started collecting minor works of art. But as brilliant as he was in ferreting out criminals, his vision for the future of the agency was limited. Six years after becoming Deputy Director he was passed over for the number one spot when "they" brought in a younger, more charismatic man. The publicists had finally arrived. Now, two years away from his 60th birthday, he was the living embodiment of the caricatured civil servant (albeit without the bad suit) at the end of a long career—- alone with a government pension, a slipping stock portfolio and an encroaching bitterness. He was no longer the "hot cop" in D.C. Looking at his half-empty glass, George tried to rally. He was still the second most powerful man at the agency and some felt he was actually *the* most powerful because he controlled everything that happened in the field. For all intent and purposes, the ATF was George's domain. Let the Director handle public relations and schmooze with Congress. That suited him just fine.

A knock on his open door frame interrupted his reverie. He turned in time to see Diana Brown sashaying in.

"You wanted to see me, sir?"

"There's too much glass in this damn town, don't you think?"

"I'm sorry?" she asked puzzled.

"Glass. First, they lock you in an office, make you stay all day. Then they put windows in the goddamn place. Eight, ten, twelve hours a day you sit here wishing you were out there."

"We could...I don't know...go for a walk," she says, trying to think of an appropriate reply.

"No, thanks. A walk, then an affair, then the end of the affair. Don't have it in me," he laughed. "Want a drink instead?"

"No thanks, darlin'," she smiled, her Savannah accent on the rise. "A drink, then another drink, then an affair, then the end of the affair... then unemployment."

George laughed. "You do have a way of making my day pleasant."

"It's a southern thing..." she drawled with a smile, then took a seat across from him, now all business.

"Where do we stand on the latest gun shipment tip? Reliable? " he asked.

"As far as I can tell. Supposed to land on a remote beach in Maine sometime this week."

"Great. I'll alert the Maine office. They can work with the Coast Guard up there."

"I'll fill Jeff in. Any idea where he is?" she asked.

"At his house in Myrtle Beach?"

"Maybe in spirit, but his body's in New York."

George was surprised. "Who told you that?"

"Well, he didn't, I can tell you that. Ran into him at Dulles on his way to southern California for some sun, fun and fishing. But, you know little ol' me, boss. Never take the word of a good lookin' man. Watched him from afar as he left the waiting area to L.A. and high-tailed it over to the LaGuardia shuttle gate. Imagine that. He lied to me."

George reacted just the way Diana had hoped.

"God damn son of a bitch!" he exploded. "I don't want some guy on a mission out there balling up my investigation. Go find him!"

"Me?"

"Yes. You're quite familiar with his personal tastes and habits, if I remember."

95

"You know, you're right. There are *way* too many windows in this damn town," she said, smiling inside.

NEW YORK CITY

Poe stood outside the 17th Precinct on East 51st Street, debating with himself. He checked his watch. Six o'clock. Finally, he made his decision. He pulled open the front door and strode into a large squad room as if he belonged there. A uniformed sergeant sat behind a reception desk typing on a computer keyboard.

"Hey, Sarge, I'm looking for Jefferson Leeds."

The sergeant slowly looked up from the screen. "How long's he been missing?"

"He works here."

"You've been misinformed."

Poe studied the sergeant a moment—- over fifty and balding, fair skin, broken nose and very angry eyes. He decided to pass on the repartee. "Where's homicide?"

"Any place somebody kills you," the sergeant replied without a trace of irony.

Poe was running out of patience. "OK, once more without the punch lines. I'm looking for a homicide detective name of Jefferson Leeds. Is he in the house?"

"I'm gonna say it again—- he doesn't work here."

"You know, if you really work on it, you could raise your consciousness level all the way up to prick," Poe snapped as he turned away from the sergeant and walked quickly out of the precinct mumbling to himself, "Wannabe comedians, that's what they are. They're all friggin' comedians."

It was seven-twenty eight by the time Poe returned to the office. Now he *knew* he was wired 'cause he was being time specific. Any other day, he would have said seven-thirtyish. He needed to calm down and think before he talked to Lorna. He hit the playback on the phone machine.

"Hi, I'm Katie Kreider and I'm getting married next month…"

"Yeh, like I really want to be there," he said to the machine as he fast-forwarded to the next message.

"Hey, sexy it's me." Carol's voice came through the machine. "Gotta cancel our date tonight. My sister's in from Boston and I promised to give her a girl's night." She dropped her voice to a husky whisper, "but you're more than welcome to come play with me later. Say around midnight?" Damn, he thought, as the next message began to play.

"My name is Bob Edelman. Have a job doing…"

Poe shut off the machine. He had no patience for this. He nervously paced the floor then went across the hall into the editing room. He turned on the lights and found a pile of tapes on the console with a note from Lorna.

Had another really bad day. The Juhola shoot was cancelled,
so I did the Fisher penthouse. Here are the tapes.
You're not going to believe them. Do me a favor and edit
and catalogue them for me, I couldn't bear to look at that
place again. Being in it for two hours was enough.
Love you, Me

Poe picked up one of the cassettes and threw it across the editing room. Every disappointment, every lost dream seemed to come to the surface and he was furious. Furious at the way he screwed up his career. Furious at Lorna and their stupid business. Furious that Carol stood him up. And, furious that he was onto a great story and had no network resources at his disposal. Damn it, I'm gonna do this, he thought. He grabbed the phone on the worktable, flipped through his Rolodex and dialed a messenger service.

He had a half hour. He fished out the original Worthington tape from the bottom of his canvas bag, placed it in an 8"x10" manila envelope and addressed it to himself in care of his Aunt Helen in Bayside. He took another deep breath, then picked up the phone and dialed again.

Ilona Joy Saari

"Yo, Poe here. We have to talk, Lorna. Call me as soon as you can. I'm in the bay. And I mean pronto. It's important."

He tried Lorna's cell. When her voice mail kicked in, he repeated his message.

He sat for a moment stewing about his next move then got up to put on some music. He tripped over his camera bag on the floor by his console chair.

"Damn."

He picked it up and tossed it onto the worktable, failing to notice that the bag hit the phone and knocked the receiver off the hook. He turned on the CD player. Coldplay spewed forth covering the phone's dial tone. He plopped down on his chair and started to wade through the tapes that his sister had so helpfully left for him.

It was seven-thirty and the setting sun was in Lorna's eyes as she turned the corner heading west, lugging her ever-present canvas bag, a video camera and a large bag of Chinese take-out. What was the point of daylight savings, she asked herself, if it made these miserably hot and humid days longer? Between the heat and work, she couldn't remember a worse week and yearned for long, dark evenings and two feet of snow. She thought she'd enjoy the Juhola shoot when she had booked it—- a quick spritz through a new recording studio, videotaping and cataloguing the pricey new equipment for their insurance company. But when she had gotten there, the shoot was postponed since most of the equipment still hadn't arrived. Hadn't music people discovered the telephone? Couldn't they have used one to call me before I schlepped all the way over there?

Her next shoot was another insurance booking. What could be bad about taping the contents of a Madison Avenue penthouse? Nothing, right? It was a disaster. Actually, the shoot wasn't a disaster, the penthouse was. In her life, Lorna had never seen such hideous possessions. From red and gold flocked wallpaper, to French and Italian furnishings upholstered in red and gold crushed velvet. It was like being in Louis XIV's decorator-challenged cousin's whorehouse. If there was

98

any justice in the design world, a tsunami would swoosh through the entire apartment, washing all of its belongings into the first available dump. Not to mention that all the way home she had the eerie feeling that she was being followed, even in Sun Luck while she was picking up her food. But every time she turned to check it out, she saw no one she recognized and no one more than once.

She finally arrived at her loft building entrance and began her nightly ritual of putting her equipment down on the sidewalk and fishing through her bag for her keys. Before she could find them, Jefferson walked up behind her and tapped her on the shoulder.

"Hey, can I help."

The Chinese food crashed to the ground as Lorna spun around and struck a karate pose. "Aggh!"

"Whoa. Jeff Leeds. 17th Precinct," he stated reassuringly as he quickly backed away and flashed his badge.

Her inner defense alarm ringing, she was still ready to kick, scratch or scream as she tried to process what he was saying. Her eyes darted from his face to his badge. Finally, she recognized him and relaxed her stance.

"Never, never, never sneak up behind a woman."

"You know karate?"

"Yeh. Took a course at the Y."

Jefferson tried to salvage the spilled Chinese food. "Hmmm, let me guess mu shu pork, beef lo mein and fried won tons."

"Well, they used to be," Lorna said as he picked up the special-sauce-soaked bag from the ground.

"It does smell good, though," she quipped trying to lighten up the situation.

He smiled. "I really am sorry. Cop's honor. At least let me help carry your stuff inside."

She shrugged. "Is this some kind of weird coincidence meeting you right smack in front of my building? Cause if it is, I have to tell you, I really hate coincidences."

"Tell you the truth I've been waiting for you."

"My turn to 'whoa.' Should I be worried?"

He smiled.

Lorna returned the smile. God, he's cute, she thought, as she again fished around her canvas bag for her keys. She handed him her cell phone, her white socks, a wallet, a credit card holder, a checkbook, a pad and pen, her bandana and a package of condoms. Realizing what she had just given him, she embarrassingly grabbed it back and threw it into her bag, then pulled out her metal lock pick and started to jimmy the lock.

"Plan B," she said as she smiled weakly.

"Sure you live here?" Jefferson asked.

"Hey, you tracked me here, didn't you?"

The door clicked opened.

"Ta da!"

Still holding the soggy take-out and eclectic contents of Lorna's canvas bag, Jefferson tried not to laugh. "Very nice. Should I ask where you learned this?"

"Don't ask, don't tell," she answered. She held open her bag and he dumped her stuff in. She entered the building, holding the door open for him. "So——- good with a corkscrew?"

He smiled again, picked up her video camera and walked in.

"First prize at the Cannes corkscrewing festival."

She groaned good-naturedly.

When they reached the front door of her loft, Lorna tripped on the welcome mat, but regained her footing before she fell to the floor.

"You all right?"

"I'm fine. Chalk it up to a personality quirk," she laughed self-consciously.

"OK," Jefferson said, sensing her embarrassment.

She shoved her hand into her canvas bag and fished around. "Oh, hell."

She dumped the bag's contents the floor, found her keys, shoved everything back into the bag and opened her door. They walked in.

Jefferson put the video camera down on a nearby table. He took in the black and white photos as he followed Lorna to the kitchen and put the take-out on the counter.

"White or red?" Lorna asked.

"Red."

Lorna pulled out a bottle of cabernet from a lower cabinet and gave it to Jefferson.

"You're on," she said as she scrounged around for a corkscrew in a drawer overflowing with every conceivable gadget *except* a corkscrew. Finally she found it.

She handed it over to him then began to wipe off the soggy cartons of food with a paper towel. Jefferson opened up a couple of upper cabinet doors until he found the wine glasses. He took out two and poured the wine.

"Well, looks like you *are* good at screwing corks," she said smiling. "Now tell me, besides scaring me to death, why are you here?"

"Chinese food?"

"Am I sharing?"

"Well, I did carry your camera."

"OK. Chopsticks or fork?"

"From the looks of it, maybe a spoon."

Lorna smiled, wondering if this was some new kind of pick-up approach or if there really was another motive for him being here. Had he really been waiting for her or had he been following her? She was about to give him the third degree when she noticed a light flickering on her answering machine. She excused herself and went to her desk. Just one message.

"Yo, Poe here. We have to talk, Lorna. Call me as soon as you can. I'm in the bay. And I mean pronto. It's important."

Jefferson watched as she hit speed dial on her phone, listened for a moment then hung up. She shrugged imperceptibly as she returned to the kitchen area and absentmindedly picked up her wine glass. She took a sip, then picked up the kitchen extension, dialed again and listened. No answer. She put the phone back on its cradle.

"You look puzzled. Poe all right?" Jefferson asked.

"I guess. He's at the office, but he's not answering the phone and the machine's not picking up. He's not even answering his cell."

"Is that unusual?"

"I don't know. We've got call waiting at the office, so if he's on the phone, he'd pick up. If he's not, the machine would. He rarely has his cell on when he's working."

She noticed a flicker of—- what? Concern? Irritation?...flash across his face.

"Probably nothing. Try again in a few minutes."

"Yeh. I will," she said.

He turned to a grouping of black and white photos of cabaret singers hanging on a near wall. "Nice pictures. Who's the photographer?" he asked as he walked over to get a closer look.

Lorna didn't hear him as she was lost in thought, worrying that her office answering machine was broken and obsessing over what else could go wrong.

Jefferson turned and realized she was miles away. "Earth to Lorna..."

"Oh. Sorry, just wondering where to go to get the best deal on a new answering machine...What were you asking?"

"Who's the photographer?"

"Me. I took them to help get a grant for a documentary on New York night life."

"And did you?"

"Yes. A small one. I've just started scouting out performers and filming them."

They stared awkwardly at the photos a bit longer.

"So how do you take your Chinese take-out? On a plate or right off the bottom of the bag?"

"I have a better idea. I've ruined your dinner, so let me feed you and when we're done we can go scout out some music."

"OK, I see what's going on. You found out where I lived so you could accost me on the street, trash my dinner and take me out on a date?"

"The truth is out."

"Weird."

"Too weird to say yes?"

"Well, I *am* hungry and I didn't have the greatest day," she said, trying to convince herself to say yes.

Jefferson leaned against a nearby pillar. "And you're still upset about seeing Lauder murdered."

"That, too. And I had a shoot cancelled today…translation, loss of income. And yesterday I was thrown out of a shoot I was dying to do on Beekman Place.

"Beekman Place?" he asked, his interest heightened.

"Yeh. Anyway, I was inside this gorgeous townhouse taping the artwork when this witch with a capital 'B' came out of nowhere and tossed me out onto the street."

"What was her problem?"

"Me. Said I wasn't supposed to be there. *She's* the one wasn't supposed to be there."

"But she lives there, no?" he asked.

"No. She's a house sitter or something."

"So, let me get this straight…You had a key, right?"

"Right."

"So you go in, perfectly legal, and this…this…Henrietta House-keeper…"

"Pauline Lawson. Like pulling teeth to get that out of her. Oh! She's making me so mad just thinking about her again!"

"Maybe we should get out of here and get something to eat before you start throwing things at me."

"I think that's an excellent idea. Just give me a second to change." Lorna headed for her bedroom area.

She disappeared behind a dividing wall.

He pulled out his cell phone and hit speed dial. "Andre, it's Jeff Leeds. Table for two in twenty minutes? Thanks."

He put the salvaged Chinese food into the refrigerator then walked to the chaise and sat down. He sipped his wine while he waited for Lorna.

Behind the partition that separated her bedroom from the rest of the loft, Lorna excitedly rifled through her closet. Something sexy, she thought. But not obvious. Something "woman of the world-ish." She pulled out a cute flower print halter-dress and held it against her. Her reflection in the over-sized mirror leaning against the wall brought a frown to her face. The wide chocolate brown molding of the 6'x4' mirror framing her image seemed to exaggerate the big pink flowers on the dress. Not the image she was going for. Too girlish. Back to the closet. A minute later she pulled out a simple Marc Jacobs black slip dress she'd found on sale at Bloomies. Perfect! Now for some sandals. She looked at the bottom of her closet. There must be a hundred pairs down there. She laughed to herself…no wonder I'm broke. She knelt down and pulled out shoe after shoe and tossed them onto the bed. She ran the gamut of designer footwear from Jimmy Choo to Keds. Finally, she found the pair she was searching for…black, strappy Manolo Blahnik sandals. Perfect! She stripped off her clothes, put on black lace panties that she considered her sexy secret, sprayed her pulse points with Gio then slipped the dress over her head. She freshened her lip gloss and tousled her hair. Without a second's thought she grabbed a few chunky sterling silver bangles and put them on her left wrist, then slid her feet into the sandals. She stood in front of the mirror and did a model's turn. Perfect. She grabbed her cell, sat down on her bed and tried Poe one more time. Still no answer.

When Lorna re-emerged Jefferson stood up and whistled. Simple, sophisticated and gorgeous, he thought, but she probably knows that. She did, although she never thought of herself as "gorgeous."

She smiled as she felt her heart racing…to where, she didn't know or care. "OK, I'm ready," she announced as she put some cash, her keys and a credit card into a small, black, vintage Chanel purse, forgetting her phone in the bedroom.

He took her arm and led her to the door. Something tingled in Lorna when he touched her.

Per Se, located on Columbus Circle was a simple but elegant room decorated in pale grays and brown, accented by sparkling chrome banisters and crisp white linens. Lorna and Jefferson sat at a table by the wall of windows overlooking Central Park sipping their after-dinner drinks. From where she sat, she could see the fireplace and imagined how the room must glow in the winter with a fire going. She listened attentively as Jefferson talked.

"So there I was, fulfilling my parents' dream…I'm about to graduate Yale Law and I get this call to meet with the mucky mucks of 'Lambertson, Jefts & Gorrick," he said with a perfect, put-on prep school accent. "When I stepped off the elevator into the mahogany paneled reception area, I thought I'd walked onto a 1940's movie set complete with leather club chairs and a cool, blonde receptionist. Before I even had a chance to sit down, another cool blonde from central casting wafted in and ushered me into a large corner office."

"Office with a view, of course."

"The Washington Monument no less," he said wryly. "Cool blonde #2 gave me some Perrier on ice with a slice of lime as I was being introduced to the all-male senior partners, all of whom talked like Kelsey Grammer in that old TV show 'Frasier.'"

"I know the sound…like marbles in their mouths," she said mimicking marbles in her mouth.

"Exactly!" he laughed. "And it was then I realized my breathing had become shallow and I was about to have an anxiety attack. I saw the mahogany-paneled walls crushing the life out of me and couldn't get out of there fast enough. When I hit the street, I sucked in long, deep breaths, waiting for my heart to stop racing. And that's how I became a cop."

They sat quietly for a moment as Jefferson played with her fingers then softly ran his hand up her bare arm. His touch was light and sensuous and the combination of the fine Napa Valley wine, incredible food and his open American charm was beginning to have an effect on her.

"You never finished your story earlier...who actually owns that townhouse you were tossed out of?" he casually asked, wanting to confirm the name he had overheard during her argument with her brother. He moved his fingers back down her arm and caressed the center of her palm wondering how much they knew, if anything.

The touch was seductive and it took her a moment to register what he had just asked.

She moved her hand away and picked up her drink. She took a sip while she looked questioningly into his eyes. "The Worthingtons. Why?"

"Just curious. More cognac?" he asked.

"No, thank you. There are two of you already. And I'm having enough trouble figuring out one of you."

Jefferson nodded to the waiter, who brought over the check.

"Why don't we get some fresh air before heading downtown?"

"Great idea. Where can we find some?" she giggled then asked herself what she was doing. *She* didn't giggle.

Jefferson laughed as he signed the check and gave it back to the waiter.

"You have an account here?"

"Doesn't everybody?" he answered with a smile.

Lorna gave him a puzzled look as they headed toward the front door, stopping briefly as Jefferson tipped the Maitre'd.

Back on the street, Lorna stood silently while Jefferson hailed a cab. They got in and he gave the driver the address of a cabaret. He took her hand as the taxi pulled into the street.

"Jeff?"

"Yes."

"How can a guy on a cop's salary afford an account at Per Se?"

"I work on commission. You gotta admit that's the best mac and cheese you can get for $350."

"And that suit," she smiled, as she stroked the fabric of his sleeve, "Armani doesn't come cheap."

"Your point?"

"My point—- you tell me you're a cop, but you eat and dress like a prince. Or a mobster."

He laughed. "Mobster?! I thought I had better taste than that." He let go of her and put out his hands, palms up, alternately lifting and lowering them, as if his hands were scales.

"Let's see…Euro-trash or John Gotti…Trash…Gotti…"

"I'm sorry. It's none of my business."

Trying to make light of her prying, she added, "Maybe you have a sugar mommy."

"And daddy," he said, amused.

"What?"

They reached a corner and the cab stopped for a light. Jefferson put his arm around her. "I have very wealthy parents and a very healthy trust fund."

He pulled her close and kissed her as they waited for the light to change. Lorna returned the kiss then suddenly pulled away.

"Whoa! When did we get on this Ferris wheel?"

The light changed and the cab began to move again. Jefferson smiled to himself. Her kiss had been warm and welcoming. He knew it would be.

Poe was still working in the editing room. He stopped, rolled his chair over to the worktable and pulled a big box of Cheez-Its from his camera bag. He struggled to pull apart the top of the wax papery, airtight bag inside the box. Why do these manufacturers make it such a pain in the ass to open these damn things? What if I was starving? I'd be dead as a doornail before I could get lifesaving sustenance into my mouth. The bag suddenly exploded open between his hands, sending Cheez-Its flying across the console. He scarfed them up and shoved a fistful into his mouth. Just as he was about to roll his chair back to the monitor, he noticed the phone off the hook.

"Shit!" He got the dial tone back and dialed Lorna's loft number.

"Hey, it's me again. Where are you? The stupid phone was off the hook. Anyway, I'm still in the bay. Call me damn it, it's important."

Frustrated, he slammed down the receiver, then tried Lorna's cell. No answer.

The west side smoky cabaret was jammed with people listening to Lady Jane, a New York cult diva with a plus-size body and an even "plusser"-size voice that filled the intimate room with deep, husky notes. Dressed in a black sequined gown, Lady tossed her long blonde mane to emphasize a lyric. The club crowd was a mish-mash of young and old sipping martinis…a lot of black, a few piercings and an assortment of tattoos on very thin women who smoked at the bar. Except for the candles on the tables and the lights on the small stage, the room was dark.

Jefferson gazed at Lorna as Lady Jane was finishing her set. Lorna turned and blushed when she saw the look on his face. He took her hand and kissed it. She smiled and turned her head back to the stage. The song ended and the crowd burst into loud applause.

Jefferson leaned toward her. "Want anything else?"

"Now, that's a question just loaded with possibilities."

"Then let's get out of here and explore those possibilities."

Jefferson paid the bill and they left. On the sidewalk, he took her in his arms and kissed her again. And, once again, after returning his kiss, she pulled away. She headed toward Sixth Avenue. He fell into step alongside her. Neither one of them said anything as they crossed Sixth then turned right, leading downtown. It was after midnight and the air was a little cooler than it had been in weeks. Lorna felt wonderful. They continued in silence for a few blocks till they reached Radio City Music Hall. Suddenly, Lorna stopped underneath the theater's marquee.

"This is my favorite building in New York," she said.

She led him over to the glass encasements filled with posters of the various stage shows.

"When I was a little girl my aunt would bring my brother and me every year to the Christmas and Easter shows. I thought the inside of the theater, in all its golden glory was the most beautiful place in the world. I never wanted to leave. So, when I was sixteen, I decided to become a Rockette. Of course, you had to be eighteen, but that didn't stop me. I had studied the requisite tap, ballet and acrobatics for twelve years so I was ready." She stopped talking as she ran her hand wistfully over the glass covering a poster of the long line of Rockettes kicking in unison.

"And?"

"And I lied about my age," she continued, "auditioned and made it."

"And they never found out?"

"Not for a whole seven days. The most exciting week of my life. I'd leave my house each morning, pretending I was going to school, then take the train into the city and walk through that stage door around the corner as if I owned it. Of course, the very first day, when I walked on stage for rehearsal, I did a very Lorna thing. I tripped over a lighting cord and crashed to the floor along with a stage lamp…major embarrassment in front of the whole company. "

Jefferson laughed, totally enjoying himself…enjoying her. "A very Lorna thing?"

"I have a tendency to fall flat on my face at the most inopportune times, though that was only a minor pratfall in a career of major flopping-on-face moments…shall I continue?"

Still laughing, he asked, "Will it hurt?"

"Only when you laugh. And you will. It really was all Clayton Baker's fault. You know the banking Bakers?"

"I do."

"Of course you do," Lorna quipped, now laughing herself. "Well, Clayton invited me to his sister's coming out party in Manhattan. You know debutantes, ball gowns, yada, yada. I was eighteen and thought I was Cinderella. My pumpkin coach was a stretch limo and when we arrived at the hotel and I saw all the paparazzi outside the hotel, I was hoping *I* would turn into a pumpkin. I never knew how blind you became when those camera lights are aimed at you. Anyway, soon I was standing in line on a mezzanine landing with a bunch of other couples in gowns and black tie waiting to be announced to everyone in the ballroom below. Announced!!! Like we were about to meet the Queen of England! Music from some orchestra was playing and I was still half blind when a dude dressed like a Nutcracker finally called out our names. We moved to the top of the stairs and as we started to walk down, my skinny three-inch heel got caught in a fold in the stair's carpet. I tried clinging to Clay's arm for balance, but my momentum was too strong and I fell head-over-heels down the stairs, landing in a silk chiffon puddle at the bottom."

Jefferson laughed even harder.

"Go ahead, I told you you'd laugh, but I was so mortified, humiliated and just totally freaked that I pretended to be unconscious until one of the deb's doctor dads came to my rescue and carried me into the ladies lounge. Six thousand years at Miss Mildred's Ballet, Tap & Acrobatic School and I couldn't manage to pirouette my way out of falling. At least my tumbling lessons proved valuable."

"So, did you ever get to the ball?" he asked.

"Oh, sure. After about an hour I mustered up the courage and left the bathroom."

"And?"

"And no one noticed except Clay who was so sweet and just pretended nothing happened as he swept me onto the dance floor."

"Ah, the manners of the 'born-to-the-manor.' So who ratted on you?" he asked.

"Ratted on me?"

"About being underage for a Rockette?"

"Oh, right," she smiled. "My wonderful Aunt Helen. It seemed my school called her to find out why I hadn't been in class."

"She didn't know you were out getting your kicks?"

Lorna smiled. "I'll ignore that. Anyway, she followed me the very next day and boy did she read me the riot act. The choreographer, too. Didn't know what hit him. You know, about hiring an under-aged girl, about me lying to everyone, yadda, yadda, yadda. Then she grabbed my arm and dragged me back to Bayside before I ever got a chance to perform in an actual stage show. I thought I'd be grounded for life. But my aunt is very cool. She understood and forgave me. I never lied to her again."

Lorna walked him the stage door then stopped. "My entrance to Never- Neverland."

Her eyes shone as she told her story.

"Sometimes when I'm really stressed, I like to wander around the empty Music Hall. It's so beautiful. Majestic, really. I know every nook and cranny of this theater…every lounge, every smoking room."

"Somebody give you a key?

"Hey, I'm a New Yorka," Lorna gushed in her best Queens accent. "I don't need no key."

"Ah, yes. Your demonstration earlier this evening."

She laughed. "Well, I would have used my key if I had found it."

Jefferson couldn't help being drawn to her and he leaned in to kiss her again. This time she didn't turn away. As their passion built, he ran his hands over her body. A couple walked by. Embarrassed, she pulled away.

"Don't you arrest people for doing this in public?"

"No," he answered huskily. They kissed again, then Jefferson stepped into the street and hailed a cab. But Lorna had other plans. She was walking east toward Rockefeller Plaza. Jefferson waved the cabbie on and followed her. When they reached the wall overlooking the plaza restaurant, she stopped and leaned over it, taking everything in. A few late-night diners lingered at candlelit tables. Above them stood the Plaza's enormous golden statue of Atlas holding the world on his shoulders, keeping everyone safe. Towering over everything, in all its deco splendor, was the beautiful RCA/NBC building.

"This is New York to me. I love to be here at night. It's when I believe anything is possible and dreams come true."

He took her hand. "Don't they?"

"I don't know."

Lorna looked searchingly into Jefferson's eyes, not trusting her feelings, but wanting to give into them anyway. This time she kissed him. They kissed a long time before she moved away.

"I think you should take me home."

He grabbed her hand and they hurried to Fifth Avenue. Miraculously, a taxi with a glowing "on duty" light appeared, racing to nowhere. Jefferson let go of Lorna's hand and waved it down. The driver slammed to a halt. Jefferson opened the door.

"Soho," he said as they climbed in and were slammed back into their seats as the taxi peeled out and headed downtown at breakneck speed. Startled, Lorna grabbed onto the armrest and started to laugh.

"You think we'll make it alive?"

Jefferson laughed. "Well, just in case we don't," he pulled her to him and kissed her. No longer wanting to stop his attentions or intentions, Lorna kissed him back with no reservations. They became more and more passionate, and he deftly slipped his hand under her dress and into her lace panties. Lorna's breathing became heavier and her yearnings stronger as his fingers teased her. She caught her breath and pushed him gently away.

"I feel like Sean Young in that movie with Kevin Costner…the limo scene," she said hoarsely. "But there's no partition to raise."

Jefferson had no intention of stopping. He buried his face in her neck and continued to kiss her as his hand moved further up her body, stopping at her bare breasts. "I don't think Costner cared," he whispered in her ear.

"Maybe not, but I do," Lorna stated firmly.

"Okay." He got the hint, leaned back against the seat and closed his eyes. He reached for her hand and held it.

"You think we should tell the cabbie exactly where we're going?"

Jefferson laughed and gave him her address.

Lorna looked at him, then out the window, calculating how long it would be before they'd be at her loft. She couldn't remember ever wanting a man as much as she wanted Jefferson.

It was only ten minutes before the cab pulled up in front of her building, but those minutes seemed like hours to her. She hurried out of the taxi, got her key out of her tiny purse in a flash and opened the front door before Jefferson had finished paying the driver. As the cab careened away, he rushed in after her and, ignoring the elevator that would take an eternity to get to her floor, they raced up the stairs, almost giddy with anticipation.

Lorna, keys still in hand, opened the door and before they finished locking it behind them, they started to undress each other in the semi-dark. Jefferson kissed her mouth and neck. She pulled off her slip dress and he slowly moved his mouth and hands down the front of her body, caressing her breasts with his lips and fingers.

The light from the little lamp she always left on surrounded her body in an amber glow. He kneeled in front of her. He slowly slid her panties, no longer her little secret, to the floor. As he kissed her stomach and teased her nipples with his fingers, she was enraptured. He pulled her down to her knees then gently pushed her back onto the floor as he hurriedly took off his pants and carefully placed his gun on the floor, an easy reach away. He pulled a condom out of his pants pocket and slipped it on. He continued to play with her body, arousing feelings in Lorna that she had never experienced. When he finally entered her, she truly thought she had died and gone to heaven, even though she was lying on her back on a hardwood floor.

Jefferson brushed a stray curl off Lorna's cheek as she lay sound asleep in his arms. He smiled as he remembered how it didn't take long before they had wanted and needed to make love again. Leaving their clothes in a heap on the floor, they had made their way to the bed—-this time, however, their lovemaking had been slower and more deliberate as they explored each other's bodies searching for ways to give each other pleasure. He looked at his watch—3:30 a.m.—then looked at Lorna, not knowing if he felt joy or regret. He didn't want to fall for her but, he thought to himself and smiled, she had literally charmed the pants off him. He gently freed himself and eased out of bed. He grabbed his clothes from the floor and quickly dressed, then picked up his gun. He looked at her sleeping face one more time, then carefully opened the front door and quietly left the loft.

The neighborhood was like a ghost town as Jefferson hurried away from Lorna's building. So much for the city that never sleeps, he thought. He half-jogged to the corner. When he saw a lone cab slowly trolling the street for an early hour fare, he hailed it and got in. The cab quickly sped away, leaving the street deserted once again.

Still in the darkened editing room, Poe was fast asleep in his chair, feet up on the editing bay console, surrounded by empty potato chip bags, an empty container of spinach dip, the empty Cheez-Its box and a couple of empty Rolling Rock beer bottles. Maria had been in to clean hours ago, but that was before his second wave of the munchies. With the monitors off, the only light in the room came from a single desk lamp on the worktable. The phone rang. He jerked awake and rolled his chair over to the table without getting out of it and answered the phone.

"Lorna?—Carol, my god!"

He looked at the time. Four AM. "I'm so sorry, doll. I fell asleep. Honest."

He listened a moment. "Of course I ate dinner." He looked around at his junk food debris. "I don't know—- some potatoes and spinach," he laughed. "No, I'm not mad you cancelled dinner. How's sister Sandy?"

He rolled himself closer to the editing console while he listened to Carol fill him in on her sister's latest career/man crisis. He grabbed a half empty bottle of Rolling Rock and knocked it back.

"So, all's well now?" he asked as his stomach growled in protest at ingesting the warm, flat beer.

"Great. Look, I'm sorry I didn't make it down to your place. Rain check for tomorrow?—- Terrific. I'm gonna pack it in and just go home and crash.—- Okay, sweetie. Love you, too."

Poe hung up the phone then dropped his empty beer bottle into a wastebasket. He grabbed a couple of sound effects tapes and climbed a ladder to put them away in the floor-to-ceiling steel racks. As he reached the top rung, he thought he heard the office front door open.

"Lorna?"

No one answered. "Of course it's not Lorna," he muttered to himself then piped up.

"Anyone there?"

Silence. He shrugged and began to line up the tapes on the top shelf. Suddenly, something made him jerk and he almost fell off the ladder. He looked down and saw a man in the shadows at the base of the ladder, his face covered by a stocking.

"Hey!"

The ladder began to jerk violently. Terror stricken, he tried to climb down, but lost his footing as the man grabbed at his pant leg and pulled. Poe crashed to the floor, slamming the back of his head on the corner of the worktable. Tapes fell off the shelves on top of him. Dazed, he tried to get up, but a gun butt smashed into his skull. He slumped to the floor, silent, as blood streamed out of his head.

The intruder had waited patiently to come back to the editing room when no one, not even the cleaning lady, would be there. His irritation at finding Poe in the editing room flushed his cheeks till they burned. When he saw him up on the ladder he'd had to make a decision—- kill him or try again another night. He had wondered if this fool had already taken the enhanced tape to the police or was keeping it under wraps while working on finding the bigger story. He had had no way of knowing. He just knew he had to search for the tape tonight. If he didn't find it, so be it. That wasn't his problem. She was gonna to be pissed, he now thought, but he had made his decision and felt no regret.

Ignoring Poe's body, he systematically began to search through the cassettes in the editing room. He piled up the few that were unlabeled and began to review them. He'd watch one for a few seconds, snatch it out of the machine and put in another, growing angrier and angrier as he failed to find the townhouse tape. He knocked the tapes to the floor in frustration. The thought crossed his mind that Poe might have changed the label and he'd have to screen every cassette in the place, but before he did that he searched the console drawers. No tapes. He pulled at the worktable drawer. Locked. He grabbed a metal letter opener from the desk and pried it open. Inside, he found the tape marked "Worthington shoot." He peeled off the label and stuck it on another cassette he picked randomly off the floor, placed it in the desk drawer then left with the unlabeled tape.

chapter

NINE

Jefferson and Lorna were making love on a private beach. The ocean waves washed over her body enhancing her sexual pleasure as he...Wait, what's that? What's that noise? This is a quiet beach! It's getting louder, louder, blaring insistently!

"Geez, stop it!" she said, then woke up with a start. She realized she was dreaming and the horn was a harsh reality. It was morning. The sun had risen and the daily traffic jams outside her window were at their toxic, noisy peak. She reached for Jefferson, but found only a pillow.

"Jeff?" she called out as she got out of bed and went to the bathroom.

"Jeff, you in there?"

Lorna knocked, then opened the door and looked in. No Jefferson. No Jefferson anywhere in the loft. So much for the morning-after "after-glow." Hurt and a little angry, she went into the kitchen and made a cup of instant coffee. She noticed the light on her answering machine and hit play as she sipped her first shot of morning caffeine.

Poe's voice was loud and clear. "Lorna, it's me again. Where are you? The stupid phone was off the hook. Anyway, I'm still in the bay. Call me damn it, it's important."

Back in the kitchen, she grabbed the receiver off the wall phone and dialed. "Hey, bro, it's six o'clock in the morning. Where are you? I tried you all last night. I'm not going to bother you if you're at Carol's, but Carol, if you're there, tell him to get his ass in gear and get to the office. Bye."

She hung up the phone, grabbed some OJ from the fridge and poured a small glass, then found the cold cuts in the meat drawer. She slapped together a bologna sandwich, with tons of mayonnaise on wonderfully white Wonder Bread. What could be better than the taste of mayo sliding on processed meat mixed with gooey bread? She took a bite then thought for the millionth time that she should try to eat more healthfully. She ripped a piece of lettuce off the head she had in the vegetable bin and stuck it in the sandwich. That's better. She turned on the television.

"Don't look at me like that. I added greens!"

Yikes, she was now defending her eating habits to a newsreader on TV. Maybe it *was* time to join junk food anonymous. She turned up the TV volume as she sat on a stool by the kitchen counter, sipping her instant coffee and eating her sandwich.

"…according to Mary Davis of the Federal Trade Commission.

In other news, the governor of New York announced last night that he will appoint State Assemblywoman, Liza Crounse to finish the term of Senator Harold 'Hap' Lauder."

Lorna stopped mid-chew and listened closely.

"Lauder was assassinated a little over two days ago by a still unidentified gunman who posed as a waiter at a Lauder political fundraiser. The assassin was killed seconds later by a uniformed policeman who mysteriously disappeared that night, along with the murder weapon."

Lorna turned down the volume and called Poe again.

"Okay, Poe...I just heard the news about the missing cop. What's going on? Is this what's so important? I don't want us to get involved. The police have our tape. That's it. Okay?" She hung up the phone, took a defiant bite of her sandwich then went into her bedroom to get ready for work.

The knock on the door awoke Jefferson from a deep sleep. He grabbed the lush white hotel robe lying at the end of the bed, threw it over his naked body and stumbled out of the bedroom, through the suite's sitting room to the front door.

"Who is it?"

"Room service."

He opened the door, allowing the waiter to roll in his breakfast cart. The smell of the fresh coffee tantalized him as he signed the check and waited for the waiter to leave before pouring a cup. He'd only had a couple of hours sleep and caffeine was just what he needed. He ignored the sugar and cream and inhaled the aroma of the rich black coffee as he took a big sip. As his mind gradually awakened, he thought of Lorna. He had to admit, she was something. Last night he couldn't keep his hands off her. She was smart, beautiful and very sexy and he would love to make love with her again, but Lorna Raven was definitely real "romance" material. Been there...done that.

Time to eat. He removed the silver dome covering his food and took a big bite of the spinach omelet. He sat down, grabbed the New York Times that came with his standing breakfast order, and started eating in earnest.

He flipped to the sports section. Damn, the Red Sox lost. Nothing else in the paper interested him, not even the latest speculations and rehash of the Lauder assassination or the mystery of the naked body found on the shore in Long Island City. His eyes roamed around the sitting room as he continued to eat. The Tribeca Grand suited him. The downstairs' atrium bar, tall potted palm trees and candles that glimmered through a wall of glass lenses excited his sense of style. He smiled...and then there's that great selection of single malt. The hotel was trendy and filled with the self-important, but he felt emotionally safe in its midst. The minimalist suites were soothing and didn't have any ghosts to haunt him.

He still loved The Mark, but that place was his past...a past filled with too many memories. He flashed on the time he and Robert had shared his two-bedroom suite while working on a tip involving a shipment of stolen art arriving in New York by freighter from France. The tip turned out to be false, but they had discovered the veal parmesan at Il Vagabondo late one night as they played bocce and drank Italian wine. Every chance they had they'd go there together, have a red sauce meal and play a few games. At times Diana would join them. He tried to remember why it had been so long since he'd been there, but he was fooling himself...he knew why. He should have known better than to let himself be vulnerable to anyone...a lover or a friend.

The bitterness overwhelmed him. He shook his head to void the memory, finished his omelet and went into the shower.

A half hour later, Jefferson swiftly walked through the Tribeca Grand lobby and out into the morning sunlight. He glanced at the ornamental street clock atop a tall iron pedestal in front of the hotel as he walked across the brick "cobblestone" sidewalk. 8:30.

Sitting in a far corner of the lobby, Diana lowered a newspaper. She dropped it on the table in front of her and followed Jefferson.

Compared to the subway station the air outside felt like an Arctic breeze to Lorna. Though the mercury only hit a mere eighty-nine degrees yesterday, the temperature in the subway was stuck in the hundreds. The air was still humid, but the weather report was optimistic, predicting a drop in the humidity and a high of ninety. Lorna laughed to herself as she walked toward her office. Ninety degrees! Hell, if the humidity came down it would seem like winter.

As she walked by Pinky's, she weighed the merits of a fried ham and egg sandwich, but wisely chose against it. Ham and egg on top of bologna and mayo all before nine o'clock in the morning just wasn't a good idea. She laughed. Wow...a halfway intelligent decision about food…what a concept. She must be happy. In fact, she couldn't remember how long it had been since she felt this good. Jeff probably just had an early shift at the precinct, she reasoned. Granted, he could have left a note, but she knew he'd call. Last night was special. Sleeping with someone on a "first date" was not her style, but this man was different…attentive, caring, and he listened.

"Not to mention, adorable, funny, handsome," she said out loud then blushed when a passerby gave her a smile. Who could resist?!

By the time she reached the front door of her office, she had replayed the prior evening two more times in her head and couldn't wait to see Jefferson again. She was surprised to find the door unlocked. Great, she thought. Poe was already here diligently at work. She entered the reception area. No lights were on.

"Poe? Are you here? I tried calling you this morning at your apartment," she yelled as she headed back toward their office. A dim light seeped out of the editing room into the hall. She walked in.

"You so busy you can't say hello?" she said. The only light in the room came from a single 60-watt desk lamp at the end of the editing console. She switched on the ceiling light. No Poe.

"Poe, are you here?"

She moved further into the room then stopped. Poe lay motionless on the floor alongside the worktable, his head in a pool of blood. She ran to him.

"Oh, my god! Poe!" she screamed.

She leaned over and touched his face.

"Oh, no, no, no, no, no. Oh, god, no."

She dropped to her knees and put her head to his chest and listened for a heartbeat. She didn't hear one. She pressed her fingers into his neck to feel for a pulse. Nothing.

"One…two…three…" she counted out loud as she pressed on his chest with both hands. Nothing.

"One…two…three." Still nothing.

She pinched his nose closed with the fingers of one hand and opened his mouth with the other. She took deep breaths and forced air into her brother's lungs. She repeated this ten times, but Poe still lay motionless. She stopped and began pressing down on his chest again.

"One…two…three…One…two…three…please, Poe, please!"

She stopped CPR and again pushed her fingertips into his neck. She felt a faint throbbing.

"Breathe! Breathe!" she screamed at him as she pulled the phone off the worktable and dialed 911. She took a deep breath and tried to be calm.

"Hello. Yes, it's my brother…someone tried to kill him. He's barely breathing! There's blood…"

She sat by Poe's body, stroking his face as she tried to concentrate on what they were asking her. When the operator's questions sunk in, she gave them her name and address.

She hung up the receiver and put her ear to his chest, taking comfort that his heart was still beating. She cradled him in her arms and began to cry.

The office door was open, as was the editing room door across the hall. Detective Zach Rosen was working with the crime scene investigators in the editing room. Zach looked more like the Yeshiva student he once was than the thirty-four-year old detective he'd become. But looks were deceiving. If Zach looked like a scholar and teacher, he moved like a boxer and talked like a gang leader. He was tough and ambitious and he loved getting the bad guys.

By the worktable, Lt. Frank Muller watched as the paramedics put Poe's body on a stretcher and wheeled him out. Lorna ran after them.

"Where are you taking him?"

"St. Luke's," a paramedic yelled out as they rushed the gurney down the hall, Lorna right behind it.

"I'm going with you."

***

Still in a state of shock, Lorna sat by Poe's bedside in the ICU, his head covered in bandages. The sound of all the beeping monitors helped her hold it together. The ER doctors had told her he was in a coma and something about his brain being swollen and having a neurosurgeon drill holes in his skull to relieve the pressure. She agreed, even though she couldn't concentrate on what they were saying. But that part was over and he was alive. That was all that mattered for now. She had to stay strong. She had to believe he'd be all right. She watched as a nurse hooked up another clear bag on a pole by the head of his bed and wondered what it was for. She sensed the nurse leaving, but had no idea that Lt. Muller had walked into the room. He eased a chair closer to the bed and sat down across from Lorna. She looked in his direction, but her eyes were unfocused.

At six-two, two-thirty, Frank Muller was an imposing man. Not fat. Not overwhelming. But imposing. His fifty-five year old face full of crevices said I'm "interesting" in a lived-in sort of way. His skin was ruddy. His cropped brown hair was streaked with gray. But, the first things you noticed were his piercing pale blue eyes, like icicles reflecting the sky. Someone once described him as a New York winter—-dark, foreboding, with a cold intelligence. There was nothing teddy-bearish about him. The fact that he only wore dark brown suits didn't help to lighten him up. But Muller, above all else, was weary. He had been a New York cop for more than thirty years and a lieutenant at the west side homicide division for the last nineteen. He'd been promoted to captain eight years ago, but turned it down—- too much paper work and way too much politicking. There wasn't much he hadn't seen and, upon reflection (something he seemed to be doing more of lately) he wished he had become an accountant. Numbers don't shoot, garrote, bludgeon or knife one another. However, from all preliminary indications, Alan Raven was the victim of an accident and not the attempted murder his sister had called in. He looked at Lorna, her clothes covered in blood, and felt the sadness emanating from her soul.

"Ms. Raven, I'm Lt. Muller."

Lorna looked at him blankly.

"Ms. Raven?"

"What?" she asked, barely cognizant of anything or anyone.

"The sooner we start the sooner I can leave."

"Start?" she asked having no idea what he was talking about.

"I need to ask you some questions," he said kindly.

"OK," she answered, her mind still not completely understanding what this stranger wanted from her.

"Can you tell me how long you and your brother have been in business?"

"Just a little over..." she faltered. Poe's smiling face flashed through mind. "I don't know, a year?"

"You're the ones got Lauder's assassination on tape. Correct?"

"Yes," Lorna now realizing who she was talking to.

"Why do I know that name Alan Raven?" the lieutenant asked.

"He used to be in news. Probably saw him on TV," she answered, trying desperately to concentrate on the questions so she could help in any way she could.

"Right. The reporter?"

"Yes."

"Fired, wasn't he?"

"Yes he was fired!" she stated defensively. "What's that got to do with anything?"

"Nothing, I'm sure. I'm sorry," he said sincerely, though if he had been fired, Muller thought, he may have been depressed enough to drink himself into a stupor. "Can you tell me the last time you saw him?"

"Yesterday around lunch time."

"And why do you think somebody wanted to kill him?"

"I was shooting a townhouse two days ago and this bitch wouldn't let me finish," Lorna declared, as if that would make sense to the lieutenant.

"What bitch would that be?"

"At the townhouse! Poe went to finish the job, but she wouldn't let him in. On the way back to the office a car tried to run him down.

124

Or was that yesterday?" She shook her head, as if to clear her brain. "Anyway, a car tried to run him down and I didn't believe him."

Muller could tell that Lorna was near hysteria.

"The tape!" she suddenly declared. "There was something on the tape, and..."

Jefferson hurried into the room. "Lorna, are you all right?"

"Jeff!" Lorna rushed into his arms and began to cry. He held her tightly as she nearly crumbled to the floor then helped her back to her chair. He ignored the blood that had rubbed off on his shirt and jeans as he bent down beside her. He held her hand while Muller waited silently for her to calm down.

"And you would be...?" he asked, trying not to be irritated.

"Jefferson Leeds, homicide."

"Really?" he asked incredulously. "From where?"

"Seventeenth."

"Out of your sandbox, aren't you?"

"I'm a friend. I had no idea. I went to Lorna's office and CSU told me what happened..."

"The tape!" Lorna repeated as she jumped up and ran out of Poe's hospital room. Jefferson and Muller followed.

"It's there somewhere. I'll show you," she said pleadingly. She grabbed Jefferson arm and dragged him down the hospital corridor. All she could think of right now was that she had to find that tape. It would explain everything and they'd find the person who did this to her brother.

Lt. Muller followed. "I'll drive."

Zach and the CSU team were finishing up when Lorna rushed into the editing room and began frantically rummaging through the tapes.

"Hey, sorry, Ms. Raven. Can't let you compromise the scene." Zach wasn't unsympathetic, but he didn't need some civilian messing up his crime scene if, in fact, this even was a crime scene.

"I know, but I have to find the tape."

"You guys finished?" Muller asked.

"Just about."

"All photos been taken?"

"Yeh."

Muller nodded at Zach.

"All right, but you have to put these on," Zach said as he gave her a pair of latex gloves. "Try not to disturb too much."

The investigators moved out of the way as Lorna put on the gloves and carefully went through the tapes on the floor, on the console and worktable. She became more and more distraught when she couldn't find what she was looking for.

"I know it's here. It has to be here."

Finally, as a last resort, she went over to the desk, opened the drawer and found the Worthington tape.

"See! Here it is!" She put it into a slot on the console and hit "play."

"There's an image on the tape. I didn't believe him, but he was convinced it was Lauder..." she said, as the monitor lit up on a wedding. The bride and groom were leaving a church while their friends showered them in confetti. She fast forwarded a bit and hit "play" again. The bride and groom were dancing. She popped the tape out and looked at the label, double-checking that it truly was the Worthington tape.

"I don't understand. This is the tape. What's going on?"

"I don't know, but are you saying someone tried to kill your brother because of Lauder?"

"No!" she shook her head again. "Yes!"

"No, yes, what?"

"This was the Worthington tape, see." She shows him the label.

"No, I don't see, Ms. Raven."

"I got a reflection off a piece of glass on a painting. Poe thought it was Lauder. But it couldn't have been since I shot it after he was assassinated. But this wedding we shot months ago..." She put the tape on the desk and started to cry.

"I know this has been devastating for you, and I know you want a reason why your brother was hurt, but from what we've seen, it appears to have been an accident. There are no signs of a struggle. Just the disarray you'd expect if someone fell off a ladder."

"It wasn't an accident," Lorna said defiantly.

As Muller and Lorna talked, Jefferson picked up the tape and noticed a second label sneaking out from under the label marking it the Worthington townhouse. He unobtrusively rubbed his finger along the nicks on the desk drawer before quietly closing it.

"Look, I'm really sorry, but right now it looks like your brother had one beer too many, fell off the ladder and hit his head on the corner of the desk here."

"He didn't fall!"

"Did you make a copy of the tape?" Jefferson asked.

"We usually do, but I was so angry after *she* threw me out...I...I just didn't. I don't think Poe did, either."

Muller watched Jefferson look around the room, checking the floor where Poe died, looking at the desk corner, at the ladder.

"Detective Leeds, thought you were just a friend?"

"Sorry. Habit," Jefferson apologized.

"Maybe you'd like to take Ms. Raven home so she can change her clothes and get back to the hospital."

"Please don't talk about me like I'm not here. I'm standing right in front of you! Or can't you see that, either."

Jefferson took her arm. "Lorna, let's go."

Lorna looked imploringly at Muller.

"We'll call you when we know anything for certain," he promised as he wrote his cell phone number on the back of his business card and handed it to her. "But, if there's anything else you remember or want to tell me, you can reach me at one of these numbers."

Lorna put the card in her shirt pocket then peeled off the latex gloves and handed them back to Zach. She grabbed her canvas bag. Her eyes fell on Poe's wind-up toys, some still on the editing console, some on the floor. She gathered them up before anyone could stop her and put them in her canvas bag. As she did, she noticed the Circle Line tape amidst the tapes and debris on the floor. Instinctively, she snuck it in her bag.

"Ready?" Jefferson asked.

She nodded and they both walked out of the editing bay.

Lorna hesitated in the hall, but Jefferson took her arm and steered her out of the office. He hurried her to the elevator, then out the building.

The CSU team had packed up their gear and was heading out of the editing bay when Diana walked into the office. Seeing Muller and Rosen there, she flashed her badge. Muller looked at it, then at Diana. "Now what the hell is ATF doing here? Is there a stash of Cuban cigars we missed?"

Diana turned on all her Savannah charm. "If there is, I certainly hope y'all share them with me."

Muller smiled. Behind the drawl he sensed that this lady was no fool. Zach couldn't keep his eyes off her.

"What do the Feds care about a guy who cracked his head open?" Zach wondered.

Muller continued to smile. Instinctively, he knew she wasn't here just because Alan Raven fell off a ladder, but her presence made him think twice about the fall being accidental.

Diana's eyes roamed the editing room. "I'm sorry. Did somebody die?" she asked innocently, ignoring Zach's question.

Now that was insincere, Muller thought, half expecting her to bat her eyes.

"A terrible accident. One of the owners of this business fell off the ladder there and cracked open his skull. Blood everywhere," he answered wryly without telling her Poe was still very much alive. At least for now.

"I'm so sorry to hear that. I wouldn't mention it to the cleaning crew," she teased, as she gave both men a two-hundred-watt smile.

Muller laughed to himself. No need for you to bat your eyes, honey, your smile's a killer. But I'm sure you know that.

"Was it the brother or the sister?" she asked.

"The brother," Zach answered.

"And the sister? Where is she?"

"You just missed her, she's..."

Muller quickly interrupted Zach. "You were about to tell us why you dropped by."

"Oh, you know us D.C. bureaucrats, we do like our busy work. Makes us feel important."

"And you're here to be busy how?"

"It seems my boss wanted a hands-on interview with the Ravens about the night Lauder was assassinated. All their prior interviews with police and other law officials, nicely typed as they were, haven't sated the hungry beast."

"Well, it seems *half* of those nicely typed written interviews are going to have to be enough, aren't they?"

"It seems so," Diana said resignedly. "Thank you so much..."

"Muller. Lt. Muller."

"Muller. And Detective..."

"Rosen," Zach answered and held out his hand to shake Diana's. "Zach Rosen."

She shook it. "Zach," she said and directed a smile just for him then walked out of the editing room.

Muller and Rosen said nothing until they heard the outer office door close.

"Put your tongue back in your mouth, Zach. She's way outta your league."

Lorna sat on her chaise in an old chenille bathrobe, her hair wet from the long hot shower she had taken to wash away Poe's blood and soothe her emotional pain. In her hand was one of Poe's wind-up toys——- a baseball. She wound it and watched the ball's little feet move frantically back and forth, its tongue darting in and out as it wound down and stopped. Jefferson came in and put a steaming mug of tea on the coffee table in front of her.

"Thank you," she said automatically. She rewound the baseball and put it on the table. The toy scurried to the edge, fell off and crashed onto a pretty pink rose woven into the pattern of the hooked rug. She watched the feet and tongue flail in the air, as if calling for help. When the toy stopped moving, Lorna broke out in tears.

"It's not fair."

"I know." Jefferson said. He sat down beside her and rubbed her shoulders.

"Don't say you know when you don't have a clue what I'm talking about, OK? I mean, just because you're rubbing my shoulders, you can't possibly know he hates suits."

"What?"

"Poe. He hates suits. Wore one maybe twice in his life and that was under threat. What if he dies? I'll have to find one to bury him in. And it's not fair that somebody who hates suits would have to spend eternity in a god damned suit!"

He stopped rubbing her shoulders and took her hand.

"Lorna, he's not going to die."

"But what if he does?"

"Then you can bury him in whatever you want to bury him in."

"With his toys?"

"He'd probably like that."

Lorna got up and started to pace. Her mind was racing. "What if the police never believe me? What if our HMO won't cover him if they think he was drunk?"

"I doubt that could happen."

"Of course it could happen. You're rich. You don't have to worry about things like that, but people are denied claims all the time." Lorna began to panic. "And what if they pay now, but he needs long-term care? They don't like long-term care. They could cut off…"

"Shhh—Shhh…" Jefferson pulled her into his arms and tried to calm her down. He stroked her hair. "Poe's not going to need long-term care. He's going to be fine."

They were quiet for a moment as he continued to hold her, then Lorna moved away up. "I have to get back to the hospital."

"I'll go with you."

"No. Please. I'd rather go alone."

"You sure?"

"Yes, I'm fine. Thank you. I've got to call my aunt."

"Anything else I can do?"

"Find the person who tried to kill him."

Jefferson kissed her cheek and headed for the door. "I'll call you later."

When he left, Lorna went to the phone and dialed.

"Aunt Helen? Hi, it's me," she said. "Yes, well, I want to see you, too."

She listened for a moment. "What package?"

"No, don't open it. Can you please bring it to Poe's apartment? I have to get some things for him. He's in the hospital."

It had been a long time since Diana had been in Soho and she resented the fact that she couldn't take the time to wander through the art galleries. But the lack of time didn't stop her from getting out of her cab blocks away from Lorna's loft. Right now she was going to enjoy walking through the streets and looking in the gallery and shop windows before facing a presumably grieving woman. A sort of "stop and smell the roses" approach to sleuthing. Or in the case of Manhattan during this heat spell, a "stop and smell the city garbage" approach. Diana laughed to herself. Hell, I'm from Savannah where it's so hot and wet orchids grow in the air. The weather here was like a spring day in Georgia.

Something caught her eye in a boutique window across the street. Even from a distance she could see it was a vintage Yves St. Laurent wool suit. It always amazed her that stores chose the dog days of summer to debut their fall clothes. But, like a moth to a flame, she couldn't get across the street fast enough to check out this wintry outfit. She put her nose close to the glass and stared at the beautiful multi-colored tweed jacket and skirt that looked to be about her size. She could just see herself in it, accented by a wonderful camel cashmere turtleneck, and decided she had to have it. She tried the door. Locked. A sign in the window told her the store was closed until further notice. Oh well, look on the bright side, darlin,' she thought, you just saved yourself some serious dollars.

Diana continued down the street, window-shopping and gallery gazing. She was surprised to see in one gallery window a collection of 19th Century Edward Curtis photographs. The whole western décor fad had been over for some time. Pictures of Native Americans and their way of life captured so beautifully by Curtis were more often relegated now to Colorado, Texas and those other cowboy states. Of course, if Ralph Lauren had featured them again in his New York store, every Park Avenue matron with a mink coat and every Westside artsy-fartsy dilettante would be snatching them up.

She checked her bearings and figured she was about half a block from Lorna's address when she saw Jefferson walk out of a building. She quickly moved into the shadow of a nearby dumpster. Out of sight, she watched as he walked past her and up the street. When he turned the corner, she headed straight for the building he'd just left. It was Lorna's. Of course, she thought.

Dressed in a fresh pair of yellow cotton pleated trousers and white tee, her canvas bag in tow, Lorna was about to leave when her doorbell rang. Thinking it was Jefferson, she opened the door without looking through the peephole.

"Did you forget some——- Oh!" she said, surprised to see a strange woman at her front door.

"Lorna Raven?"

"Yes."

Diana took out her badge and showed it to her.

"Diana Brown from the ATF," she announced——- no fanfare——- no Georgian accent.

"ATF?"

"Alcohol, Tobacco and Firearms."

"I know what the ATF is," Lorna said, angry at the intrusion and anxious to leave. "Why are you here?"

"I'm investigating Senator Lauder's murder."

Lorna just stared at her, taking in her short, sophisticated haircut and her expensive, lightweight black power suit. She briefly wondered how this woman got into her building then decided it wasn't important. Someone must have been leaving and inadvertently let her in.

"May I come in?" Diana asked.

"Well, I'm not exactly in the mood to..."

"I know. I stopped by your office. Lt. Muller told me what happened. I'm so sorry for your loss."

"Loss?" Lorna asked, confused.

Diana gently pushed on the door, opening it wider, giving her a better view of the inside. Lorna barely noticed.

"Did he tell you it was an accident?"

"Yes," Diana answered as she easily moved past Lorna and into the loft.

"Well, it wasn't! Someone tried to kill him."

"*Tried* to kill him?" Diana's face revealed nothing even though she just realized Poe was still alive, a fact that Lt. Muller purposely neglected to tell her.

"Yes! Over a damn tape!"

"What tape? The tape you made on the Circle Line?"

"No. Another tape."

"There's another tape?"

"Well, not anymore."

"I'm sorry, why don't we start at the beginning." Diana casually sat down on one of the slip-covered chairs. Lorna looked at her. Who is this woman sitting in my loft as if she belonged here, she wondered.

"Look Ms..."

"Diana," she answered, then quickly continued, "Does this have anything to do with the tape you made of the Lauder shooting?"

"No. It was an insurance job." Lorna dropped her canvas bag on the floor and resumed her seat on the chaise. "A tape I made in somebody's townhouse."

"Want to tell me about it?"

"Why should I?"

"Well, for one thing, I won't dismiss your brother's injuries as a freak accident."

Lorna continued to look at her. Maybe this woman *would* believe her. Maybe she would look for the person who tried to kill Poe. With nothing to lose, she made the decision to tell Diana everything, no matter how foolish it may sound. She glanced at her watch. Carol was still teaching summer school so Lorna had some time before she went to her apartment to tell her what happened. She could see her, then meet Helen before she heard about Poe on the local news. In less than ten minutes, without a single interruption from Diana, Lorna spouted her litany about the Worthington townhouse, Pauline Lawson, the reflection on the glass, Poe's suspicions about Lauder, the near hit-and-run, finding him unconscious in a pool of blood, then going to St. Luke's and seeing him lying in that hospital bed in a coma, hooked up to all sorts of monitors.

"Then Jefferson brought me home so I could change," her voice faltered. "Poe's blood was all over me."

Diana sympathetically reached out and took Lorna's hand. "Jefferson?" she asked.

"Jefferson Leeds from the 17th Precinct. Haven't you met him yet?"

"Never heard of him," Diana lied.

"He's working on the Lauder assassination, too."

"Well, there're quite a few of us working on the case. Haven't met them all. Now, about the tape—- the town house tape. Did your brother ever make that image clear enough to see who it was?" she asked, fishing to see if Poe had confided anything more than suspicions to his sister.

"I don't know. Maybe. But he wouldn't have told me and now the tape is gone."

"Gone?"

"Yes. It was marked the townhouse tape. But it wasn't. I think whoever tried to kill my brother stole it."

Lorna noticed the mug of tea Jefferson had brought her. Her hands shook as she picked it up off the coffee table and took a sip. It's still warm, she thought, as Diana sat silently, waiting for her to continue.

"I'm always trying to keep him from spinning his webs to get at a story. Reminding him he was out of the news business. But, he just ignores me. He's like a damned spider—- you know what I mean?'

Diana nodded sympathetically.

"You sweep away the web and an hour later there's another one," Lorna continued.

She put her tea cup down and stood up. "Now I really have to get back to the hospital."

"I'll see what I can find out about your brother's accident," Diana told her then gently prodded Lorna to tell her all she remembered about the night Lauder was murdered. But Lorna was done talking, so Diana took out a business card and wrote down a number. "I'm staying at The Mark. Here's the number. And my cell. If you think of anything else, call me." She handed Lorna the card.

"O.K."

"And again, I'm very sorry about your brother."

"Thank you."

Lorna saw her out then went to her window. When she saw Diana leave the building and turn the corner she grabbed her canvas bag and rushed out.

Jefferson stood in the shadows across the street from the Worthington townhouse. He looked at his watch and was about to leave when the front door opened. Pauline walked out, locked the front door and headed south. He followed. A cab drove by but she ignored it as she reached Mitchell Place, turned right and continued down the street. She stopped in front of the Beekman Tower Hotel. Jefferson was right behind her as she stepped into the elevator and pushed the button for the twenty-sixth floor.

She gave him a perfunctory look as the doors closed and he made no move to push any of the floor's buttons. He smiled and shrugged. The elevator quickly moved up and came to a stop. The doors opened to the Top Of The Tower restaurant, an art deco room bathed in mauve and cocoa. Its walls of windows and terrace dining boasted a near 360 degree view of the Manhattan skyline. As they stepped off the elevator, Jefferson wouldn't have been surprised to see Humphrey Bogart in bowtie and tails or Jean Harlow in a white, satin slip dress sitting at the bar sipping gin and bitters. Pauline gave him another look as they entered the room.

"I hear they do a mean Cobb salad," Jefferson said, smiling charmingly at her.

She ignored him and immediately joined a man sitting at a window table smoking a thin brown cigarette. A drink was waiting for her. Dressed impeccably in an expensive Italian navy suit, beautifully tailored deep blue shirt and yellow silk tie, the man oozed a continental background. The French cigarette cemented the image. She waved a waiter away when he approached the table with a menu.

Jefferson sat at the mottled granite bar and ordered a tomato juice. The bartender reached for a glass behind the bar where royal blue panels on the wall lighted the liquor bottles in a wall recess. He poured the juice and placed it in front of Jefferson

"The smoker. Any idea who he is?"

"Who's asking?"

Jefferson put a twenty on the bar. "Mr. Jackson."

"He's attached to the embassy of one of those new East European countries."

"Which one?"

He looked at Jefferson, who put another "Jackson" on the bar.

"Not really sure. One of those countries with twenty-seven letters and no vowels, but he's got a distinct Russian accent."

The elevator door opened again and Lou Edwards, dressed in a tan summer suit, stepped out and hurried past the bar. Jefferson immediately recognized him as the cop who shot Lauder's assassin. He watched as Edwards joined Pauline and the "multi-consonanted Eastern European" Russian.

"Now that we're all here, we can talk some business," the Russian said. "But, first. Our friend is doing well?"

Pauline watched as he stubbed out his cigarette and lit a fresh one with a slim gold Dunhill lighter.

"He's doing a lot better now that we got him out of the townhouse," she answered as she waved away the smoke in her face. "When are you going to get him out of the country?"

"Soon," Lou promised. "We're making new arrangements."

Lou's promise did nothing to ease Pauline's stress. As cigarette smoke hovered in front of her she felt fear creeping up her spine. She didn't know which would suffocate her first. Everything was falling apart. Why did I listen to Hap and confront that annoying girl? Pauline thought. She didn't even know I was there. She certainly didn't know *he* was. So what if she had gotten his image on that glass? By the time she figured it out, he'd have been long gone and no one would have ever known about me. Instead that reporter showed up. Who's next? The Russian exhaled another cloud, causing Pauline to cough. She picked up her napkin and waved it in the air.

"In case you hadn't heard, it's against the law to smoke in New York restaurants," she said to him.

"You say without a trace of irony," he smiled. "But not to worry, this establishment has given up trying to infringe on my right of free expression. I spend too much money dining here."

Back in the moment, she ignored him, and got down to business. "Are your people on their way to Maine?"

Ilona Joy Saari

"Unfortunately, it seems your ATF has recently decided to guard Maine shores from foreign invasion."

"What? Then cancel everything," Pauline ordered. "Hap can't handle anymore complications." Hell, *I* can't handle anymore complications, she thought to herself. "It's time to cut our losses."

The Russian took a long drag on his cigarette, exhaled slowly then put it out. "But *we* sent them to Maine."

He smiled. "They were figuring it out anyway so we confirmed their suspicions," he continued with obvious pride in the way they were playing this high stakes game. "And now we can proceed without any misadventure."

"No. It's getting too risky. We must cancel," Pauline said emphatically.

"What's life without a little risk?" he said, not expecting an answer. "Besides, there would be losses. And those losses would be ours."

"I don't care."

"But we do. We want our final payment and your people can't pay that if they don't deliver our merchandise to their buyers and get their payment."

Pauline put her hands in her lap to hide their tremors. She needed to appear calm and in control. She willed her hands to stop trembling. They did. She picked up her glass and sipped her drink.

"All right. What's the new plan?" she asked.

"Have you been to Long Island this time of year?" the Russian asked.

"Frequently," Pauline answered sarcastically.

"A lovely place, wouldn't you say?"

"Long Island is, of course, long," she said sarcastically. "Care to be more specific?"

"Past the Hamptons…a small secluded beach. Even the locals have trouble finding it. It should be the perfect place for our final shipment. Mr. Edwards and I can discuss the particulars later."

"Fine," Pauline said, resignedly. "And he can fill you in on all the details from our end. I trust everything will go smoothly."

138

"Absolutely. And, unlike my schizophrenic country, I am always at your service.

Pauline got up and shook his hand.

"Gentlemen," she said, then shook Lou's hand and walked through the restaurant past Jefferson and into the elevator which hadn't moved since Lou's arrival.

Lorna stood outside Carol's apartment. She'd been there for ten minutes, her own sorrow keeping her from inflicting the same pain on someone else. The longer it took her to tell Carol, the longer Carol would be happy. But it was getting late and she had to meet her aunt at Poe's apartment. She knocked on the door. A few seconds later, Carol opened it, smiling.

"Lorna. Hi. I just got in and was about to grade some papers. You're the perfect excuse not to. Come in."

"Thanks."

Lorna entered and Carol closed the door behind them.

She always enjoyed being in Carol's apartment. It was a happy, cheerful place. The living room was so full of color—- deep yellow walls, glossy white woodwork, floral and striped fabrics of rich blues and greens. Lorna noticed a large color photo of Poe and Carol hanging over a faux fireplace, dominating the room. In the photo, Poe stood rigidly "posing" as they did in old tintypes. His left arm was around Carol, who was laughing.

"I finally saved enough pennies to have it blown-up and framed. I can't believe how much good framing costs these days."

"It looks great," Lorna told her.

"Well, it's our Poe. Always joking around."

Lorna stared at the picture.

"Lorna, what is it? Carol asked as Lorna sat down on the couch and started to cry.

As if on autopilot, Lorna navigated her way to Poe's apartment in an old brownstone on West 22nd. It was a great space...a small, two-bedroom apartment on the ground floor with a charming walled-in brick patio and a working fireplace in the living room. For Poe, however, the apartment's best feature was that it was only a minute's walk from the Chelsea Diner, one of his favorite places for breakfast, even if breakfast was two in the morning. She fished in her canvas bag for her key ring which included one for Poe's front door. Of course she couldn't find it. She jiggled the bag. She heard them. The keys were in there. Frustrated, she stuck her hand deep inside and fingered around the bottom touching everything but her keys. She struggled to keep calm as she jiggled the bag again trying to pinpoint their location. She shoved her hand back into the bag grabbing at everything she touched. No keys. A wave of fury flooded over her. She wanted to scream and scream. Instead, she swung her bag against Poe's front door over and over again till her arms ached and the bag's contents spilled onto the floor. Her mini-rage over, she found the keys and shoved everything else back into the bag. Deep breaths, she said to herself. Deep breaths. She let herself in.

Once in the small entryway, she stood immobile for a moment as she looked into the living room. A brown corduroy sectional and a world-weary steamer trunk used as a coffee table were the room's main furnishings. Original movies posters covered the white walls. On the fireplace mantle was a framed photograph of herself and Poe as children straddling their two-wheelers.

She walked into the room and sat on the couch. Her heart was breaking. To escape the pain she focused on a large poster of the old Cecil B. DeMille movie "The Greatest Show On Earth," and, for a brief moment, considered running away to the circus.

She smiled thinking how their shared love of the old classic movies had begun. They were just kids in elementary school when Aunt Helen had first rented one of her favorite old movies and the three of them had curled up on the sofa together to watch. It became their Sunday night family tradition. If only she could turn back the clock.

She went into Poe's bedroom and opened his closet. Hanging neatly were faded blue work shirts, flannel shirts, a couple of dress

140

shirts and a brown corduroy jacket that looked like it was made from the leftover fabric of his sectional. She stared at the jacket wondering why she never knew he liked brown. On the closet door was a collection of vintage ties. His favorite was a1950's Marilyn Monroe that Lorna had found at a thrift shop in the East Village. On a shelf in the closet was a battered suitcase. She pulled it down and threw it on the bed, opened it then went back to the closet, grabbed a work shirt and a pair of jeans and folded them into the suitcase. She pulled out some underwear, a couple of tees and PJ bottoms from a drawer, then found his shaving stuff in the bathroom. Once everything was packed, she brought the suitcase into the living room

The door buzzed, startling her.

"Who is it?"

"It's me, sweetheart," Helen's voice came through the door.

Lorna opened it and threw her arms around her aunt, who dropped the manila envelope she was carrying. Helen held her close then steered her niece to the sectional.

Lorna desperately tried to hold back her tears as she explained to her aunt in more detail about what happened to Poe and his condition. Then Lorna put her arms around her and the two of them clung to each other as they wept. It was a long time before either of them could speak.

"We had an argument," Lorna finally said through her tears. "That's the last thing—- we were arguing."

Helen tried to collect herself so she could comfort her niece. "Sweetheart, you're always arguing. That's how you love each other… you argue."

"I yelled at him to stop trying to recapture his career! What was I thinking?"

"It's OK, I'm sure he yelled at you, too. Just tell me what happened."

"I know, but…" Lorna stopped when she saw the manila envelope on the entry floor. She bolted over and snatched it up.

"What's this?" she asked.

Ilona Joy Saari

"What I told you about on the phone," Helen answered. "A messenger dropped it off. Addressed to Poe, in care of me."

Lorna opened it. Inside she found the Worthington townhouse cassette.

"A tape? He sends himself a tape?" Helen asked, not really expecting an answer.

Lorna laughed, despite herself. "He just couldn't help himself. He had to follow the story. You know what, Aunt Helen, there's so much I have to do I can't go to the hospital right now. I've packed a few things. Will you take them to him? When he wakes up he might need something."

"Of course, sweetheart. I'll just call Carol first."

"I've already seen her. She's probably at St. Luke's already."

"Good."

Lorna sat on the sofa again and buried her head in her hands. Helen surrounded her with her arms, holding her close. Lorna went limp and allowed Helen's love and care to surround her. The thought that *she* should be comforting Helen the way her aunt had always comforted her entered her mind, but she couldn't. She had reverted back to that little girl, finding solace and a safe haven in her aunt's arms. As Helen lovingly stroked her niece's hair, Lorna felt tears fall on her forehead. Where, she wondered, does this loving woman find the strength to deal with her own pain and still give me the consolation I need?

Lorna pulled herself together and smiled when she saw a little typewriter wind-up toy. She picked it up and gave it to Helen. A look of determination crossed her face. "Bring him this to remind him he has a story to write."

Helen knew that look. "Yes, yes, of course. Don't you do anything crazy."

"No, no. Of course not."

"Lorna, why don't you just come with me to the hospital, dear. I'm worried about you."

"I can't…I'll be fine. I'll call you later," Lorna promised.

"OK, sweetheart, but I'll see you there later. Right?"

142

Helen hugged Lorna and they both teared up again.

"I'll be there as soon as I can. I love you," Lorna whispered.

"I love you, too, my precious girl."

Lorna kissed her aunt then handed her Poe's suitcase and led her to the front door. As soon as Helen left, she grabbed the tape and ran to Poe's tape player and TV. She played it and saw the Worthington tape cued to the image on the Chagall.

"What, Poe? What?"

She removed the tape then remembered the Circle Line tape she had taken from the editing room. When she pulled it out of her bag, she noticed for the first time a piece of paper taped to the cassette with numbers written on it: 00:04:28...00:07:17, 00:08:23.

"Time codes," she said out loud.

She put the tape into the VCR and found the first time code. She saw Senator Lauder standing on deck of the Circle Line boat.

"What are you telling me, Poe?" she asked the television screen.

She took out the tape and put the Worthington dub back in the VCR. She froze the picture on the image on the Chagall. She stared at it. Suddenly, she ran into the tiny second bedroom Poe used as his office and rolled out another TV and tape player perched on an old tea cart. She set the second television as close to the living room set as the cable wires allowed. She brought up the Circle Line tape and froze the image on the Chagall. She touched the image of the silhouette then touched the image of the Senator. She pulled her cell phone out of her bag, found the international phone number she was looking for and dialed. She listened to the ring on the other end as she stared at the two TV screens. A woman finally answered.

"Yes, I'd like to speak to Mrs. Kathryn Worthington, please... Yes, I'll hold."

While she waited, Lorna fiddled with the Circle Line tape, stopping when she saw Senator Lauder at the dinner dais. He removed a couple of pieces of paper from his pocket and began his stump speech.

"Thank you all for coming here tonight," Lauder started.

Lorna turned down the volume as he continued to talk.

"Yes. Yes, Mrs. Worthington? My name's Lorna Raven, I'm sorry to bother you like this, but did you get my previous message?"

"No? Oh. I work with American Fidelity Insurance…"

She listened a moment. "No, no there's no problem. It's just that I've been videotaping the contents of your townhouse as you requested but, well, your house sitter didn't think…"

Lorna was interrupted. "You don't have a house sitter? Are you sure? Her name's Pauline Lawson."

"Oh, so you *do* know her."

Lorna sighed as she held the phone away from her ear. "M'am, you don't need to tell me every charity board you're on together. I just want to verify that she doesn't have permission to stay in your home."

Kathryn Worthington confirmed what Lorna had just figured out.

"Thank you, Mrs. Worthington. No, there's nothing to worry about. Hope you and Mr. Worthington are having a wonderful safari. Goodbye now."

Lorna hung up and looked at the TV screen as Lauder continued his speech. She turned up the volume.

"…I want all Americans to feel as safe in their homes as I do in mine. Thank you."

Applause erupted from the fundraising crowd. Lorna fast-forwarded to the next time code on the list. On the screen a uniformed policeman pulled his gun on the waiter who had shot the Senator.

"Freeze! Police!" the cop yelled.

Lorna watched as the waiter stopped and turned, his hands slightly raised. The cop fired. She stopped and rewound the tape, then played it again.

"Freeze! Police!"

The cop shot the assassin again. Lorna stopped, rewound and played it again, this time hitting the slo-mo button.

"Freeze! Police!"

Again the assassin stopped and turned, his hands slightly raised. The cop fired. A confused look crossed the waiter's face before he died. Lorna froze the tape on a close-up of the waiter.

"Oh, my God! He was surrendering!"

She went to Poe's desk and found a magnifying glass, then back to the television screens. She re-ran the cop's moves before he shot the waiter, then she froze the tape. Using the magnifying glass she made out his precinct and badge number and called information for the telephone number. She called the precinct, pretending to be a reporter and asked to speak to the officer involved in the death of Senator Lauder's assassin. She was finally transferred to a desk sergeant. After repeating her request, he told her he didn't have a clue what she was talking about. Lorna explained herself more precisely and read him the cop's badge number. The desk sergeant, with an annoyed sigh, told her that someone was putting one over on her because no such number existed at that precinct. Stunned, Lorna hung up. What the hell was going on? And what did Poe know? She fast-forwarded to the next time code.

"8:23...8:23," she said impatiently. She stopped the tape at 8:23 then gasped, not believing her eyes. Stunned, she closed her eyes for a moment then opened them again and stared at the monitor. There on the screen dressed in an elegant tuxedo was Jefferson Leeds!

"Jeff?"

She watched Jefferson on screen as he did nothing but observe. She rewound the tape and watched him again. Nothing was making any sense. She grabbed Lt. Muller's card from her wallet and dialed his number. "Lt. Muller, please."

"Well, when do you expect him?" she asked, then listened. "Yes, this is Lorna Raven. Would you please get a message to him to meet me at the Beekman Place townhouse in an hour? It's very important. Thank you."

She dialed Muller's cell. No answer. She cut the connection and then found Diana's card in her wallet and dialed her cell. Diana's voice mail picked up. "Diana, this is Lorna Raven. I need you to meet me at the Worthington townhouse as soon as possible. It's very important. I'm on my way there now."

Before leaving, she rewound the Circle Line tape and replayed it again, watching the cop shoot the waiter. This time she let the tape run a bit longer and saw him bend over the waiter's body. He felt for a pulse as people scurried around in the background. During the chaos of this second shooting Poe must have been distracted because the picture on the monitor suddenly became crooked. But in the corner of the frame Lorna saw the cop feel around the floor, pick something up, put it in his ankle holster and cover it with his pant leg. It didn't take a seasoned detective to figure out that the cop had surreptitiously taken the waiter's weapon. She ejected the tapes, threw them into her canvas bag and rushed out the door.

chapter

TEN

The intense heat and humidity were back with a vengeance, but Lorna barely felt it as she paced back and forth across the street from the Worthington townhouse. She noticed beads of sweat sliding off her stainless wristband as she checked the time. Five-thirty. She'd been pacing for almost forty minutes. No Muller and no Diana. She was tired of waiting. She crossed the street and knocked on the front door. No answer. She knocked again. She waited. Nothing. She pulled the key from her pocket and went in. She checked the security system. It was off.

"Hello? Anybody home?" she yelled. No response.

She cautiously walked down the long entrance foyer past the Chinese red lacquer table she remembered from her first visit. The house was eerily still and hot. Hot! Right! She didn't feel that Arctic air that had nearly frozen her toes off. The air-conditioner wasn't on and judging by the heat in the house, it had been off a long time. She cautiously walked into the living room.

"Hello? Anybody? Ms. Lawson?"

Silence. She caught her reflection in the glass covering the Chagall painting and stared at it for a moment.

"Pauline?"

Still no answer. She left the living room and went into the sunroom. No signs of life. The drapes were closed and the room was pristine...not a floral cushion out of place.

Lorna peeked into the kitchen, took a deep breath and walked in. It was immaculate. Not a stain on the white subway tile back splashes or white marble counter tops. Not a dirty dish in the white porcelain farm sink. Not a crumb on the black and white tile floor. Not a fingerprint on the stainless Sub-Zero or Wolf six-burner stove. How could it be so spotless? Don't they even nuke popcorn in here?

Suddenly, Lorna saw Poe lying on the kitchen floor, red blood splashed everywhere against the sparkling white. She gagged and ran from the room and back into the foyer. She sat down on that same delicate bamboo chair she had used when she was forced to put white socks on her freezing toes. She took a deep breath then shook her head trying to clear her brain and get back on track.

She found the stairs to the upper floor and slowly walked up.

"Hello...Ms. Lawson..." she called out.

"Pauline. It's me, your favorite videographer..."

She reached the second floor and walked down the long hall, opening doors along the way. First door—a chute to the laundry room below. Second door—an empty bedroom filled with country antiques. Third door—another empty bedroom. Lorna's mind drifted for a second as she wondered what profession allowed Mr. Worthington to live like this. Banker or bank robber? Same thing, she thought. She opened the fourth door and found yet another empty bedroom, this one furnished with bunk beds, computer stations and toys. Must be for the grandkids. Behind another door was a linen closet.

She froze. What was that noise? A door closing? Her heart jumped in her chest as she held her breath and listened. Silence. Probably came from outside or just one of those loud creaks that old houses have. All she knew now was that the house she couldn't wait to videotape was beginning to give her the creeps. Of course, any house would give her the creeps if she was snooping around it looking for clues to an attempted murder.

She quietly hurried down the hall and opened the last door to find a huge master bedroom beautifully decorated with dark mahogany furniture and crisp, white monogrammed bed linens. Pauline had to sleep somewhere and Lorna assumed that she would have chosen only the best.

She walked over to the bureaus and marveled how everything was arranged so perfectly…a place for everything and everything in its place. Lorna thought *she* was neat and orderly, but she paled in the organization department next to Kathryn Worthington.

She peeked into the marble master bath. Perfect, again. The towels looked freshly laundered. The sinks, shower and tub were clean and dry.

Why in the midst of tragedy do people think of the silliest things? Lorna laughed to herself as she imagined the imperious Pauline Lawson running around the house in a formless housedress and apron, scrubbing and dusting.

Under the circumstances, she certainly wouldn't have called in a maid service.

Why did she leave, though? Because of me? Because of Poe? And where did she go? Did she leave with the man whose image she had gotten on tape? Nothing made sense unless that man was Lauder.

An uneasy chill swept over her and Lorna couldn't get out of the house fast enough. She left the bedroom and hurried down the back stairwell finding herself once again in the large kitchen. She stopped for a minute to get her bearings.

Suddenly, someone grabbed her arm, twisting it behind her back! She screamed, and turned to see the cop from the Lauder tape leering down at her.

She struggled to get free, but his grip was like a vice. She kicked him in the shin, doing more damage to her sandaled toes than to his leg. The kick, however, diverted his attention long enough for her to grab a heavy decorative bowl off the kitchen island and smash it into his forehead, forcing him to loosen his hold.

She jerked away, ran out of the kitchen and down the hall. In her panic, she fumbled with the front door.

She turned and saw the cop, slightly dazed with blood trickling from his forehead, barreling after her.

Finally she got the door open and rushed out to the street.

As she ran down Beekman Place, Lou Edwards calmly left the townhouse pressing a handkerchief on his forehead to stop the bleeding. He methodically closed the door behind him and hurriedly walked after her. He picked up his pace when he realized no one else was on the street.

Lorna frantically looked for someone…*anyone* she could ask for help. She searched the street for a car she could jump in front of or a taxi she could hail, but the area was eerily empty of traffic.

She came across an outdoor staircase framed by old-fashioned street lanterns. She ran down the stairs. Halfway down, the stairs forked. If she veered to the right she'd end up trapped in a small, deserted park with no other exit. If she bore left, she'd end up on a footbridge over the FDR Drive leading to the East River's edge. Though terrified, she remembered the police were still dragging the river for Lauder's body. As she ran across the footbridge in search of help, Edwards reached the top of the staircase. The traffic on the highway noisily sped along below her.

When she reached the other side, she looked over her shoulder and saw that he still stood, like a sentinel at the top of the staircase, watching, dabbing his forehead.

Ha…made him bleed, she thought, then realized she probably only made him angrier. If no one was on this side of the highway to help her, her only other escape would be to run onto the parkway.

Lorna rushed down the footbridge stairs and onto the river's edge walkway, dotted with park benches. Police and FBI boats were in the water, but there appeared to be no policemen or agents on the shoreline. Her thoughts were racing. He was hiding…waiting for her to come downstairs. Damn it, how did he know she was in the house?!

In the distance she saw two men walking toward her. Hoping they were federal agents, she ran toward them.

"Excuse me. Excuse me," she called out as they got nearer. "Excuse me."

"Yes?" a man dressed in chinos and khaki polo shirt answered.

"Are you FBI?" Lorna asked.

The two men laughed. "Nope, CPA. Here in the Big Apple for a convention," chinos answered.

Her eyes searched the waterfront for anyone that could be an FBI agent or a NYC cop, but everyone seemed to be out on the boats. These out-of-town accountants would have to do. They looked "pressed" and preppy enough to be Feds, especially the one in a lightweight cream suit, but she needed to put on an act for the man out to kill her.

"CPA's, huh?" she said animatedly then pointed up in Edwards's direction. "What brings you to the waterfront, the east side skyline?" Her mind was racing…Who was this man chasing her? She no longer believed he was really a cop. If I'm lucky, she thought, maybe he'll think these guys are part of the police search team and I'm telling them about him.

"Nah," chinos laughed. "Just thought we'd come down and watch the hunt for a U.S. Senator's body. Something to tell our friends back home."

"Yeh, it's pretty wild," she answered nonchalantly, trying to cover her fear. "Like being at a movie."

No one said anything as they walked toward the footbridge.

"Look, I'm sorry to bother you," Lorna said, not knowing if these men would back away from her if she told them a killer was chasing her, "but there's a creepy guy following me and it's scaring the hell out of me." She was tap-dancing like crazy now, hoping to appeal to their chivalry. "Would you mind if I just tagged along for a while?"

"Where is this guy, I'll take care of him?" the man in the cream suit asked.

"He's right up there," Lorna answered this time pointing directly at the top of the stairs high up on the other side of the footbridge. When they looked up, no one was there.

"He *was* there, honest," Lorna said almost pleadingly. "Please, will you guys just walk me to First Avenue? I can catch a cab home there."

Sensing she was telling the truth, chinos took her arm in his.

"Sure, thing. I'm Kevin. My friend here, Mr. *'I'll take care of him,'* is Mike."

"And I'm...Susie." She didn't know why she gave a false name. Just seemed like the thing to do.

She smiled in relief as they made their way up the staircase and onto the footbridge. In front of them was New York's breathtaking skyline, the United Nations building just a few blocks away. Lorna shivered, thinking how this was the same view everyone was enjoying the night Lauder was shot and took a header into the river.

As they made their way up the stairs on the other side of the footbridge, down Beekman Place and finally First Avenue, Lorna stayed alert, searching for signs of that bogus cop.

The men stayed with her as she desperately tried to find an empty cab. No luck. Not wanting to leave her alone, they insisted on walking her to the subway at Lexington Avenue. She thanked them profusely and said good bye.

She hurried down the stairs into the station constantly looking over her shoulder for the man who was chasing her. He was nowhere to be seen. She heaved a sigh of relief. All she wanted to do now was go to the hospital and see her brother.

***

The station platform was jammed with people. Lorna felt safe in the late rush hour crowd as she pushed her way closer to the tracks. It was hot and claustrophobic, but what better place to hide than in a mass of humanity? I'll be just fine once I get on that train, she told herself, and let out a sigh of relief when she heard the noise of an approaching train in the distance. She inched her way closer to the edge of the platform. She didn't care if it was an express or a local...she was getting on that train.

Suddenly she felt a hand on her back deliberately pushing her forward! She screamed as she fell onto the tracks close to the platform wall. Nothing's broken, she managed to think, as she quickly scrambled to her feet. The sound of the train grew louder as it neared the station. She jumped up trying to grab the platform ledge so she could pull herself back up, but she couldn't hold on. A stabbing pain shot through her ankle as she fell back onto the track. Panicked, she looked for a crevice, a nook, anywhere she could squeeze herself into and hide from the train.

An arm reached out to her as if the hand of God had broken through the heavens. Her heart was pounding with fear as she reached up and grabbed it. The train came into view at the far end of the station. Its lights on the tracks almost blinded her. Another hand latched onto the back of her shirt and yanked her up onto the platform as the train came to a screeching halt right next to her. Moments later, as she lay on the cement floor in shock, the train pulled out of the station.

A crowd gathered around Lorna, but the people seemed blurry, and moved soundlessly in slow motion. She looked up as her savior hovered over her. At first she only saw a Columbia University tee and huge diamond studs. But then her eyes gazed into warm, sympathetic brown eyes. She thought he was Jay Z and wondered why someone so rich and famous was riding the subways. Where was Beyonce? Her brain began to focus and she realized that he was younger than Jay Z, even younger than *she* was...maybe only eighteen or nineteen. He had

153

Ilona Joy Saari

flawless ebony skin, with handsome features. His tall, muscular body was covered with bling. Lorna had never seen anyone so beautiful. She tried to thank him, but no words came out. He knelt down beside her.

"Hey, you okay?" he asked soothingly as he lightly brushed a few of her unruly curls away from her face. A chill ran through her body. She knew she wasn't okay. *He* was here somewhere…she just couldn't see him. But she nodded "yes" as tears ran down her face. The young man enveloped her in his arms. "It's all right. It's all right."

"Thank you," she finally managed, the shock beginning to wear off.

"No sweat." He took a handkerchief out of the back pocket of his cargo pants and began to gently wipe the dirt and soot off Lorna's arms. He smiled. "Missed my train. Had to fill the time doin' something, right?"

She managed a smile.

A young woman in a floral sundress muttered, "Where are the damn transit cops when you need 'em?"

Lorna looked up and saw a crowd of people staring down at her. Suddenly, she felt as if she were suffocating. The walls of the subway station began to close in. She needed to escape before she had a panic attack. She winced as she stood up with the help of her savior. "I have to get out of here," she whispered to him.

Another train was pulling into the station as "Jay Z, Jr." guided her through the mass of humanity on the platform and walked her to the stairway exit. She put her arms around him and hugged him tightly. "You're the most beautiful knight in shining bling a girl could ever wish for." She kissed him lightly on the cheek.

He smiled. "Yeh, long as you don't call me your "white knight."

Lorna managed a laugh, then, ignoring her sore ankle, she hurried up the station stairs and onto the street.

She scrambled down Lexington, bumping into people as she tried to lose herself in the street crowd, oblivious to the pain in her ankle and the bleeding scrapes and bruises on her arms and the blood blotting the left knee of her yellow trousers. She turned around and there *he* was a

154

half a block away coming toward her. No longer bleeding, he pulled out a gun with a silencer from inside his windbreaker.

Now is not the time to lose it, she told herself. She fumbled in her canvas bag as she stepped into the street to look for a taxi. Finally, she pulled out her cell phone and dialed 911. When she turned around again she saw that he was less than twenty yards behind her.

"Hello, hello," she yelled into the phone, but the traffic noise was so loud she heard nothing on the other end. "Help me, please!"

A taxi pulled up a few feet in front of her. A female passenger slowly got out as Lorna made a mad dash for the open cab door. She got there just as a middle-aged businessman was about to get in. She blocked the doorway with her canvas bag.

"I'm sorry, this is mine," Lorna stated with authority as she pulled him away from the cab.

"Like hell it is, lady. I've been standing here..."

Lorna body-checked him to the ground when he tried to get in, losing her cell phone in the process. She dove into the taxi.

"Go, go, go, go, go!"

The driver recognized a frightened woman when he saw one. He peeled away from the curb before Lorna had time to close the door. The left rear wheel of the cab scrunched her cell phone to pieces. As the cab pulled into the traffic, Edwards had reached the door. He grabbed the handle, but it was wrenched out of his hand as the taxi swerved and picked up speed. Lorna pulled the door shut then turned and looked out the taxi's back window just in time to see her assailant tuck his gun into the small of his back and out of sight. No one on the sidewalk seemed to notice. Just a few New Yorkers fighting for a cab.

As the cab made its way down Lexington Avenue, Lorna breathed a sigh of relief, forcing back the tears that were rushing to the surface.

"Chinatown, please."

chapter

ELEVEN

Jefferson came out of the shower and grabbed one of the thick, white bath towels. As he ran it over his body, he wondered why the over-priced, over-decorated health club he went to in D.C. stocked those towels that had velour on one side. It was pretentious luxury… nouveau riche towels, he thought to himself…not to mention that the velour was non-absorbent, defeating the whole purpose of a towel in the first place.

The steam in the bathroom had dissipated and he looked into the mirror over the pedestal sink to see if he needed a shave. He decided he did and ran an electric razor over his face. He splashed on some Lagerfeld and went into the bedroom to dress. As he threw on a pair of faded jeans and a long sleeve, black linen shirt he wondered where Lorna was. Was she still in her loft or was she at the hospital? Will her brother's brush with death make her less open, keeping him from finding out exactly what she knew or *thought* she knew? He hoped not.

Despite himself, he was beginning to care for her and didn't want to hurt her or see her hurt.

He slipped his bare feet into his well-worn, highly polished black, slipper-like leather loafers and went into the living room. Before he took his shower, Jefferson had set up his computer and had started a Google search of Pauline Lawson. When he looked at his computer screen, there were at least ten sites that included her. He started clicking into each site. The first two just listed her pedigree...Pauline Lawson, 47, born to a middle-class family outside of Madison, Wisconsin. A graduate of the University of Pennsylvania, she moved to D.C., met and married an older, wealthy oil lobbyist who had the good grace to die a year later leaving Pauline with a great deal of money. Having majored in the romance languages at Penn, Pauline was able to move easily within the town's international community, charming more than one foreign diplomat. She was on the board of many charitable foundations, traveled often and, as gossip had it, had many benevolent "friends." She never remarried.

Most of the sites had even less information, but on one, Jefferson found pictures from years earlier of an eastern European fundraiser for Romanian orphans. In one photo Pauline was sitting at a table with Lauder and his wife, Kipper, all three smiling for the camera. The blurb under the photo described Pauline as a Washington socialite. A second photo showed three people in what seemed to be an intimate conversation. Two were Lauder and Pauline, the third Jefferson recognized as the cigarette smoking Russian Pauline had met with earlier. Another site had a more recent photo taken at a Russian Embassy party in D.C. In the foreground were Pauline, the Lauders, the cigarette smoking Russian and Jefferson's boss, ATF Deputy Director George Fowler dressed in an expensive tuxedo. Jefferson zoomed in on Fowler's image. Behind him, barely visible, was Diana.

***

The private gym Diana used when in New York was fully equipped and had large windows overlooking the hustle of the city. Diana was staring out a window as she jogged on the treadmill trying to work off her frustration. The day hadn't gone as planned. Why was Jeff in the middle of this whole Lauder thing? Because of Robert? She had to stay focused and figure out what to do before George found him and things got more out of hand. Just as she picked up her pace, her Blackberry rang. Barely sweating and in total control of her breathing, she answered her phone.

"Hello."

Speak of the devil, she thought as she listened a moment.

"Well, hi there, George," she said filling her voice with all the molasses she could muster. She slowed the tread and began walking at a clipped pace.

"Whoa. Calm down, darlin'!" she said, cutting him off. "Remember your blood pressure." She listened for a minute.

"George," she interrupted.

"George! I told you I'd find Jefferson, now didn't I?" she cajoled. "When I do, you'll be the first to know."

She rang off, stopped her cardio workout and went over to the leg curl machine. Well, it wasn't a total lie, she thought. I don't have a clue where he is right now.

As she worked the apparatus, she felt the tightening of her thigh muscles...the "burn." She liked the feeling. She also liked the definition it gave her lean legs. Runners' legs.

She looked around the gym as her thoughts lingered on Jefferson, the membership for which he had paid. How many times had she used it? A hundred? A thousand? How many times had she stayed at The Mark? She supposed it was silly to keep coming back to that hotel after their break-up, but she wasn't sentimental. The Mark suited her. She liked the understated luxury that the agency paid for. And, she liked the location...walking distance to the park, Barney's, Polo and other trendy Madison Avenue shops, not to mention some great clubs and restaurants. What more could a girl ask for? Of course, the trick was how to keep all these "perks" after the agency stopped paying for them. But, she was working on that. No way was she going back to the life she had in Savannah. She was *not* a "one bedroom, walk-up flat" type of girl. And she was savvy enough to know that as her looks faded, she wouldn't be able to rely on "the kindness of strangers."

She finished her workout and wiped down her moist arms and legs with a towel. Time to shower and take care of what has now clearly become the Jefferson problem.

Jefferson sat in front of the computer. Having a government clearance was a wonderful thing. He now knew where Pauline kept her every dime. Where Hap and Kipper Lauder banked, their complete portfolio and the real estate she owned. Alone, the Senator wasn't worth much. Both figuratively and, apparently, literally. Everything was in Kipper's name. He typed in one more name. George Fowler…then typed in his boss' address and occupation. After entering his clearance access code once again, the information on the screen changed. He scrolled through Fowler's bank records and stock holdings.

"Ah, George," he said out loud. "You gotta sue your financial advisor. No more Cuban cigars for you."

Finished with his research, he shut off his computer. It's show time, he thought, as he grabbed his hotel key and left the suite.

Lorna paid the cab driver and hobbled through the crowded, narrow streets of Chinatown past cramped souvenir shops and simple storefront restaurants, looking for a public telephone. Her ankle was slightly swollen, but she didn't think it was sprained. She needed to call someone for help…Jefferson, Diana, Lt. Muller…someone! But every phone she found was either out of order or had been vandalized. She walked the familiar streets just a neighborhood away from her loft, desperately wishing she could go home. She turned onto Elizabeth Street as she kept searching for a phone. No luck. Across the street, however, was the 0-5 police precinct. Alone and scared, she had nothing to lose. She walked in.

Sitting behind a tall counter-like reception desk was a large woman in a sergeant's uniform reading a romance novel. Her nametag pinned on her blue shirt read: Sgt. Theresa Fontana.

"Excuse me," Lorna said trying to get her attention. "Excuse me! Sgt. Fontana!"

Fontana reluctantly looked up from her book. "Yeh? What'd ya want?"

"I'm sorry to bother you, but someone is trying to kill me."

"Really?" Fontana asked, her eyebrows raised.

"Yes, really." She held up her bruised arms as proof.

Fontana got up from her seat and came around the desk.

"Follow me," she said as she led Lorna into the precinct bullpen to a middle-aged man dressed in crumpled brown slacks and a yellow golf shirt sitting at one of the institutional gray metal desks.

"Harry, this lady says someone's trying to kill her," Fontana announced to the man.

"Lady, this is Detective Harry Goldstein, one of New York's finest," she continued. "I'm sure he'll be glad to help you."

Lorna wasn't too sure about that. Harry Goldstein had the look of a man bored with his job and bored with life.

"Sit," he said, as Fontana, having done her job, went back to her desk and opened her bodice-ripping book without another word.

"So, who are you and who's trying to kill you?"

"My name is Lorna Raven, I'm a videographer."

"A what?"

"A videographer...I take videos of events..."

"Yeh, yeh, okay, I get it. Who wants to kill a videographer? You make some woman look too fat on camera or somethin.' She out for revenge?" he asked, not even attempting to stifle his laugh.

"No," Lorna answered, trying not to get upset or angry. "The man who wants to kill me is the cop who killed Sen. Lauder's assassin.

He pushed me onto the subway tracks at the Lex and 53rd station. See."
She again held up her arms as proof then pointed to her bloody pant leg.

"He pushed you onto subway tracks?" Goldstein asked incredulously as his eyes took in the dirt on her tee shirt as well as the dirt and blood on her pants and the cuts on her arms.

"Yes."

"At Lex and 53rd?"

"Yes."

"And you came all the way down to Chinatown to report this?"

"He chased me out of the subway station! I had to grab a cab to get away from him! Lorna realized that he wasn't buying a word she said, but she continued anyway. "And I don't think he's really a cop. I tried to find him, but I don't know his name and his badge number doesn't exist. I think he tried to kill my brother."

"OK, let's see if I got this right. An unnamed cop who might not be a cop who killed Lauder's killer, may have tried to kill your brother and *did* try to kill you in a subway station in mid-town. Is that how it plays?" he asked as he looked at her now as if she just escaped the loony bin. "Are you sure you just didn't fall off a curb trying to hail a cab?"

"Yes, I'm sure," Lorna answered curtly.

"I see. And you want me to find this unnamed cop who might not be a cop and arrest him for the attempted murder of you and your brother."

"Yes. You can talk to Lt. Muller..."

"Well, I'm sure I can, but you see we got a problem," he interrupted her again. "If I don't got a name or address or witnesses, I got nothing to go on. But, you know what?"

"What?" she asked, believing he was now just humoring her.

"I believe something did happen to you so," his voice softened a bit, "I'm gonna type up a complaint. You can sign it and I'll file it. Then if you ever find the name of this cop who's not a cop, you come back here and we can go from there. For now I suggest you go home and get some rest."

Lorna didn't know if she should cry, hit him or just grab his gun and shoot Harry Goldstein right between the eyes in his sneering face. Instead she just said, "Fine."

Goldstein filled in the form in his desk computer. "Person issuing the complaint, Lorna Raven, like the bird, right?"

"Right."

"Name of the alleged attacker unknown."

Lorna sat in the chair afraid to move because if she did she really might become violent.

Goldstein continued to talk and type. "Address of alleged attacker unknown."

Finally he finished, printed out a copy and handed it to Lorna to sign. She looked at the useless piece of paper, refusing to cry. She signed it, got up and walked out of the station without even saying goodbye.

"Hey, Fontana, come here," yelled Goldstein. "Another Lauder nut. This one's story's a real winner."

Lorna had been sitting in Madam Nu's for an hour trying to control the waves of panic that washed over her. She nursed a pot of tea and picked at the pepper beef she had ordered. No one in the restaurant took notice of her battered arms or dirty, bloody clothes.

She took another sip of tea. As soon as it's dark, I'm going home, she decided. I can clean up and call someone for help.

Aunt Helen popped into her head. She must be frantic that I'm not at the hospital, but I can't go there. What if he's there waiting for me there? Oh, my God!, she thought, panic rising in her throat. I have to warn Aunt Helen and Carol! They can't leave Poe alone. Not till I can get him police protection!

She looked out the window. It was finally dark. Time to go home.

Lorna crept along the alley behind her building, constantly looking over her shoulder. Moving through the shadows, she made her way to the fire escape leading up to her loft. She double-checked to make sure no one was around then jumped up to grab the pull-down ladder. She couldn't reach it. She spotted a lone garbage can alongside a dumpster. It was filled to the brim and smelled of rotting road kill, but she didn't have an alternative. The can was heavy but not unmovable. She pushed with all her might, struggling and sweating in the heat, and finally shoved it down the alley and under the fire escape. Nearly gagging on the stench, she swatted away a hoard of flies feasting on the decayed food. She turned the lid upside down to give herself a level platform to stand on. Her ankle throbbed as she climbed on top of the can, grabbed the ladder and pulled it down.

Headlights turned into the alleyway. She quickly climbed up to the first level and pulled the ladder up after her. The car inched its way toward her. She held her breath and pressed her body against the building. I'm invisible! I'm invisible, she said over and over in her mind as the car moved closer to her. An alley light shined on the front windshield. Two passengers. A guy and a girl about her age. Her heart stopped racing. No killer cop. No scary people. She let our her breath as the car passed below and continued down the alley.

Before anything or anyone else came, she quickly climbed up the fire escape to her own window. She grabbed her lock-picking tool from her canvas bag and picked open the wire window cage that she had installed to protect her from the bad guys. She peered through the window. As always, the lamp on her desk was on but it didn't give off enough light to see every nook and cranny of the loft. She waited a moment. Nothing moved. It seemed safe to go in.

She took her soiled white bandana out of her bag, wrapped it around her hand and made a fist. She'd have forty-five seconds after breaking the glass to climb through the window and turn off her alarm. Taking a deep breath, Lorna punched the window with everything she had. It shattered more easily than she expected. She knocked away shards of glass that stuck out of the window frame with her wrapped fist then eased herself onto the sill.

She jumped down into the loft, landing on her good ankle and limped quickly to the alarm, but it was already off. Didn't I turn it on? she wondered. I was in such a state when I left, maybe I forgot. She carefully looked around, unaware of a shadowy figure quickly moving behind a decorative screen. Nothing seemed out of place, but her instincts told her that she needed to leave as soon as possible.

Her hand hurt like hell. She unwrapped the bandana and carefully massaged her fingers and palm. Nothing broken. She waved it in the air in an attempt to shake away the pain. No time for more than that cursory cure, but she did want to wash her subway wounds.

She went into her bathroom and flipped on the light. She stripped off her clothes, leaving them in a pile on the tile floor then ran hot water in the sink. She soaked her washcloth. The scrapes and bruises on her arms cleaned up quickly, but the gash on her knee was deeper and the dried blood was difficult to wash away. Not to mention it really stung.

"Ouch, ouch, ouch," she said over and over again as she gingerly wiped her knee. She was not a pain person. She dropped the washcloth into the sink, grabbed a tube of Neosporin from the medicine cabinet and dabbed some on her wounds. She then found a very large bandage and placed it on her knee.

Satisfied that her wounds were clean and antiseptic, Lorna checked out her ankle. It was still puffy, a bit black and blue and tender to the touch, but the pain was minimal. She popped two Motrins into her mouth with a gulp of water, washed her face and left the bathroom, taking the bottle of Motrin with her.

Behind a screen, the intruder watched as Lorna threw the pills in her bag then hurried to the closet. In the dim light, she put on fresh underwear, jeans and a clean white tee shirt. She then fished through her bag and pulled out Lt. Muller's business card. As she punched in the number, she briefly wished she had Poe's ability to remember numbers. Then a woman's voice answered, announcing the precinct.

"Lt. Muller, please."

Ilona Joy Saari

Learning that Lt. Muller had gone for the day, she left her name and said she'd try again later. She didn't trust leaving a more detailed message at the precinct. She dialed Muller's cell and got his voice mail.

"Lt. Muller? This is Lorna Raven," she announced, trying to be calm and sound rational. "The cop who shot Lauder's assassin is trying to kill me. I've lost my cell and I'm afraid to stay in my loft or office, so I'll have to call again. Please put a police guard on my brother. You have to believe me. He's really in danger." She hung up. At a loss, she called information and asked to be connected to the 17th Precinct. While she waited, she wondered how it was that she could have gone out with a man, slept with him and not have his phone number. Why didn't he *do* something when Lauder was shot!?

"17th Precinct."

"Hello, yes, ah...is Detective Jefferson Leeds there?" she asked this latest police operator.

"Please hold."

After a moment, the operator came back on and told her there was no detective by that name at the 17th.

"Of course there is," Lorna argued. "He's in homicide."

The operator repeated that Jefferson Leeds was not a detective at the 17th, homicide or otherwise. Trying to be helpful, he suggested she try another precinct. Near tears, Lorna asked him if there was some sort of computer list of all homicide detectives in Manhattan. If so, could he please look it up for her. It was important. Sensing her desperation, he agreed and put her on hold again. Though he was gone less than a minute it felt like days to Lorna as her heart beat in her chest like those ominous drums that always come up in movie moments like this. He came back and the news was not what she wanted to hear...no listing for a detective Jefferson Leeds anywhere.

Hurt, confused and feeling betrayed, she thanked the operator and put down the receiver as the intruder came out from behind the screen. He soundlessly inched his way toward her. She stood immobile by her desk, not knowing what to do next. There was one last person

166

she could try. She grabbed her bag and pulled out Diana's card. The intruder inched closer to her as she picked up the phone again and dialed.

"Diana Brown, please."

The intruder, now less than ten feet behind her, stopped short and quickly retreated back into the shadows behind the screen.

No one answered in Diana's room. The hotel operator returned and asked if Lorna would like to leave a message on her voice mail.

"Yes," Lorna answered then waited for the tone. "Diana, it's Lorna Raven again. I don't have my cell," she continued. "Some cop tried to kill me. Jefferson's not a cop and I don't know who else to call." She slammed the phone down. She dialed Diana's cell and got another voice mail message.

"What?!? Doesn't anybody have their cells on in this town?!" she screamed into the phone, then continued in a normal voice. "Diana, it's Lorna. I'm leaving my loft before someone kills me. I'll call you back." But before she left she had to warn Aunt Helen and Carol.

Lorna tried her aunt's cell first. No answer. She then tried Carol's.

"Carol? It's me. How's Poe?" She listened as Carol told her there was no change in Poe's condition and that she had just sent Helen home to get some rest. Worried that Poe might be left alone in his room, Lorna told her not to leave him alone.

"Make sure you know the doctors and nurses who come into the room," she said trying not to get emotional. "And please be careful. I love you."

The intruder watched as Lorna went to her dresser and pulled out another tee and some panties from a drawer and tossed them into her canvas bag.

She hurried into the kitchen and opened the pantry door. After moving around soup cans, spaghetti sauce jars and an inordinate amount of baked bean cans, she found what she was looking for...a phony can of Campbell's condensed tomato soup. She unscrewed the bottom, took out a wad of money and stuffed it in a jean pocket.

She grabbed her canvas bag, climbed up on the window sill and back out the broken window. As she disappeared down the fire escape, Jefferson came out from behind the screen, just as the phone began to ring.

"Hi, you've reached my machine. You know the drill."

"Lorna, you there? Pick up," Diana's voice echoed in the loft. "Damn. I didn't hear my phone——- traffic noise," she continued as her voice trailed off.

Lt. Muller sat in the restaurant wondering why he had let his sister talk him into this blind date. He could hear her words now. "Frank, you don't have to marry her...just have a cocktail...break some bread." Finally he had called the woman, the bread was broken and he was studying the menu. He learned that she was a corporate lawyer who didn't eat meat or poultry because of the excess hormones injected into the animals. Nor did she eat cheese and cream sauces which she termed "artery cloggers." She was very thin. She did like fine wine, though.

As they waited for their first course, he watched as a man at a nearby table talked incessantly on his cell phone, ignoring his female dinner companion, who looked miserable. He empathized. He hated when people talked on their phones in restaurants, especially since most people dismissed their respectful restaurant "voices" when on their cells, allowing anyone within a hundred yards to hear everything they had to say. It was just plain rude...rude to the people sitting at the table with them and rude to the other diners who could care less about their business.

"Frank?" his date asked trying to regain his attention.

"I'm sorry. What did you ask me?"

"I was just wondering if you ever wanted to be something other than a homicide detective."

He'd been asked that many times over the years and his answer was always the same. "Didn't have the talent to pitch for the Yankees or be a rock star," he smiled, "that left the family business. I don't think it ever occurred to me to do anything else."

"And now with twenty-twenty hindsight would you have made the same choice?"

Interesting, he thought. Most people didn't bother with a follow up question.

"Good question," he said as his cell phone vibrated against his rib cage. "Ah, excuse me." He took the phone out and checked to see who was calling. He didn't recognize the number, but since this was strictly an emergency phone, it had to be business.

"I'm sorry, I have to take this. I'll be right back." He took the napkin off his lap and dropped it on the table as he stood up. "If the food comes, please don't wait."

"I hope it's nothing serious," she said as he left the table and headed toward the men's room. He walked by the man who still hadn't stopped talking on his cell and wondered when his dinner partner was going to dump her pasta over his head.

As he weaved through the tables, he saw his waiter walking toward his table with his steamed mussels. His stomach growled and he hoped this call was nothing serious. His date was pleasant enough even with her food issues, and he loved steamed mussels.

When he entered the bathroom decorated like some faux British "men's" club, he saw another man at a sink, washing his hands. He hated to talk "shop" in a public place so he waited until the man left. As soon as he was alone he flipped open his phone, punched in his password and listened.

"Damn," he said out loud when he heard Lorna's two messages. He immediately dialed the precinct and ordered a uniform over to St. Luke's. He didn't know why, but he trusted Lorna's instincts. Her calls had unsettled him and even the thought of steamed mussels didn't entice him to stay for dinner. He would be miserable company wondering how he had missed the calls. He needed to get back to the precinct to see if he could track Lorna down. He walked out of the men's room and back to his table. He didn't sit down.

"I'm so sorry," he told the woman waiting for his return. "An emergency at the station. I have to get back."

"But, Frank, at least eat your mussels…"

"I'm sorry."

"I'm sorry, too," she said as she slid her chair back preparing to get up.

"Please stay," he continued. "Enjoy your meal. I'll take care of the bill before I leave."

Without waiting for a response, Lt. Muller walked away, found the waiter and gave him two one hundred dollar bills to cover dinner and an expensive bottle of wine he'd ordered to undercut his guilt. Out of eyesight, he waited to make sure the waiter delivered the wine then left. The restaurant was only a few blocks from the station house. He hurriedly walked down the street, rationalizing in the back of his mind that his date would have much more fun eating a great meal and sipping good wine without him. He just wouldn't be able to stop worrying about this Lorna thing.

When he walked into the station the desk clerk handed him his messages, which included two more from Lorna. He hadn't understood all Lorna had said on his voice mail, but it was apparent she was in trouble. He read the two messages. The earlier one wanted him to meet her at a Beekman Place townhouse.

Why? he wondered. What does a house on the east side have to do with her brother falling off a ladder? He stared out his glass-enclosed office into the precinct bullpen, still amazed after all these years how busy it always was, no matter what the time. Crime never sleeps. Nor, apparently, could he.

He listened to Lorna's second message on his cell again and grew alarmed. Where was she? He checked her file and realized that the last number Lorna had called from was her *home* phone. What the hell. He dialed the number. Maybe she was too afraid to answer her phone. Her machine answered.

"Lorna, this is Lt. Muller returning your call. If you're there, please pick up." He waited a few moments. The machine clicked off. Frustrated, he cradled the receiver as Detective Zach Rosen walked into his office.

"Thought you had a dinner date or something."

"Or something," Muller said matter-of-factly. "Got a disturbing call from Lorna Raven and came back here to see if I could track her down."

"And?"

"No luck."

"Well, I had some and decided to follow up. This whole Lauder thing? The guy who filmed his murder is in ICU...it bugged me, so I did some head-butting quid pro quo with my FBI contact. Get this. The cop that shot Lauder's assassin...he's an *ex*-cop. Name's Lou Edwards. He was thrown off the force about three years ago."

"What for?"

"Killing his partner."

"And he's still walking and talking on the streets of New York?"

"Word has it Lou's partner found out something dirty on him and had to be shut up. No one could prove it."

"Then what the hell was he doing in uniform on that boat?"

"According to my friend, Internal Affairs thinks he's a gun for hire, a paid assassin. They figured that was what his partner found out. Probably socked away a big retirement account somewhere in the Caymans."

"So we got a hit man hired to hit a hit man," Muller said. "Do we file that under irony?"

"Might be a good place."

"Since you're on a roll, have you found out who that bogus detective is, yet?" Muller asked.

"Nope. No one anywhere has ever heard of Jefferson Leeds."

"Naturally. And according to this report," Muller said as he held up a sheet of paper he took from the file, "the fingerprints he left in Raven's office are not on file anywhere. No arrest record, no military record, no driver's license anywhere in our glorious fifty states, no nothing. Not even a social security card."

"Must be from Mars."

"Or Washington, if he's not some terrorist mole from who knows where. Find out who the hell he is and what he has to do with all this."

"Can I go home first and take a nap?"

"A short one," Muller answered as Zach walked out of the office. "Then find that ex-cop." Muller then picked up his phone and called dispatch to make sure a uniform had been sent to the hospital.

Carol dozed in a chair next to Poe's bed, lulled asleep by the beeping monitors. Lou Edwards hovered in the doorway and watched her sleep. He took out his gun, the silencer attached and was about to take aim when he heard footsteps coming up behind him. He quickly put the gun away and turned to see a uniformed cop approaching.

"Hey, what're ya doing?" the cop asked, his hand reaching for his gun. "Visiting hours are over."

"Sorry," Lou answered in a contrite voice. "I'm looking for my wife's room. I musta gotten turned 'round when I came out of the john."

"No problem," the cop said relaxing his arm away from his holster.

Lou nodded and walked down the hall as the cop took up his sentry post outside Poe's room.

Lorna stayed in the shadows as she walked through her neighborhood, clueless as to where she could hide. She had wanted to wait and call her aunt when Helen got to Bayside, but was afraid to stay in her loft a minute longer. She'd call her as soon as she settled in somewhere. But where? She couldn't go to Bayside in case "they" were watching the house. She was pretty certain someone would be waiting for her at the hospital, and she didn't dare risk putting a friend in danger. She could go to a hotel, but would have to use her credit card. Nope, can't do that. She had read enough crime novels and seen enough police procedural shows to know that credit card charges could be traced. And since she didn't know who the enemy was, she had no idea how sophisticated they were in tracking down their prey...her.

Having made it out of her loft without incident, she was feeling an immediate "danger reprieve" and realized she was hungry. Hunger pangs were attacking her stomach full force and she wished she had finished the pepper beef. A hole-in-the-wall newspaper/convenience store was just down the block. She looked around. No one seemed to be following her so she ducked in and bought a super-size bag of Cheese Doritos to tide her over.

She thought longingly of the homemade macaroni and cheese casserole Helen always made when she went there for dinner and tore into her Doritos with a vengeance.

She shook her head in an effort to banish all thoughts of warm, inviting, fat-gram-laden comfort food and concentrated on what she should do next. She needed help. Lt. Muller was unreachable. Maybe a good thing, she thought. Wasn't one of those boys in blue trying to kill her?

She shoved a fist full of chips into her mouth. Brain food. As she chomped down, savoring the unique "cheesy" flavor, the solution came to her. She now knew where she had to go. She knew whom she needed to trust.

With a clear vision, she continued to munch her chips as she rushed down the street to an uptown subway station. Before entering, she checked again to see who was behind her. No one seemed threatening. She quickly ran down the stairs, zipped through the turnstile with her metro card and waited for the train. She searched the crowd. No familiar faces. No killer cop about to jump out at her. But the memory of almost being squashed by a moving, screeching, trillion-ton train was all too vivid and she cautiously stayed well back from the platform's ledge. She let out a sigh of relief when the subway pulled in and no one had tried to shove her onto the tracks. It was getting late and, like all New Yorkers, Lorna knew that the end cars would have fewer people. She wanted to be surrounded by humanity, safety in numbers and all that, so she got into a middle car and found a seat. As the train moved out of the station, her hands began to shake as hours of tension escaped her body.

She thought about what had happened. Someone had tried to murder Poe. A cop had tried to kill her—- twice! Jefferson had lied to her. He wasn't a detective at the 17th Precinct. How could she have been so attracted to him? How could she have felt so safe in his arms? It was a few minutes before she felt the tears stinging her cheeks. Not a single passenger noticed.

Lorna wiped her face with the back of her hand and took solace in her bag of Doritos. Well worth the $2.49, she thought.

She finished off the chips just as the train pulled into the Lexington/ 59th Street station.

Thinking she should take a diversionary tactic, she darted up from her seat, scurried past the straphangers and made it out of the subway car just as its doors were closing. To make doubly and triply sure no one was following her, she went into Bloomingdale's and wandered around, losing herself in the crowd.

She took the escalator to lingerie, figuring there was no way a killer cop could stalk her into *this* department undetected. Her mind wandered a moment when she noticed a white cotton bra-and-panties set by Calvin Klein.

Someone moved behind her. She turned abruptly, frightening the poor salesgirl who had come to help her. The woman backed off and Lorna scanned the area. No threatening men in view.

Feeling secure that she had avoided her attacker, she left Bloomingdale's. Rather than go back underground and take another subway, she would walk the twenty odd blocks to The Mark Hotel on Madison and 77th… fewer dark places for someone to jump her…more places for her to escape into…easier for her to run if she needed to.

When she reached The Mark, she cautiously entered the lobby and immediately went to the house phone and asked for Diana Brown. Again, she was given Diana's voice mail.

"Diana, this is Lorna Raven again. I'm downstairs in the lobby. I need to talk to you."

She hung up and approached the registration desk. A clerk was angrily mumbling to himself as he typed something into a computer.

She excused herself for interrupting. He ignored her. She politely excused herself again, this time a bit louder. He stopped typing, smiled and gave her his benign attention. She smiled back, wondering how he could so easily go from aggravation to accommodation. She asked him for pen and paper. After he returned to his computer, she began writing her note: "Diana, I'm in the lobby. I found the tape I told you about. Lorna." She folded the note and gave it to the clerk to put in Diana's message box.

Feeling better now that she had taken control of her situation, Lorna sat on one of the peach velvet club chairs that were placed in a conversation grouping by a wall featuring a mural of primary colors. Crayons standing at attention, she thought. Copper, silver and gold spheres hung on an adjacent wall. She would wait for Diana as long as it took, positive that Diana would be the one who could help her.

She picked a discarded newspaper off a chrome side table and tried to concentrate on the day's news, but was way too keyed up.

She kept reading the same sentence over and over again. Every time someone walked into the hotel or off the elevator, she looked up.

Resigned to her waiting fate, she would pass the time taking in her surroundings.

She hadn't been in this five star hotel since it finished its renovations from restrained old-world elegance to a sophisticated 21st century version of 1940's minimalism. The black and white striped marble floor made a bold statement against the cream walls, blond woods, chrome accents and simple modern gray velvet benches, but the striking change made her feel alien in a strange land. Even the neighborhood of gilded-age mansions and townhouses that was once a source of wonder made her feel like Alice after she fell down the rabbit hole. The city was no longer Lorna's magical place, but a place of fear.

An hour later, Lorna came out of the ladies room just as Diana walked into the lobby. She was about to wave, but quickly put her arm down when she saw Jefferson enter the hotel right behind her.

"Diana," he called out.

Diana turned around. "Darlin,' there you are. I've been looking *everywhere* for you," she smiled, then gave him a very non-platonic kiss.

Stunned, Lorna quickly ducked behind a column, the only shelter in sight. She thought about going back into the bathroom, but was afraid she'd be seen. She gritted her teeth holding back her rage as she watched this "touching" reunion.

Jefferson pulled away and firmly grabbed Diana's shoulders.

"What the hell are you doing here?" he practically hissed in her car.

Oblivious to the tension, the desk clerk interrupted.

"A message for you, Ms. Brown," he said as he handed over Lorna's note.

"You just hold that thought, sugar," Diana drawled, as she smiled at Jefferson, then opened and read the note. "Oh, my god!" she gasped, her accent totally gone. She frantically looked around the lobby but didn't see Lorna. She ran outside to search the street but came back a moment later.

"And to think my kisses used to make your toes curl," he said sarcastically.

"I've missed us," she answered coyly, shifting emotional gears. She ran her fingers tantalizingly down his face.

"Really," he said dryly. "It's only been two years..."

"...Four days an' twenty-two hours," she quipped, her accent returning.

"And, of course, for old times' sake, you're going to let me read that note now aren't you *darling*'," Jefferson said, as he took her arm and led her into the bar.

As soon as they disappeared from the lobby, Lorna snuck out of the hotel and hurried down the street in a complete state of confusion.

The Mark bar which had once been a study in old, eclectic European design with dark mahogany paneled walls, Chinese lamps and wing chairs upholstered in textured floral fabrics was now a futuristic space encased in rosewood walls in a diamond pattern with sconces that looked like lighted buttons tufting the wood. Jefferson hadn't been here in years and was taken aback by its transformation. He went over to the space-age chrome bar and ordered drinks, then he and Diana sat down on brown and white animal spotted lounge chairs at an intimate table in a corner of the room. He stared intensely into her eyes, making her uncomfortable. She "blinked" first.

"Still single malt I see," she said breaking their silence. "How'd you know I'd be here?"

"I'm either psychic or you've become predictable."

The waiter brought their drinks...Jefferson's scotch, neat. Diana's Grey Goose martini, three olives.

"Even with all the changes, this place has a lot of memories," Diana said as she savored a sip of her drink.

He looked at her beautiful face bathed in the glow of the table's lighted candle and tried to dismiss the pain and anger he still felt for her. He couldn't.

"Really? I don't remember a thing."

"I think we're being a tad disingenuous, wouldn't you say?"

"The royal 'we' can be as disingenuous as we wish."

"Suite 628. The Jeff and Diana suite?"

"Don't you mean the 'fill in the blank' and Diana suite," Jefferson said pointedly.

"I don't deserve that."

"Few people in life get what they deserve."

"Bitterness becomes you," she said. "Makes you appear all dark and brooding. It's sexy."

"You haven't answered my questions, Diana."

"Which questions, darlin'? The reason I miss you?"

"You know sometimes you're just not clever enough. Hand over the note."

Diana held the note in her hand, but before Jefferson could snatch it from her she used the candle on the table to burn it, singeing her fingers in the process. She didn't flinch.

"I see you still have a high threshold for pain."

Diana took another sip of her martini then popped an olive into her mouth.

"I want to know Diana...why *are* you here?" he all but demanded.

"George had a hunch."

"A hunch?"

"Yes."

"Just rolled over next to you in bed one morning and said, hey 'Diana, I want you to follow a hunch?'"

"Sorry, darlin,' not my type."

"Really? He's a definite rung up your career ladder. Above Robert. Way above me."

"Is that what you think? That I used Robert?"

Jefferson swirled the scotch in his glass then drank it down. "He never got over you."

"No, Jeff, he never got over the fact that I was capable of doing things without him."

They stared at each other, their history smothering them like a burial shroud.

"Don't you think I miss him, too? I was devastated when I heard." Diana spoke softly.

"I don't know what you think anymore. I don't think I ever did," he stated coolly.

"For what it's worth, you were never a rung on my ladder."

"Why don't we just let sleeping dogs lie, OK?"

"Fine." She finished her martini and olives and got up to leave, slowly leaning forward right into Jefferson's face. His eyes betrayed no emotion.

"Speaking of sleeping," she whispered as she lightly kissed him on the lips. He felt his muscles stiffen. His hands felt like ice.

"Who are you sleeping with these days?" she asked in a taunting manner. "That pretty little videographer?"

"Don't have a clue what you're talking about," he answered, his tone flat and controlled.

"Oh, darlin,' *we're* being disingenuous again," she said, still only inches from his face. She backed away.

"Fowler knows you're here mucking with the investigation. Sleeping with a pretty little thing to relieve the tension is just part of your charm, if I recall."

"What's he want, Diana?

"Your ass. He wants your ass back in Washington."

chapter

TWELVE

After sneaking out of the Mark Hotel, a confused and frightened Lorna ran down the street not knowing what to do or where to go. Out of breath, she stopped and leaned against the wall of a building, clutching her stomach. "Breathe," she said to herself over and over again till her heart stopped racing and her lungs took in air at a normal pace. Images of making love with Jefferson ran through her mind as Diana's voice whispered in her memory, "never heard of him."

She knew she needed to find someplace to think...somewhere safe until she could figure out what was going on. One option was to ride the subway until morning, but that brought out an involuntary laugh. Safe in the wee hours of the morning in a New York subway? Hardly. The only place that would make her feel safe, she knew, was home...not *her* home, but *home* home. She'd be careful. She'd make sure no one followed her. She was going home to Bayside.

***

The rhythmic movement of the Long Island Railroad train had lulled Lorna into a fitful sleep. A sudden jerk woke her up and for a moment she had no idea where she was. Then she recognized the lights of a passing building and realized the next stop was hers. About a dozen people were in the car...some snoozing, some reading, others just staring into space. Through the back door window she saw a man leave the car behind hers. He stepped onto the platform that joined his car with hers. She watched him adjust his glasses then peer into her car. They locked eyes just before he yanked the door open and entered. Around forty, dressed in jeans and a short sleeve plaid shirt hanging loosely outside his pants, he took a seat across from her. When she diverted her eyes, she felt him staring at her. When she turned to look at him again, he quickly looked at something else. Her mind raced. Who was he? Why was he staring at her? Was there a gun hidden in his waistband under all that plaid? Her heart began to race as the train pulled into the station. She looked at the man again as the train jerked to a stop. His eyes seemed dead as he held her stare for a second then dropped his gaze to the floor as the doors opened.

Afraid he would follow her, she waited until the last second then dashed out of the car, heaving a sigh of relief when the doors closed behind her and no one else from the train was on the platform. She looked inside the car as it pulled away. The man smiled slightly as their eyes met again, causing a shiver to run up her spine. She knew she was being irrational, but what could she expect after the day she'd had? The guy was probably just some jerk looking to psych her out to pass the time til he got home to his internet porn in Little Neck. She checked her watch. Eleven twenty. Aunt Helen must be home by now.

She took a deep breath. The air was thick with humidity, but after being in the cold, air-conditioned railroad car it didn't bother her. She usually walked the mile or so from the station to her old house, but she was in a rush to feel her aunt's comforting arms surrounding her. She hurried over to the taxi stand and felt almost light-hearted when she saw a lone cab parked out front. This was a good sign, she thought. It didn't matter that the cab looked like it had starred in every low-budget smash and crash car chase movie in the history of "cinema." She didn't miss a beat as she quickly jumped into the broken down, un-air-conditioned car and rolled down the window, letting the humid air spill over her face as they took off.

As they headed down 35th Avenue and turned onto her aunt's street, her survival instincts kicked in and she told the driver to pull in front of a split-level house two blocks away. She quickly paid and got out, then slowly walked up the flagstone path leading to her neighbor's front door.

As soon as the cab was out of sight, she moved into the shadows and made her way down the street toward her aunt's house.

Half a block away, she hid behind an ancient oak tree and looked longingly at her childhood home, a three-story brick structure with white trimmed windows, black shutters and a black front door. The yard and driveway were defined by thick green hedges bordering the sidewalk and large bushes of blue hydrangeas under the front sunroom windows.

She wanted to run into the house and yell, "I'm home, Auntie Helen" like she did as a little girl, but suppressed the urge.

She looked around the neighborhood to make sure nothing seemed out of place or "wrong." The street was quiet…a few parked cars…not a soul in sight.

She took a step out of her hiding place when a flicker of light caressed the corner of her eye.

She quickly moved back behind the tree and searched the street for the light source. There it was again, a tiny golden glow moving up and down in the tan, four-door sedan parked across the street and a few yards up from her aunt's house.

She watched the light as it continued to move up and down in the passenger's seat. Someone was sitting in the car smoking a cigarette. Though there was a street light on the corner, Lorna couldn't see anything or anyone in the car…just the glow of the cigarette.

Suddenly, the driver's door opened and a man got out, looked around, then leaned against the car and stretched his hamstrings, back and shoulders. In less than thirty seconds he was back in the car. It doesn't take years of detective training to know that there were two men in the car and that they weren't waiting for a tow truck or a pizza delivery. They were watching her home. The home she grew up in, happy and loved. The home they would violate if they knew she was there.

Not knowing how many others were watching the house, she wasn't going to chance sneaking into the backyard and climbing through a window.

As quickly and quietly as she could, using the night shadows as cover, she moved away from the house, turned the corner and ran up the adjacent street.

Her mind filled with "what ifs." What if she hadn't had the taxi let her off down the street? What if she'd just pulled up in front of the house and Aunt Helen had run out to greet her? What if? What if? She knew what if. They'd both be dead.

She stopped running and walked at a brisk pace. She had to get back to the LIRR station and catch the first train back to the city.

What if they get tired of staking out her house and find her walking on the street? Panicked, she spun around looking for the tan sedan, then shook her head thinking she'd better stop with the "what ifs," but still stay alert.

When she reached 35th Avenue and Bell Boulevard, she saw a number Q13 bus ease its way toward the bus stop. Perfect!

She ran, and by the time it opened its doors and let out a lone male passenger, Lorna was there to jump in.

She fished her metro card out of her canvas bag and slid it in the machine attached to the coin drop. As the machine spit it back out, she saw on the little screen that she only had ten dollars left on the card.

"Damn," she said under her breath, realizing she'd have to buy a new card soon.

She retrieved the card and took a seat in the rear of the bus, her back to the sidewalk in case anyone was walking down the street looking for her. As the bus pulled away from the curb and moved down Bell, she noticed for the first time that she was its only passenger.

Lorna had made the decision to forget the LIRR. She'd take the bus all the way to Flushing and catch the IRT into the city. But first she had to call and reassure her aunt. As the bus turned on Northern Blvd., she got up from her seat and walked up to the driver.

"Excuse me."

"Yeh."

"I need to call my aunt and I've lost my cell. Do you have one I could use for just a minute?"

He took his eyes off the road and gave her "a look," then turned his attention back to his driving.

"Please, it's local," she said pleadingly. "I'm late and I was supposed to be there for dinner hours ago. Mac and cheese, my favorite! With Velveeta!" She knew she was about to start rambling, so she took a deep breath and continued calmly. "Please. I know she's probably worried sick."

He thought for a moment, then took pity on her, unclipped the phone off his belt and handed it to her.

"Make it short," he ordered trying to sound gruffer than he was as he stopped for a red light.

Lorna took a seat half-way down the aisle and dialed. "Aunt Helen, it's me."

She listened for a minute. "No, no. I'm fine. Really. I just got to the hospital," she lied. "I'm sorry I didn't call earlier, but I lost my cell. I'm using Carol's."

The light had changed and the bus moved forward as Lorna continued her conversation.

"Please don't be upset, I didn't mean to worry you."

"What man? What did you tell him?" she asked after her aunt told her some nice man had "dropped by" an hour or so ago looking for her and apologizing for the late night intrusion.

"No, no. It's all right. Probably just another reporter wanting to interview me about Lauder's death," she vamped, realizing the man at the door was probably one of the men watching the house.

The driver turned and gave Lorna another "look," this one of impatience as she listened to her aunt, unable to get a word in edge-wise.

"I'm sorry, Aunt Helen, I really shouldn't be using a phone in the ICU," she said to continue the charade. "I'll call you tomorrow," she promised. "I love you."

She handed the phone back to the driver. "Thank you."

The man grunted as he clipped his cell back onto his belt then stepped on the gas, causing her to lose her balance and throwing her into a seat.

Jefferson couldn't sleep. He got out of bed, wrapped the white terry robe around his naked body and went into the living room of his hotel suite. He turned on the television and flipped through the channels, trying not to remember. Finally, he shut off the TV and poured himself a scotch. If he couldn't block out the memories, he decided he might as well give in and wallow in them. He wondered if he still loved her as he sat down on the couch and sipped his drink.

Diana had flattened Jefferson like a steamroller. He hated that cliché, but he couldn't think of any other way to describe her impact on him. She was smart, funny, sophisticated, daring and so beautiful. Not an approachable beauty like Lorna, but regal...almost untouchable. Strange that she had seemed so unattainable even when he had been making love to her, but maybe not. Maybe that was what had drawn him to her.

Jefferson remembered how he had researched everything about her the minute they had parted after their first night together. He had been bewitched and needed to know what made this woman tick. It hadn't been easy, but eventually he was able to hack his way into her agency file. He'd found out that Diana had excelled at everything...the physical challenges, as well as the mental. But her childhood read like a bad Tennessee Williams' play.

Born and bred in Savannah, Diana's mother had been a renowned madam. Her father, ironically, was the chief of police as well as her mother's longtime lover. And, of course, he was married with three other children.

From the minute Diana was old enough to understand who her parents were she had distanced herself from them. When she had finally confided in Jefferson about her past, she told him how she despised her father's hypocrisy and her mother's need for his protection. Diana had vowed never to need a man to survive. She was going to run with the bulls on her own terms and she became very adept at stepping around the bullshit, even at the same time men showered her with favors, which she heartily accepted.

After getting a full scholarship to Vassar, Diana left home for good. "An east coast education in one of the original "sister" schools," she once laughingly told him, "to add some polish."

After Vassar came Columbia Law, again on scholarship. It was there, according to her file, that she was recruited by the ATF. The file never mentioned, nor could it, that she was no ideologue. Flag and country held no interest for her. It was the thrill of the chase…the chance to beat the boys in their own game that made the offer appealing to her.

It hadn't taken Diana long to conquer Washington. Men had flocked to her and she thrived. They took her to Paris for dinner and to banquets at the White House. And she reveled in the high-life. They told her secrets that she had no qualms about using to further her career. But, she had never been with any one man for longer than a few months until she'd met Jefferson.

For two years they had done everything together, had even shared cases, and when they hadn't been working or making love, they had traveled the world. Jefferson had had no idea that he could love someone so completely, but he could never quite make himself propose marriage. He knew that money, lots of it, was important to her and he was not sure if that included *his* money.

Jefferson got up and made himself another drink, four fingers, neat, then returned to the sofa for more wallowing.

Two years ago, Diana had been out of the country for three weeks following a drug smuggling lead and he was feeling restless. Robert Stainbrook, a rising star in the agency and Jefferson's best friend, had recently stopped a major terrorist plot out of the New York office and he had yet to congratulate him. What better way to celebrate Robert's good work than in person, Jefferson had thought at the time. He had no open investigations, so why not just fly to New York and surprise him?

He had grabbed the keycard to his private suite in The Mark Hotel, packed an overnight bag and took a cab to Dulles. Three hours later he pulled up in front of the hotel, excited about being in New York... looking forward to seeing his friend.

He had walked quickly through the lobby and waited patiently for the elevator. Maybe they'd head over to Il Vagabondo for a game or two of bocce, some veal parmesan and sautéed spinach, with a great bottle of Chianti.

His mouth was watering by the time he had gotten to the front door of his suite. A "Do Not Disturb" sign was hanging on the door-knob.

Since he paid to keep this suite for himself alone, alarm bells had gone off in his head. The only other person with a keycard was Diana, and she was in Europe. He had pulled out his gun and unlocked the door.

Quietly, he had entered the living room. A room service cart covered with half-eaten food stood by the couch. A man's jacket and tie were in a heap on a chair. He had picked up a tan silk blouse off the floor. The smell of a perfume he knew so well lingered in the fabric. His mind had reeled as he tried to ignore the obvious.

Familiar noises of passion came from the bedroom. Gun pointed straight ahead, he had forced himself to go into the room. In his bed was the love of his life having sex with his best friend. They had stopped when they realized he was there watching them.

No one had said a word. Jefferson had lowered his gun and walked out of the suite.

Diana kept up the affair with Robert for six months after that. Then, one night in Rome after a romantic dinner and passionate love-making, she had quietly gotten out bed, leaving a sleeping Robert alone in their hotel room. When he had awakened, he knew it was over. He didn't even try to call her. After a two week bender, Robert had returned to the States to mend his fences with Jefferson.

Jefferson began to doze off as the image of Diana in bed reaching out to him slowly morphed into Lorna. Before he fell asleep, he wondered what a shrink would say about that.

LONG ISLAND—ONE A.M.

The light from a full moon was glistening off the ocean as several Eastern European men made their way to the shore of a deserted Long Island beach in two motor launches loaded with large crates. Three miles out, a large yacht drifted. Waiting on the beach were "corn fed" red-blooded white American males and a large truck. As the boats cut their motors and landed on the shore, Lou Edwards rode up in a dune buggy to supervise the unloading.

The Americans unloaded the crates. Lou used a crowbar to help open them and check their contents. Inside were dozens of AK47s and boxes of ammunition. Satisfied with the delivery, an American pulled an attaché out of the truck and handed it to Lou. Lou gave it to one of the Europeans who opened it. The case was filled with untraceable American currency. He quickly counted the money and, satisfied that it was all there, snapped the attaché shut. He and his men got back into the launches and sped out to sea. Not one word was spoken during the whole ten minute exchange.

Lou watched as the men boarded the yacht. As the boat moved off the horizon, he got back into his dune buggy and drove down the beach. He pulled behind a large grassy sand dune about a mile away. He shut off the engine and stepped out of the dune buggy. Grabbing a pair of binoculars, he climbed the dune and lay down on his stomach on the sand, hidden by the tall grass, as he watched the men load the truck. Looking through the binoculars, Lou searched the beach access road that the truck had used to get to the shoreline, then focused on the truck. The driver got into the cab and started the engine as the last crate was lifted on.

Suddenly, floodlights lit up the area as eight police jeeps came barreling down the access road and onto the beach. The driver of the truck leaned out of the cab firing an automatic weapon as the other men pulled out guns and shot at the police.

The police returned fire as the truck started to move forward, but the jeeps surrounded it, keeping the truck from getting to the road or from racing down the beach.

Lou watched as two of the men were hit as they tried climbing into the truck. Bullets blasted through the windshield of the cab, hitting the driver in the face. He slumped over the steering wheel as the truck engine kept running, its wheels spinning deeper and deeper in the sand. The battle was over in less than five minutes.

As the police handcuffed the men and loaded them into their jeeps, Lou wiped down his dune buggy of any fingerprints. Satisfied, he took off his deck loafers and wiggled his toes in the cool sand. Carrying his shoes in one hand, he quietly made his way down the beach in the opposite direction from the battleground to another road access where his car was parked two miles away from the action.

NEW YORK CITY

Lorna stared out a window at the tunnel walls as the subway train pulled into Grand Central and jerked to a stop. Though she was in a middle car, she was its only passenger. She reluctantly left the train and walked onto the platform. Not knowing what she was going to do next, she followed the few people who had been in other cars to the escalator. Soon she was in the cavernous main terminal. She looked up at the vaulted ceiling painted the color of an evening sky, and wondered how the artists were able to paint the gilded constellations onto the interior of this massive dome.

She walked past the famous brass clock atop the information booth and looked for an empty seat. Every square inch on every bench was taken. Standing in the middle of the terminal, she watched the people going to and from the various tracks, amazed at how busy it was after midnight.

Not far from her a woman stood impatiently under the clock, ironically checking her watch every few minutes.

Suddenly, the woman smiled and waved frantically as she rushed into the arms of a man entering the terminal. Like a "diamonds are for-ever" commercial, the man picked her up and swung her around in the air as she kissed him over and over again, reminding Lorna that there actually were people in the world who were happy.

She turned away from the lovers as a homeless man approached her, his hand outstretched. He quickly backed away when he saw the tears streaming down her face. Misery, apparently, did not love com-pany.

Amid all this human activity in the city she loved, Lorna had never felt so tired...so alone.

Exhausted, with no idea where to go, she found a space against a wall near some college students who sat on their duffel bags waiting for their train to be called. She lay down on the cold floor and curled up into a fetal position, using her canvas bag as her pillow.

.

chapter

THIRTEEN

"Rise and shine, princess," a voice echoed in her head. "Rise and shine."

Who is that? she thought. It's not time for school yet. Hold on, someone's shaking me. Aunt Helen never shakes me.

"Come on honey, get your ass out of here. The worker bees are about to swarm."

A rough tug on her pant leg woke Lorna with a start. She opened her eyes and looked straight into the face of a uniformed policewoman.

"Get movin,' doll."

Lorna scrambled to her feet, grabbed her canvas bag and headed for the ladies room. As she passed the brass clock she saw that it was only five in the morning.

A cleaning woman was mopping the bathroom as she entered. A good sign, she thought, as she headed straight into a stall. She hated public toilets, but was happy to see *and* smell the fact that the seats had just been cleaned. When she came out of the stall, the cleaning woman was gone and she had the bathroom to herself. She ran hot water in the sink then yanked off her tee shirt, dunked it in the water and used it to wash up. She pulled the clean tee from her canvas bag and put it on. She stripped off her jeans and panties and continued her sponge bath. When she finished, she put on fresh underpants and stepped back into her jeans. She shoved the worn panties and wet tee into the trash bin, then grabbed her bag and walked back into the terminal. In the few minutes it took to freshen up, Lorna decided that she had to risk sneaking into her office.

One thing about traveling the subway and walking the streets at the crack of dawn...no crowds. It also made it easier to spot a potential killer.

Arriving at her office building, she decided against the elevator and walked up the six flights. Like a kid looking both ways before stepping off the curb, she stuck her head out of the stairwell and looked all around before venturing into the hallway.

She cautiously made her way down the hall, listening for any threatening sounds. As usual, the other office doors were closed, with no sounds of life coming from behind them. For the millionth time, Lorna wondered if she and Poe were the only tenants on the floor. Just to be safe, she searched for her keys *before* she walked down the hall.

As she reached her office, she looked over her shoulder to make sure no one had entered the corridor behind her. She unlocked the door and entered the office. She stood in the reception area for a moment still listening for any unusual sounds. Nothing. She went down the office hall and into the editing room.

Exhausted from fear, tension and little sleep, Lorna let her canvas bag just slide off her shoulder where it thudded to the floor. Without thinking she picked up one of Poe's toys that she had missed earlier, a miniature Godzilla. She wound it up and sent it scooting across the console table, sparks "flaming" from its mouth. She stared at it, mesmerized for a moment, then remembered why she was in the editing

194

room. Someone had tried to murder her brother. Someone was trying to kill *her*. Why?

She grabbed the Worthington tape out of her canvas bag and put it in an editing machine. She pulled up the shot of the silhouette on the Chagall and started playing with the dials and buttons, isolating and enlarging the image. Physically depleted by fear and lack of sleep, her body put up with this for about fifteen minutes before rebelling. Her eyes grew heavy. By the sixteenth minute she was asleep in her chair.

In his office, Lt. Muller sipped his coffee as he read the paper. That morning ritual was broken when one of his detectives stuck her head in.

"Got a minute, Frank?"

"Sure, got lots of 'em. Take two," he answered smiling. He liked this woman. Sara Kelly had transferred from Boston a year ago and he loved her no frills, take charge attitude. Early forties. Divorced. No kids. She was smart, good at what she did, and they had fallen into a pattern of having drinks after work two or three nights a week. Some nights they even had dinner. He hadn't really enjoyed a woman's company since his wife had died four years ago, but he enjoyed Sara's easy way. It didn't hurt that he also was attracted to the bold gray streak in her black hair that framed her handsome face and her tall, regal bearing. He was never a dater and felt awkward around most women. Last night's fiasco proved it. As nice as his blind date was, and she *did* seem nice, he would have jumped at any chance to get out of that restaurant—and he did. But, not with Sara. With her, he often thought about expanding their friendship into something more meaningful. Whether he followed up on that idea or not, one thing he knew...no more blind dates.

She dropped a file onto his desk. "Results on that Alan Raven guy."

"And?"

"Well, according to his doctors, if you don't count the laws of nature, you got an accident. Otherwise you got yourself an attempted murder."

"And if we just follow the law?"

"Then we still have an attempted murder," she answered. "There's a second wound on the back of Raven's head. Couldn't have been made by the desk, unless he smashed his head twice on the corner. Those laws of nature, specifically gravity, seem to dismiss this as unlikely. From what the doctors tell me, my guess the second wound was caused by a blunt instrument…a hammer or gun butt."

"Definitely against the laws of nature," he said as he picked up his phone and dialed.

Lorna was still asleep in the chair, her head on the editing bay console. A car horn honked outside, startling her awake. The bay clock read 8:00. Shit! She slapped herself a couple of times then rushed into the reception area to check the front door. Locked. Relieved, she went into the bathroom and brushed her teeth. She gingerly cleaned her cut-up knee and changed the bandage. She stared at herself in the mirror.

"My god, any more strung-out you could be a model," she sarcastically told herself. She splashed water on her face and tried to do something with her unruly hair. Within seconds she gave up. To hell with it. The office phone started to ring. If it hadn't, she might have heard the sound of someone picking the front door lock.

Lorna waited, but whoever was calling this early in the morning hung up before her machine could answer. She went into the main office and grabbed a baseball cap from the coat rack and put it on. As she walked back into the editing room the phone started ringing again. This time it rang long enough for the answering machine to click in and Lorna's voice filled the room.

Someone quietly stood in the hall listening.

"Hi, you've reached the office of Raven's Video. Please leave a message after the beep." The machine beeped.

"Ms. Raven, this is Lt. Muller. Are you there? I've been trying to find you. I put a guard outside your brother's room as a precaution, but just learned you were right, someone did try to kill him. He..."

Lorna snatched up the extension in the editing room. "Didn't I tell you?! Didn't I tell you?! And now they're trying to kill me! And it's all because of Lauder," she rattled on, barely taking a breath. "He's alive and Poe knew it and I have the evidence and..."

Muller interrupted and asked if she knew who was trying to kill her. She told him how the cop from the Circle Line tried pushing her in front of a train and chased her with a gun.

He filled her in and told her the "cop's" name.

"So why don't you just arrest this Lou Edwards guy?" she blurted out.

Muller assured her that they were looking for him, then asked that she come to the station and tell him everything she knew. No way! she thought. Edwards is a killer ex-cop, Jefferson *isn't* a cop, Diana may or may not be an ATF agent and lied about knowing Jefferson. Why should she trust Muller or anyone who says they're in law enforcement?

She told him she wanted to meet him someplace open. Someplace familiar. She thought of St. Patrick's Cathedral across the street from Rockefeller Center. From there they could go somewhere safe and talk.

"I'll meet you on the steps of St. Pat's at noon," she said.

Muller tried to convince her that she would be safer coming to him, but soon realized she was too frightened, and agreed to meet her at the cathedral. The steps of the church with hoards of people milling about should be safe enough until he could figure out what was going on.

He heaved a world-weary sigh. "Fine. St. Pat's at noon."

She hung up the phone, ejected the Worthington tape and put it back in her canvas bag as Jefferson walked in behind her.

"Good morning."

She screamed and dropped her bag.

"How long have you been there?" she demanded.

"Just walked in," Jefferson lied. "What's wrong?"

"Apart from breaking into my office and scaring ten years off my life, what could be wrong?" she said trying to make light of the situation. She grabbed her bag and slowly made for the door. Suddenly she tried to bolt past him. He grabbed her arm. She struggled to get away, but his grasp was too tight. He pulled her toward him and grabbed her other arm. His fingers dug painfully into her flesh just above her elbows.

"I saw you on the tape. On the boat. You were there!" she said as she continued to struggle.

"Lorna, calm down," he ordered.

"I will not calm down! Lauder's alive and you know it, and you're not a cop...and——-" she abruptly stopped talking as her mind raced and her eyes widened in terror. "You're the one!" She knew she should shut up, but couldn't stop herself. Why did she always have to talk non-stop when she was nervous or scared? She twisted violently, freeing herself of his grasp. Jefferson quickly moved to block the doorway forcing her to back further into the editing bay.

She stared at him. "You tried to kill Poe," she said, choking back her emotions. Her mind was racing, remembering that night. "Oh, my god! It was right after you slept with me."

"Lorna, please. I didn't try to kill him. I'm sorry I had to lie to you..."

She breathed heavily as she looked at the man she had made love with so passionately. He approached her cautiously, quietly, a lion tamer approaching an angry cat.

"...I'm with the ATF," he continued in a soothing voice. "Lauder was part of a gun smuggling operation I was investigating. He staged his own death when he knew he was about to be exposed."

Lorna, her back against the worktable, wasn't buying any of this. She reached behind her, searching for something. Her hand touched a large, weighted tape dispenser.

"You've got to believe me. I had nothing to do with what happened to your brother," he stated firmly as he reached for her.

She snatched up the dispenser and quickly dodged him only to slam into one of the tall steel racks, dislodging a crate of videotapes from the top shelf.

Jefferson saw the crate about to fall on her. He rushed to push her away as she lunged at him, smashing the tape dispenser onto his skull with all her strength. Stunned, he staggered backward and slumped to his knees as the crate crashed to the floor, hitting him in the shoulder. He tried to get back onto his feet, but banged into the worktable. He braced himself as he waited for the dizziness to pass.

Lorna raced out of the editing room, down the hall and into the reception area. She opened the door and ran down the corridor. Reaching the elevator, she frantically pushed the button. The door opened.

As she stepped into the car, Jefferson ran out of the office and down the hall toward her.

She repeatedly hit the "close" button. Please, please, please close, she begged the Gods. She held her breath as he came closer and closer.

"Lorna, stop!" Jefferson pleaded, "You've got to let me explain." Just as he reached the elevator, the door closed.

My heart's going to explode out of my chest, Lorna thought, as the car seemed to inch its way down to the lobby. She prayed there would be no stops along the way.

Abruptly, the elevator stopped on the first floor. The door opened and she ran across the marble floor, through the old deco doors and onto the sidewalk.

Inside the building Jefferson raced out of the stairwell and into the lobby.

Just as he hit the street, Lorna ducked into the lobby of the neighboring building. She knew she had to hide.

Across the lobby she saw two men stepping into the elevator. She made a dash for it, jumped in and wedged herself behind them.

Before the door closed, she saw Jefferson through the building's glass front doors. He stopped in front and glanced into the empty lobby.

Ilona Joy Saari

She almost let out a cry when she thought he was looking directly at her, but felt almost giddy when she realized he didn't see her hidden behind the two men.

As he turned his back to her and looked up and down the street in frustration, the elevator door closed.

Lt. Muller was about to leave the station when his office phone rang. He debated about answering it, but thinking it might be Lorna Raven, he grabbed it.

"Muller."

He listened as the caller identified herself. His stomach gave a nervous tumble when he realized it was Diana Brown. The thought that something had happened to Lorna flashed through his mind. He pulled open his desk drawer and reached for a roll of Tums. But, Diana just wanted to know if he had heard from Lorna. Relieved, he threw the Tums back into the drawer. He listened as she explained that she'd been trying Lorna at her home phone, office phone and cell with no luck. She sounded concerned.

"She's hiding," Muller told her.

"Hiding from what?"

"From the people who tried to kill her brother."

"What?" Diana asked. "I thought his fall was an accident."

"His doctors think otherwise."

"If this is related to the Lauder assassination, we have to find her."

"Even if this is *not* related to the Lauder assassination, we'd have to find her. But she's found," he told her. "I spoke to her earlier and I'm meeting her at St. Pat's in a little while, then taking her someplace safe until we can figure this all out. I'll call you when she's settled. You can interview her then." Muller hung up the receiver and hurried out of his office before there was another interruption.

After escaping from Jefferson, Lorna decided to hide in plain sight until her meeting with Lt. Muller. She had a few hours to kill so, limping slightly, she cut across Central Park on foot to the east side and took the Fifth Avenue bus downtown. She was relieved that the bus wasn't that crowded and gratefully collapsed into a seat. It felt good to get off her feet. Her ankle was throbbing just enough to be uncomfortable. She fished out the Motrin from her canvas bag and swallowed two. The bus slowly made its way downtown. At 57th Street she decided to get off.

On the street, she checked her surroundings. No one seemed to be following her. She headed down Fifth toward the cathedral, stopping for a moment to look in Tiffany's windows. Pencil-slim Audrey Hepburn in her pencil-slim, black floor-length gown, with strands of pearls and a long cigarette holder popped into her head as it did every time she walked by the store.

She wished she could have breakfast in Tiffany's, or at least Audrey's cup of coffee. Right now she was more hungry than frightened and the movie triggered another memory. She knew exactly where she was going to wait. Falling into step with other pedestrians, Lorna hurried down Fifth to 51st Street, directly across from St. Pat's. She made a quick left and walked to the building numbered 5, The Prime Burger coffee shop.

The breakfast rush was over, leaving many of the blond wood seats in the front of the restaurant empty. Arranged in horseshoe shaped "rows," these attached chairs were nicknamed "box seats." Each one had an individual swinging tray which reminded her of the tray on a baby's highchair. She preferred these "singleton" seats over sitting on a stool at the counter and only sat at the tables in the back if she was with someone. Her stomach growled as she inhaled the smells of deep frying onions and grilled beef. She quickly chose a box seat facing the big front window and entrance. A waiter wearing the coffee shop's uniform of white jacket and bow tie brought her a menu, but she didn't need it. She immediately ordered a rare cheeseburger, onion rings and a diet coke. She kept her eye on the coffee shop's entrance while she thought about how she found this place.

Ilona Joy Saari

The first time she saw the movie "Breakfast At Tiffany's" she and her college roommate, Candace, had rented the DVD. Because the movie showed the New York Public Library and other real New York locations, Candace wondered if the coffee shop, called Hamburger Heaven in the movie, really existed. It didn't take long for them to find out. Though the name had been changed, everything else remained the same. The burgers were delicious, maybe Lorna's favorite in all Manhattan, the onion rings and steak fries, perfect, and the sweet potato pie was the best she'd ever eaten.

Why, she wondered, for the millionth time did she always think about food when she was stressed? She should be trying to figure out how to help Lt. Muller find Poe's attacker. She needed to concentrate. As she went over all that had happened in her mind, her waiter brought her "brunch." One bite of the cheeseburger and her mind tripped lightly back to Holly Golightly.

Jefferson sat in the back pew of St. Patrick's Cathedral waiting for twelve o'clock. He watched as people arrived for the noon mass. If he were a praying man, he'd pray that Lorna hadn't canceled her meeting with Muller or changed their meeting place. He was pretty sure she didn't know that he'd overheard her conversation, but he wouldn't bet his life on it.

He looked around the church as various parishioners, tourists and city dwellers lighted candles and prayed at the small altars running along the interior side walls. The church's gothic architecture with its spires that towered more than three hundred feet was awesome, but it was the ornate interior that Jefferson loved the most. Sitting in this place surrounded by dark woods, stained glass windows and religious art gave him a sense of peace, unlike the colder, modern, teak wood Lutheran church he had gone to as a child.

His attention turned to the front of the church as the altar boys in their white robes came out to light the main altar's candles. The mass was about to start. He checked his watch. One minute to twelve. He looked around the church one last time then headed outside.

Lorna came out the coffee shop and surreptitiously walked to the corner of Fifth and 51st. She scanned the noontime crowd for Lt. Muller and felt a rush of relief when she spotted him artfully jaywalking across Fifth Avenue toward the cathedral. She didn't see Jefferson standing in the shadows at the top of the church's steps. Nor did she see Diana waiting under an awning in front of Saks Fifth Avenue across 50th Street. As Muller climbed the cement stairs, Lorna dodged traffic as she rushed across the street. The Motrin had finally dulled the pain in her ankle and she felt almost weightless as she walked toward the person she believed would help end her nightmare. Her need to be with her brother was overwhelming, but she knew she had to survive first and that meant finding the person responsible for putting him in the hospital.

She by-passed a few people sitting on the steps eating lunch as she climbed her way toward her savior. She didn't notice Lou Edwards among the luncheon crowd. He casually ate an apple as he watched Lorna approach the lieutenant. Just as she reached Muller, Lou stood up. He dropped the apple core and slowly moved toward them. When he was ten feet behind Lorna, he pulled a gun from under his shirt.

Jefferson saw it and yelled Lorna's name. Startled people on the steps looked up at him as he rushed down toward Lorna who turned to him and didn't see Lou point his weapon directly at her. A flash of sunlight off the gun hit Muller in the eyes as he saw Lou move menacingly toward Lorna. Instinctively, he moved in front of her just as Lou lunged forward. He felt the barrel of Lou's gun jab into his ribs as Lou pulled the trigger. The bullet smashed through Muller's chest. His last thought before he collapsed against Lorna was that his assassin seemed surprised he had shot him instead of her. Lorna tried to hold him up, but he slid to the ground, lifeless.

"Oh, my god!" Lorna gasped as the people around her screamed. A businessman ran over to her as she stood helplessly. Amid the chaos she saw Lou quickly shove his gun back into his waist band under his shirt and melt into the crowd. Panicked, she rushed down the cathedral steps and onto Fifth Avenue.

"Stop her!" screamed the businessman. "Someone stop her. She just shot this guy!" No one did anything as she ran onto the avenue.

Lou moved through the crowd calmly and totally unnoticed. He hurried down the steps after Lorna. Jefferson pushed through the stunned bystanders, waving his badge. He reached Muller and checked his neck for a pulse as the businessman kept mumbling that a woman did it.

"Call 911," Jefferson ordered. When the businessman pulled out his cell phone and dialed for help, Jefferson took after Lorna and Lou. He saw Lorna run into Rockefeller Plaza with Lou not far behind. He raced down the steps and into the traffic. A taxi screeched, barely missing him as he ran across the avenue.

The light turned green as Diana stepped off the curb and followed them.

Lorna ran around the wall that surrounded the Rockefeller Plaza ice skating rink and restaurant, the place where she had first kissed Jefferson. She crossed the street and went into the eastside entrance of the RCA/NBC building. Lou was less than half a block behind her.

Inside the skyscraper, the lunch crowd choked the long tunnel-like lobby. Halfway down the lobby Joe, a shoeshine man, was plying his trade for a customer who sat in an elevated chair. He was cranky. It'd been a slow morning and his last customer had stiffed him. As he grabbed a shammy he couldn't help but notice Lorna frantically pushing her way through the mass of humanity trying to reach the elevator bank.

Ten feet in front of her, people were cramming into an open elevator. She lunged forward. "Hold it!" she yelled just as the doors shut in her face. Another elevator opened and a stream of people got out. Lorna tried to get in. She turned her head and saw Lou enter the building. He stopped and looked for her in the crowd. She abandoned the elevator bank and headed for the west side exit at the other end of the lobby, frantically checking behind her.

Joe watched her closely as she ran through the crowd past him. He saw the fear on her face. He hated to see a woman in trouble and suspected someone was chasing her. He absentmindedly buffed his customer's brown wing-tips as he scanned the faces in the lobby. He spotted Lou coming toward him, bobbing and weaving in the crowd, eyes fixed on his prey, and made a snap judgment. He didn't like the man and he was in just the mood to show him how much.

Lou was now only a few feet away when Joe deliberately kicked his big wooden kit into Lou's legs causing Lou to trip and crash to the floor.

"Ah, shit man, sorry," he said, trying not to smile. "I got this nasty twitch."

Lou got up in time to see Lorna run out the far exit and disappear. He grabbed Joe by the collar and shook him. Terrified, Joe's customer threw a ten on the seat and took off just as Jefferson entered the east side of the lobby. He spotted Lou and rushed toward him.

"Hey, I said sorry, man," Joe said with mock innocence as he looked directly into Lou's eyes.

Lou shoved Joe into the wall then charged after Lorna. Jefferson followed.

The smile that Joe had been holding back finally broke out on his face as he pocketed the ten. He was in a much better mood.

Outside, Lorna ran down the sidewalk toward Radio City Music Hall. She stopped at a side door of the theater and searched her canvas bag for her lock pick. Tears of frustration and downright terror stung her cheeks as she fumbled in her bag, knowing that she only had a minute before Lou found her and she'd probably never get the door open in time. But she had to try. Finally, she felt her pick. She quickly pulled it out and started on the door's lower lock. She had opened this stage door many times before when the dead bolt wasn't on and prayed that someone had left it off. She felt the lower lock 'click' and pulled at the door. It didn't budge.

Ilona Joy Saari

Lou appeared at the corner just as the door banged opened and a stream of dancers flowed out, engulfing her in their midst. She grabbed the door to keep it from shutting. She wanted to sneak in unnoticed, but the dancers began to walk off in different directions and Lou spotted her. He moved quickly up the street as Lorna slipped into the theater and pulled at the heavy door, *willing* it to close. She knew how a deer felt when caught in the headlights when Lou, only a few feet away, stared into her eyes. He reached out to grab her just as the door slammed in his face. Now dispersed up and down the block, not a single dancer noticed them.

Safely inside, Lorna leaned against a wall shaking uncontrollably as she listened to Lou angrily pull at the door.

Jefferson rushed out of the RCA/NBC building as an enraged Lou hurried down the street. He saw Lou dash up to the theater's front entrance and pull on the door. It was locked.

Hugging the buildings, Jefferson moved closer. Lou banged angrily on the door. After a moment, a maintenance man opened it. Lou flashed a badge then pushed his way past the befuddled worker. Before the stunned maintenance man could close the door, Jefferson ran up, flashed his own badge and entered the theater.

Lorna knew that Lou would somehow get into the theater, so she had to hide. She climbed the back staircase up to the second mezzanine. She opened a door and cautiously went onto its outer ring that overlooked the Grand Foyer. On her hands and knees, out of sight from below, she crawled up to the railing and peered over the top. Lou slowly walked up the lobby's expansive staircase that had always reminded her of the staircase in "Gone With the Wind," the one that Rhett climbed as he carried Scarlett to their bedroom. She quickly ducked down as Lou stopped and looked up at the balcony rings. He stood there a moment, carefully turning around on the step, searching the rings for any signs of Lorna. She held her breath. When nothing caught his eye, Lou headed back down the stairs and into the theater's cavernous auditorium.

206

Lorna inched her way to the nearest door leading to the third mezzanine. She climbed the stairs and entered the outer ring. On all fours again, she made her way to the first set of doors that led to the mezzanine seats. She entered and crawled down the steps to the first row. Crouched in a ball on the floor in front of the first-row seats, she peered over the mezzanine's low wall. Below, Lou held a gun by his side as he walked down an orchestra aisle. From her high vantage, he seemed less threatening in the auditorium's curving space and sweeping golden proscenium arches. Just as he reached the stage, the sound of a door opening reverberated throughout the theater. He turned and fired, the bullet narrowly missing Diana who had just entered the auditorium. Lorna covered her mouth to suppress a cry.

"Son of a bitch!" Diana gasped as she ducked behind the last row of the orchestra.

Lorna's heart began to pound when Jefferson suddenly lunged out from behind the thick gold stage curtains and leapt onto Lou. They struggled as Diana rushed down the aisle, her gun drawn. Jefferson punched Lou in the gut, smashing him to the floor. Lou's head slammed into the armrest of one of the red velvet seats, knocking him cold. Diana picked up Lou's gun and held it on him just as Jefferson looked up and saw Lorna duck out of sight.

"Watch him," he barked at Diana, then ran back up the aisle and out of the auditorium. Back in the Grand Foyer, Jefferson raced up the main staircase to the third mezzanine, barely noticing the terrified maintenance man hiding behind the refreshment counter. He hurried around the outer ring and threw open each set of doors leading to the theater seats. No Lorna.

After leaving the mezzanine, Lorna cautiously went down the back staircase to another level then weaved her way through a few small lounges, her footsteps muffled by the thick leaf and geometric designed carpets. In other circumstances, she had marveled at the elegance of the various rooms and the mixture of marble and gold, foil and chrome…

the deep reds, greens and golds of the plush rugs and elegant furniture...but today the theater's beauty escaped her. Having made her way to a long forgotten, out-of-the-way smoking room, she hid behind a tall, upholstered easy chair. She turned off the lamp on the chair's Bakelite end table. She knew Jefferson was searching for her, but didn't think he'd find her here. He's probably looking in all the ladies rooms and lounges, she thought. This room wasn't easy to find. Because she knew the theater so well, she knew she had a slight advantage. For the moment, she couldn't think of a safer place.

When Jefferson finished his search of the lower lobby's bathrooms and lounges, he made a sweeping search of the shallow mezzanines and their outer rings. No sign of Lorna. He knew *she* knew every nook and cranny of the theater and that he probably wouldn't find her, so he returned to the auditorium. Diana and Lou were nowhere in sight. He took out his gun and slowly walked down the center aisle, scanning each row of seats. When he reached the first row, he found Diana lying on the floor, lip bleeding.

"What happened," he asked as he helped her to her feet.

"Right cross," she quipped.

"His gun?"

"Gone with him," she answered, dropping her eyelids in embarrassment.

Jefferson handed her his handkerchief. "Lip's bleeding."

She daubed away the blood as he stared at her.

"What?!" she asked.

He kept staring at her. Annoyed, she shoved the handkerchief into his hip pocket, smoothed out her clothing and walked up the aisle and out of the auditorium. He looked at the spot where she'd been lying and wondered why she wasn't dead. Or why Lou wasn't dead. As he walked back up the aisle, he kept looking over his shoulder. Something wasn't right, but he just couldn't put his finger on what was bothering him. He pushed open the doors to the Grand Foyer, walked past the sweeping staircase and leaned over the snack counter.

"You can come out now," he said to the maintenance worker still crouched in a fetal position behind it. Then he left.

On the street outside, he couldn't shake the feeling that he was missing something. He watched Diana walk down Sixth Avenue. She seemed to be in a hurry. He wanted to know why, so he followed.

Lorna had been crouched down behind the chair for twenty minutes. Her knees were killing her and her thigh muscles were burning. Oddly enough, her ankle no longer hurt. Maybe it was because everything else about her legs hurt more. Whatever the reason, she couldn't stay in this position for another second. Surely it was safe to come out from hiding. If not she'd figure it out then. She stood slowly and stretched her aching muscles, then cautiously left the smoking room, retracing her steps to the back staircase. As she walked through one of the thirty small lobbies she remained alert, listening for any signs of Jefferson or anyone else. Everything was quiet…peaceful even. She made her way to the stage door and let herself out of the theater, turning west toward the nearest uptown bus stop.

It always amazed Jefferson how he was able to follow almost anyone almost anywhere. Diana was a trained agent, yet she seemed to have no idea that he was behind her as she walked toward Central Park talking on her cell. She seemed angry. When she reached 59th Street, she hailed a cab. Maybe he was born under a lucky "tail your prey" god, because immediately after she got into her taxi, another one drove up. He jumped in, wondering if today was the day he should play the lottery.

"Follow that cab," he said to the driver, who looked at Jefferson skeptically in his rear view mirror.

"Is there a problem?" Jefferson snapped impatiently as Diana's taxi moved down the street while his taxi hadn't budged. It was obvious this driver was not thrilled with Jefferson's request. He was about to pull out his badge when the cabbie hesitantly turned on his meter and pulled into the street.

Ilona Joy Saari

Slowly the cabs headed to the eastside and Jefferson wondered if Diana was just going back to her hotel. Wherever she was going, he would follow. He had no other plan.

Jefferson's mind wandered from Diana to Lorna. He had to admire Lorna's resourcefulness. She had certainly outwitted him...twice. And in one day. He wondered what their relationship would have been if they had met under different circumstances. She was beautiful and he enjoyed making love to her. He had to admit that she was getting to him. He smiled. Diana was right on the mark when she guessed that he had slept with her. Since his relationship with Diana he had made it a habit to seduce the beautiful women he was investigating. It became a part of his being...a game he played to ward off thoughts of love, hearth and home. Beautiful women became his drug of choice. He enjoyed the seduction. He enjoyed the sex. And he enjoyed walking away. The image of Diana in bed with Robert flashed across his mind and all his feelings for Lorna disappeared in the pain that image still inflicted.

More than Diana, though, he had missed Robert and was glad they had reconciled their friendship. He remembered how Robert had shown up at his doorstep after Diana had left him, his eyes full of regret. He had let him in and the two sat in Jefferson's library sipping 18 year-old scotch and smoking fat Havanas. They drank and smoked all night in silence. Shortly after the sun had come up, he had brewed a pot of French roast, made some scrambled eggs and bacon and had spoken his first words to Robert in six months, "Eve Harrington, Catherine Tramell, Matty Walker."

"What?" Robert asked, hung over and totally confused.

"Anne Baxter, Sharon Stone, Kathleen Turner."

A big smile crossed Robert's face. "Cold stone bitches," he laughed.

"Yup, they're everywhere."

Jefferson smiled at the memory as his cab turned south and headed downtown. Obviously Diana was not going back to The Mark. But where? What was she up to? Was she headed for Lorna's loft?

210

Jefferson was still trying to figure it out when her taxi pulled up in front of a clothing boutique next door to an Avis office.

"Don't stop," he ordered his driver, "just slowly drive by and pull up to the curb half-way down the block." The cabbie did as he was told. Jefferson watched Diana's cab through the back window. When he saw her leave the taxi and enter the boutique, he paid the driver and got out. He moved into the shadow of a nearby building as Diana came back out then entered the car rental office. Jeff swore at himself for letting the cab go. Fifteen minutes later, Diana drove out of the Avis garage in a gray Lexus. Jefferson moved covertly into the street in search of a taxi, but his tailing god had abandoned him. There wasn't an empty cab in sight.

chapter

FOURTEEN

The west side squad room was bustling with activity as homicide detectives interviewed the witnesses to the shooting at St. Patrick's cathedral.

Though Muller didn't die in his precinct, his partner insisted that the 20th lead the investigation. Zach sat at his desk questioning the businessman who had called 911.

"Well, yeh, that's what I'm saying," the businessman said, annoyed that he had to repeat himself. "It had to be that woman standing right in front of 'im. She shot him then hightailed it outta there with some other guy right on her heels."

"Wouldn't you hightail it out of there if someone was shot dead right in front of you?"

"Someone *was* shot dead right in front of me."

"Point taken," Zach said, still not convinced that Lorna should be a suspect. "But panicking is one thing," he continued. "Murdering a cop is a whole other ballgame."

"Yeh, well who else coulda shot him?"

Unnoticed, Lorna walked into the precinct and approached the desk sergeant who was talking on the phone.

"Hey, read my lips you bureaucratic asshole," the desk sergeant growled, "Muller punched his clock in *this* house, *this* house is doing the investigation. End of story." He slammed the phone down.

"Excuse me," Lorna said trying to get his attention.

The inter-office desk phone buzzed. The sergeant answered. "What?" He listened a minute as Lorna waited impatiently.

"You wanna put out an APB on Lorna Raven?"

Lorna's heart began to race as she stared at the sergeant.

Suddenly she heard somebody yell, "That's her! She's the one shot that cop!"

Lorna turned and saw Zach jump out of his seat and hurry toward her.

Frightened, she bolted out the front door.

"Wait," Zach yelled. "Ms. Raven, wait!"

She didn't hear him as she was already racing down the street.

Zach and several other cops dashed out of the building after her.

"Police! Stop!" one of them shouted as she ducked into an alley. She saw a delivery truck pull away from a loading dock and raced to catch it. She hopped onto the back bumper. The police turned into the alley as Lorna held on tightly. The truck picked up speed, increasing the distance between her and the cops.

Suddenly, the truck slammed to a stop at the corner and she fell to the pavement. She scrambled to her feet, ran around the corner and down the street as fast as she could, looking for someplace to hide. Gasping for air, she raced into a coffee shop, past a waitress and into the kitchen. She ran through the narrow kitchen, startling the short order cook, and into a little back room containing a slop sink. Seconds later, she heard the police run into the coffee shop. She moved to the nearby back door, pushed it open, then immediately slammed it shut. She then slipped into a broom closet next to the slop sink, quietly closing the door behind her.

Lorna held a hand over her mouth as she tried to catch her breath and listen to the cops question the coffee shop's waitress and its one patron who sat at the counter.

"Woman come in here in a hurry?" an officer asked her.

"Ran right out the back door," the waitress answered.

The cops walked into the kitchen and the short order cook pointed to the back door. She heard a cop walk into the little room, hesitate a minute, then go out the back door. She waited, wondering what to do, not knowing if he'd return and dramatically throw open the door shouting "Aha!" She stifled an involuntary laugh at the image. Now was not the time for nervous giggles. Her shaking hand brushed a spider web. She jerked it back and wiped it on her jeans, trying not to feel totally creeped out.

Though the closet wasn't completely dark due to the light seeping in around the door jamb, she still needed to press the little dial that lighted up the face of her Timex. If no one found her in five minutes, she'd leave. Watching the minutes tick away was tedious and she tried not to think about her aching body. As soon as she got out of this closet with its stinky mops, buckets and brooms, she was going to take a dozen Motrin. If only she could find someplace to take a long, hot bath!

Finally the longest five minutes she'd ever experienced ended. She was about to leave the closet when she heard footsteps coming toward her. They stopped right outside the closet door. She picked up a broom and watched as the light seeping through the crack around the door highlighted the turning doorknob. Panicked, she pulled the broom back ready to slam it into whoever was on the other side of the door. The door opened and Lorna lashed out with the broom, knocking a box of cleanser off the shelf above her. The white powder spilled all over her. The waitress screamed, jumped back and narrowly missed getting hit by the broom and the cleanser.

"Jesus, Mary and Joseph, you scared the living daylights out of me! What are you doing here?"

Lorna focused on her for the first time. The woman was dressed in black polyester slacks and a white blouse. A soiled white half-apron was tied around her waist. Over the shirt pocket was a plastic name-tag that read: "Dot." She guessed the waitress' age at around sixty and though she had an edge that was enhanced by her short bleached blonde hair, heavy eye makeup and purple fingernails, Lorna felt a warmth about her.

"I got lost!?" she answered, going for an improbable joke as she looked around, nervously ready to bolt in case Dot screamed for the police.

"They're gone," Dot assured her.

Lorna stepped out of the closet as Dot grabbed a clean dish towel out of a wall cabinet and handed it to her. Lorna bent over, tossed her hair forward and tried to rub the cleanser out with the towel. When she finished, she looked at her reflection in a dusty mirror hanging over the slop sink.

"Didn't help much, did it?" she said as she smiled half-heartedly. She stared at herself for a moment longer, then shyly pulled off her tee shirt and shook it vigorously. Satisfied that she got as much cleanser out of the tee as she could, she put it back on then used the towel to brush off her jeans.

"What'ya do doll, kill someone?"

"They think so," Lorna answered almost in a whisper.

The waitress just stared at her, compelling Lorna to explain.

"My brother was almost murdered and now someone is trying to kill me," she began, then took a deep breath. "I went to meet with the policeman I thought would help me, but he was shot by a cop…. Well, I don't think he's really a cop, but he *was* a cop when he killed Senator Lauder's assassin, who really wasn't an assassin since no one died and now they think I'm the one who shot the real cop."

Praying this girl hadn't escaped from an asylum, Dot took pity on her. She grabbed Lorna's arm and walked her into the coffee shop. No one else was there. "I think your brain needs nourishment. I couldn't follow a word you were saying, but I doubt you're any kind of cop killer."

She gently shoved Lorna onto a counter stool. A second later, two teenaged girls walked in and slid into one of the blue vinyl booths.

"Jose, make this girl a tuna sandwich, will ya?" Dot yelled to the short order cook.

"No, really, it's all right, I'm…" Lorna protested.

"You hungry?" the waitress asked.

"No. I couldn't eat." When was the last time she ever said *that*, she thought.

"Then have a coke. My treat. I haven't had this much excitement since my ex had his gall bladder removed." She put some ice in a glass, filled it with soda and put it on the counter in front of Lorna.

"Thanks."

Dot gave her a thumbs-up then went over to the girls and took their order.

Lorna pulled a compact out of her canvas bag and examined her face more closely. She still had a sprinkling of cleanser around her nose and near her hairline. In the recesses of her bag, she found a little packet containing a moist towelette. She tore it open and wiped away the remaining cleanser.

Dot, back behind the counter, turned on a small television bolted to the wall as she gave the food orders to Jose.

"Better wash that hair soon it's gonna smell like Bab-O."

"Bab-O?"

"Way before your time, honey."

As Lorna took a sip of her soda, her attention was diverted to a special news report from the television.

"…the naked man found dead on the shores of Roosevelt Island has been identified as Chuck Moss, a former Navy SEAL and resident of Washington D. C. He had been shot in the heart, but no further information has been released as to why Mr. Moss may have been on Roosevelt Island, or whether his murder is at all connected to Senator Lauder's assassination. We now go back to the nation's capital and the memorial service for Senator Harold 'Hap' Lauder, where reporter Bob Sederholm has some late-breaking news. Bob?"

"We've just learned that Senator Lauder's alleged assassin was not a mid-east terrorist," Sederholm reported, "but a young Greek-American man from the Bronx, a short twenty minutes away from the Lauder estate in Larchmont. It appears that the assassin was studying acting at the famed Actors' Studio…"

"Gives new meaning to the "method," Dot stated sarcastically as she turned the volume down.

Kipper Lauder appeared on the screen, leaving the church as the memorial service came to a close.

"Would you mind turning that back up a bit?" Lorna asked Dot as she took another sip of coke.

"Sure, honey." Dot turned up the volume.

The anchor was once again on camera. "Senator Lauder's wife, Kathryn 'Kipper' Lauder, has been in seclusion with her children at her townhouse in Georgetown. While we watch the various dignitaries leave the church we can't help but note the irony that a man who voted against gun control was killed by a handgun."

Lorna watched intently as the video cut to Lauder giving a speech at a campaign rally.

"…and that's why my anti-crime bill is the most important issue in Congress today," Lauder said, his voice rising for effect. "I want all Americans to feel as safe in their homes as I do in mine. Thank you."

Lorna recognized the speech as the same one he gave on the Circle Line.

"Of course. Home!" she said to herself.

Suddenly, Lorna knew what she was going to do next and felt exhilarated that she now had a plan.

"Dot, do you have a pay phone in here?"

"It's not working, but I gotta a cell you can use," she answered as she dropped off two orders of French fries and two Sprites to the teen girls. "Just hold on a sec." When she finished, she took her cell phone out of an apron pocket and handed it to Lorna.

Lorna punched in a number and waited.

"Broderick?" she said in a half whisper. "Hey, it's me. I need you to get my digital camera and meet me at Lincoln Center as soon as possible." She listened for a moment. "That late? Okay, okay. And I need some cash...as much as you can get your hands on."

She listened some more. "I promise. I'll explain when I see you. Oh, and Broderick, please make sure you aren't followed." She hung up and handed the phone back to Dot.

"Thanks."

"You gonna be all right?" Dot asked her, concerned.

"I hope so."

Before leaving the coffee shop, Dot checked to make sure no cops were lingering outside. The coast was clear. Emotionally wrought, Lorna impulsively hugged Dot, wishing she could stay safe in her arms forever.

"Thank you. Thank you for everything," she whispered in her ear.

"Are you sure you wanna go out there?" Dot asked. "You can hang here a little longer. Maybe come home with me after my shift."

"Thanks, but I'm sure. I have to go."

Dot wrote down her address and phone number on a piece of paper and handed it to Lorna. "In case you need a safe place to hide."

Lorna put the piece of paper into a jeans pocket then clung to Dot. At that moment, Lorna was tempted to take her up on her offer. Reluctantly, she let Dot go and left the coffee shop. As she walked down the street nervously searching for Lou, Jefferson, Diana and the police, she realized that she had to do something about her appearance. She could no longer count on anyone helping her. There's no way they'd believe that Lauder was alive or that he had had someone try to kill her brother and her, and had a police detective murdered. Who would? The whole world saw the Senator shot at point blank range and fall into the East River. Hell, she didn't believe the story and she was living it...so it was up to her to figure everything out before she was arrested or killed.

She made her way to Columbus Avenue, hoping to find a neighborhood beauty salon. She did. Michelangelo's. She peeked in the window of the small storefront shop and saw two empty chairs and one stylist sitting in a tiny reception area reading the National Enquirer. Perfect.

The walls were sponged a faded aqua and decorated with huge posters of renaissance art in ornate gilt-edged frames. A large crystal chandelier with little gold shades separated the stylists' chairs and the wash and hairdryer area. The décor was overwhelming for such a little space.

The stylist jumped up from his chair and gave Lorna a quick once over.

"Oh, my god, honey, your hair! There's schmutz in it."

"Schmutz?"

"You know. Gunk."

She touched her hair and remembered. "Oh, right. It was a fight to the finish, but the can of cleanser won," she said, forcing a laugh. "I need you to get it out."

"No problemo. Follow me," he said as he walked her to the sink in the rear of the shop. "By the way, my name's Michael, proud owner of this thriving establishment."

Lorna smiled. "Hi, I'm Lor...Dot."

They reached the wash area and Michael handed her a purple smock. "You can change over there, Dot."

She turned and saw a tall, three-paneled screen in the back corner painted with various shades of pink roses, puffy clouds and cherubs. Behind the screen she pulled off her tee and hung it on a hook in the wall, put on the smock then went back to the sink.

"Michael, I want you to cut and bleach my hair."

"Are you nuts?" he asked as he leaned her back and began washing out the cleanser.

"Probably. But I just broke up with my boyfriend and I need a fresh start," she lied, trying to keep her mood light, "and there's that old cliché about blondes having more fun."

"And you want more fun?"

"*Some* fun would be a nice change," she answered wistfully as she closed her eyes and slowly let go of her tension while his fingers massaged her scalp. As the hot water ran through her hair and seeped into her pores, her neck and shoulders relaxed. She thought of an old movie she once saw that put a kicking and screaming mental patient into a hot tub. Over the tub a medicinally white canvas was strapped down covering the patient and trapping her in the hot water. Only the patient's head was visible...like a woman waiting to be guillotined. Right now she'd trade places with that patient in a heartbeat.

The water had stopped and Michael wrapped her head in a towel as he brought her seat upright. "OK, honey, time to find your inner blonde."

They walked over to one of the styling chairs and Lorna sat down. He handed her a color chart with at least a dozen variations of blonde.

"Pick one."

She did...a very, very light honey color that wouldn't fight her complexion or draw attention to herself. She looked in the mirror at her deep, rich auburn hair and hoped she'd live long enough to see it grow back.

As Michael sectioned her hair and applied the slimy color gook, he regaled her with stories about his boyhood in Maine, his years working in trendy salons that closed as fast as they opened and how he had finally found someone to back him in his own shop and he didn't even have to sleep with him. He went on and on about the crime she was committing by bleaching her gorgeous hair color. Most women need highlights, weaves or just plain dye jobs, he explained, but she was the exception. As much as she appreciated the compliment, she made it clear she wasn't going to change her mind.

When it was time to cut her hair which, when wet, was down past her bra line, she told him to cut it to her shoulders. She wanted to leave it just long enough to put up in a pony tail, twist or knot.

As Michael cut and worked his magic with a blow dryer and flat-iron, Lorna stared at her reflection and tried to concentrate on his superficial chatter. She wanted desperately to get lost in his arias on hair product and the latest celebrity scandal, but she couldn't stop thinking of Poe or Lt. Muller. His voice faded into the background like Muzak as images of Poe lying in a pool of blood and Lt. Muller falling into her, dying, took over her thoughts.

"Voila!" Michael exclaimed in triumph.

"What?" she asked startled back to the present.

"Look. You're still gorgeous, if I say so myself."

Lorna look in the mirror, surprised at how different she looked. Very blonde. Pin straight hair. Blunt cut in the back just hitting her below the shoulders with trendy chopped layers on the sides.

"If blondes really have more fun, honey, you're gonna be exhausted," he said with a wink and a giggle.

She gave him a half-hearted smile, left the chair and went to the back of the salon to change into her tee. When she was finished dressing, she walked to the front of the shop.

"Master Card or Visa?" Michael asked.

"Cash."

"Cash?!" No one pays cash anymore, kiddo, unless they're traveling 'incognito.' You're not a spy, are you?" he asked conspiratorially.

"Hardly," Lorna smiled. She took out the bills she'd taken from her soup can. "More like a very maxed-out card. What's the damage?"

"One fifty," he answered.

She hated to use her money, but she didn't want her card purchases traced to this shop. Sort of defeats the purpose of a disguise, she thought, if "they" found out what it was.

She counted out one hundred and eighty dollars and handed it to him.

"Thanks again, Michael," she said, then gave him a big smile as she flipped her hair like a model in a Revlon commercial. "I love the new me!"

She left the shop and immediately headed for a little women's boutique Michael had told her about. She needed to get out of her tee and jeans to complete her transformation.

***

When Lorna had called Broderick he wasn't at his office. He was in bed but he hadn't been sleeping. Next to him was wonderfully long, lithe and naked Becky. He liked her. He liked the fact that she had been charmed by Poe's eccentricities and that she'd been saddened when he'd been hurt. She even went with him to the hospital when he went to give Carol a break. He liked the fact that Lorna had liked her and that she had liked Lorna. And he liked the fact that she wasn't a "girlie" girl but a grounded woman who didn't need a man to make her whole. It didn't hurt that she was great in bed.

He had debated about answering his cell, which could end this fantasy afternoon of lovemaking, but when he had seen that it was Lorna, he knew he had to. He wanted to be there for her in her time of need, but at the time, had no idea just how *needy* she was going to be. He had listened to her whispered voice make her requests, but got more than a little anxious when she had warned him not to be followed. What was going on? Why couldn't she just go and get her digital camera? And cash? Why did she need a bunch of cash?

Reluctantly, he had told Becky he had to leave to help out a friend. Lorna had made him so nervous, he was afraid to tell her who the friend was. He had quickly showered, dressed, and headed uptown to Lorna's office, all the while looking over his shoulder, for *what* he didn't know. Who was that woman in the red shorts sitting at the bus stop? And who was that guy in the bicycle shirt looking in a shop window across the street?

A half-hour later, he was walking down the hall toward his friend's office. The first thing he noticed was the front door. It was wide open. "Oh, shit," he muttered under his breath as he anxiously walked in.

OK, good, he thought, nothing seemed amiss in the reception area. Feeling a sense of relief, he called out bravely. "Hello, anybody here?" No answer.

Emboldened by the silence, he walked down the short hall and into the main office area. Another wave of relief ran through him. No boogiemen lurking in the shadows. The room looked the same as it always did. He checked the desk and the large armoire that Lorna and Poe used to store office supplies. No cameras. He walked across the hall and entered the editing room.

"Oh, my god," he gasped aloud when he first saw the toppled crate and scattered reels and videotapes. Kicking some aside to make a path, he went to the worktable to look for the camera. On the floor was the huge pool of dried blood. The sight of Poe's blood made him gag and stumble into a chair. He hung his head between his knees to keep from vomiting, but he wasn't able to stop the tears. The vision of his friend lying bleeding on the floor was more than he could bear. Five minutes passed before he could pull himself together. He found the camera in a case on the floor and got the hell out of the office.

As he walked down the hall he heard a door close, then footsteps coming up behind him. He turned and saw a guy about his age dressed in faded jeans and a black linen shirt. He had no idea who he was. Still shaken over the sight of Poe's blood, his heart began to beat wildly as he reached the elevator. He impatiently pushed the button. As he listened to the elevator move up the shaft, Jefferson came up alongside him. Lorna's voice whispered in his head not to let anyone follow him. His fear peaked and he was about to run to the stairs when the elevator door opened. Jefferson got in and faced him. A bead of sweat formed above his upper lip as he hesitated. Feeling like a fool standing there in a near panic, he shrugged off his fear and joined Jefferson in the elevator. The door closed. As the car made its way down the six flights to the lobby, Broderick rubbed his hands, his nerve endings tingling. When the elevator bounced to a stop and the door opened, he felt nearly ecstatic that he hadn't been shot or knifed or god knows what.

Back outside, he held his breath while he watched the guy walk down the street. He sucked in the humid air as if it were the last air he would ever breathe. Jefferson disappeared around a corner and Broderick laughed at how he'd let his imagination run away with him. Poe's accident and Lorna's paranoid warning had freaked him out, but he would finish his mission. His guard down, he neglected to notice the man in the bicycle shirt...the one that he *had* noticed earlier...follow him to the subway.

He went to his office and raided petty cash. Next up was the ATM. He withdrew all the money he had in his checking account. All told, he collected close to three thousand dollars. She better have a damn good reason for putting me through this, he thought, then immediately felt guilty for being angry at her.

As she walked down the street, Lorna kept looking at her reflection in the store and restaurant windows. She felt new and invigorated. Almost invisible, until she saw a cop standing at the corner. Suddenly she felt conspicuous, as if everybody in New York had a finger pointed at *her*. She wasn't that far from Muller's station and figured this cop was from that precinct. He'd be on the lookout for her. Should she turn around and walk in the other direction, or would that send up a red flag? What should she do? Too late, he was looking at her. But, as she returned his gaze, she realized he really wasn't seeing her, not Lorna Raven. He was seeing some anonymous blonde woman. Lorna Raven *was* invisible. She chanced a smile as she walked past him and crossed the street. He smiled back.

Two blocks later, she found the boutique. She couldn't wait to get out of her dirty tee and jeans, but first she needed to hide her hair. She fished out her emergency bandana and a rubber band from her canvas bag. After twisting her hair into a knot, she covered her head with the bandana. She'd probably have to use her credit card, which meant she could be traced, so she didn't want the salesgirl to be able to tell anyone asking about her that she was now a blonde.

Inside the boutique, Lorna kept to herself as she looked through the selections. The clothes were beautiful. And, they weren't cheap. She immediately found three pairs of drape-y linen trousers in her size...black, white and camel. She also chose a white polo shirt, a standard white tee and a cropped white linen camp shirt. Colors that don't

Ilona Joy Saari

attract attention. Not wanting to risk any unnecessary conversation, she quietly went into a dressing room and tried on the clothes. Everything fit, so she decided on the camel pants and white polo. She really didn't want to put her cleanser-riddled jeans and tee back on, but knew she had to. If she came out of the dressing room in the boutique's clothes and asked for the tags to be cut out, the salesgirl might not only remember *her*, but the clothes, too. That would certainly defeat the whole purpose of buying a new outfit.

Dressed in her old clothes, she left the dressing room and handed the salesgirl her credit card. She knew she was taking a chance, but she didn't know how much money Broderick would be able to raise and she couldn't afford to run out of cash. She only had a couple of hundred left after paying Michael.

While the salesgirl wrote up her bill, Lorna eyed a selection of sneakers and sandals. She found a pair of cute white Polo sneakers, slipped off her shoes and tried them on. Perfect fit and comfortable.

She gave them to the salesgirl who added them to the bill. Lorna signed the receipt, hoping that by the time the police traced her credit card, she would have found Lauder and that Poe's attacker and Muller's killer would've been arrested.

The salesgirl bagged her new outfit and Lorna left the boutique. As she walked south down Columbus Avenue she looked at her watch. Five o'clock.

chapter

FIFTEEN

Broderick was late. Lorna, her hair still covered by the bandana, had been sitting on the fountain rim between the New York State Theater and Avery Fisher Hall for more than an hour. Finally she spotted him entering Lincoln Center plaza, her camera hanging from his shoulder. She didn't want to wave and draw attention to herself. But it didn't take long for Broderick to find her and join her on the fountain rim.

"What's with the *schmata*? Your disguise?" he asked trying to make light of the situation. She ignored the effort.

"Where the hell have you been?" she asked, sounding more strident than she wanted to.

"With much more pleasant company, I assure you," he answered, a little annoyed with her attitude. Hadn't he dropped everything to come to her aid?

"Any trouble getting into my office?" she asked all business-like.

"Trouble? Why should I have any trouble? The police left every damn door in the place wide open. It's a wonder you have any equipment left."

He slid the camera off his shoulder and handed it to her.

Lorna took the camera out of the case and dropped it into her canvas bag. She put the case on the ground.

"So don't thank me, but you better tell me what the hell is going on," he continued.

"I'm sorry," she said, her voice smothered in sadness. "Thank you."

"Forget the thank you, give it up."

"Poe didn't fall off the ladder by accident, Brod. Someone walked right into our editing room, smashed him in the head and left him for dead. Then they murdered Lt. Muller and now they're trying to kill me."

"What? Who the hell are 'they'?"

"I don't know," she answered. Her voice was so soft he could barely hear her.

"For god's sake, Lorna, go to the police."

"I can't. The police think *I* killed the lieutenant."

"That's insane."

"I know. But there's a witness who thinks he saw me shoot him. I don't know how long I'm going to be hiding, but I can't let them find me right now."

"I don't get it. Just explain…"

"Please, Brod, you have to trust me on this. Please."

"OK."

"Promise you won't tell anyone you saw me."

"Promise."

"Did you bring the cash?"

Broderick handed her the envelope containing the money. She threw it into her canvas bag then leaned over and kissed him on the cheek.

"I love you, kiddo," she whispered in his ear, then stood up again.

"Where are you going?"

"To try and get the picture they're killing people for."

As Lorna was about to walk from the fountain she spotted Jefferson standing by the Metropolitan Opera House, watching her.

"Oh, no," she said out loud, alerting Broderick.

Panicked, she looked around for an escape route.

"What? What's going on?"

Lorna didn't answer. She saw a large group of women leaving the plaza. She grabbed her bags and hurried to join them.

Broderick's eyes darted around Lincoln Center. He saw Jefferson and remembered him as the man from the elevator. He'd been followed. Then, out of the corner of his eye, he recognized the man in the bicycle shirt. Had both men been following him? Broderick had no idea who either of these men were, but "bicycle shirt" was pushing through the crowd trying to get to Lorna before she could leave the plaza. Instinctively, he knew he had to stop him and ran toward him.

Jefferson saw where Broderick was headed and immediately recognized Lou. He knew he had to do something, fast. Within seconds he reached Lou, grabbed his arm and spun him around.

Broderick, no more than fifteen feet away, stopped in his tracks when he saw Lou's gun fall to the ground. Lou and Jefferson struggled. Lou tried to get his gun, but Jefferson managed to kick it away just as Lou smashed his fist into Jefferson's stomach. Jefferson stumbled backward giving Lou just enough time to slip away. Barely able to straighten up, Jefferson picked up the gun and shoved it into his belt as he took off after him.

The few people in the plaza who had stopped and watched the fight quickly left the scene, but Broderick stood frozen on the spot. His every pulse was beating wildly as he looked for Lorna. But, she was gone. Disappeared. He let out a sigh of relief. If *he* couldn't see her, then the other men couldn't, either. At least that was what he convinced himself as he forced his body to move. He walked back to the fountain. His knees were weak and he needed to sit down. He threw up into the fountain. This was *not* how he wanted his day to go.

***

After escaping from Lincoln Plaza, Lorna ducked into a crowded café across the street and immediately went to the ladies room. Thankfully, it was a single washroom and double thankfully, it was empty. She sighed with relief. There was no way she wanted to be "out in the open," waiting outside the bathroom door. Jefferson might come in at any moment.

Inside, she locked the door, stripped off her clothes and, with a cool wet paper towel, quickly wiped away the day's sweat and any remaining cleanser that had seeped through her clothes and onto her body. She splashed her face with cold water then changed into her new linen pants, shirt and sneakers. She dabbed on some lip gloss and took off the bandana, letting her straight blonde hair fall to her shoulders.

Her transformation was finished. Taking Dot's note out of her jeans pocket, she threw her dirty clothes and shoes into the boutique shopping bag and shoved it into the trash bin. She cautiously went back into the café. No one gave her a second look and Jefferson wasn't in sight, so she decided to take a chance and leave. She needed to get away from here and find a place to hide for the night. Though daylight was fading, she put on her sunglasses and started walking uptown. Dot's address clutched in her fist, she turned east and away from the crowds surrounding the Lincoln Center area.

With Lorna nowhere to be found, Jefferson was determined to follow Lou. He had no idea where Lorna would go next, but if he stayed on Lou's tail, he believed Lou might eventually lead him back to her. It was obvious that Lou had been following Broderick. He's good, Jefferson thought, acknowledging to himself that he missed spotting him when he started following Broderick at Lorna's office. And, if he's that good at tailing someone, he's probably just as good at spotting a tail. Jefferson knew that he'd have to be careful if he didn't want to lose him.

Staying a good distance behind, he moved in and out of doorways and shadows whenever he could. After a few blocks, Lou seemed to ease up, but Jefferson didn't want to get too close. He thought of following him from across the street, but trashed the idea…too easy being spotted from that angle. Staying directly behind him was the best way to remain undetected. Lou would have to turn completely around to get a really good look at anyone behind him. That would give Jefferson enough time to slip into a doorway or bend out of sight between parked cars.

As they continued to walk uptown, the neighborhood became more residential. Jefferson stopped when he saw Lou go into a Korean market on the next corner. The delivery truck parked a few yards ahead of him would serve as cover while he waited for Lou. Ten minutes later, Lou came out of the market carrying a bag of groceries. Jefferson smiled to himself as he realized that Lou was about to go somewhere nearby and settle in for the night.

At the corner, Lou turned west. Halfway down the block he pulled out some keys and let himself into a nondescript 1930's walkup. Jefferson waited a few moments, then went over to the building's front door, opened it and entered a little cubicle. He read the names on the buzzer, trying to guess which apartment was Lou's. No name triggered a connection. He looked through the leaded glass window in the second door leading to a vestibule and saw mailboxes and a worn marble staircase leading up to the other floors. He tried the door. Locked. He debated whether to ring a buzzer or two at random, thinking someone might buzz him in automatically, but decided against it. It really wasn't Lou he wanted to confront. At least not yet. He needed to find Lorna or Lou's bosses, whoever came first and, for now, Lou was his only ticket to finding any of them.

He went back outside and cased the area. Though the temperature had cooled off a few degrees, the humidity was stuck on sky high, so standing sentry outside Lou's building for hours was not going to cut it. Stakeouts were for kids, he laughed to himself, unless you can do them in someplace comfortable, like an air-conditioned car. He decided the best way to keep an eye on Lou's front door was from the little deli in an old walk-up across the street. If Lou didn't come back

Ilona Joy Saari

out by the time it closed, he would have to continue his stakeout from the street, but right now he was hot and cranky.

As he walked into the deli he noticed the sign in the window: "Open until midnight." Jefferson walked in and sat down at an empty table by the window. The deli owner, a seventy-two year old Romanian immigrant was helping a few customers from behind the counter. They paid and left. Jefferson held the door open for them, then closed it behind them and stood there, letting the air-conditioning condition him. The deli owner stared at him, waiting for him to sit down or come up to the counter. Jefferson stared back.

"No loitering here," he told Jefferson.

Jefferson approached the counter. He calmly took out his phony New York City detective shield and surreptitiously showed it to the owner, pretending he didn't want anyone else in the deli to know he was a cop.

"I'm not loitering," he whispered.

Fearful of police, no matter what country they were from, the deli owner backed off. With eyes lowered, he picked up some carving knives and began cleaning them.

Lorna turned the corner onto West 88th looking for Dot's address just as Dot came out of a brownstone basement apartment and hailed a cab. As Dot opened the door and got in, Lorna yelled out to her as she raced down the street, but her voice got lost in the never ending city din. She picked up speed and waved frantically, as she tried to catch up with the taxi, but as her luck would have it, the traffic light turned green just as the cab reached the corner. It picked up speed as it turned left and careened down West End Avenue. She didn't know whether to cry or laugh so she just let out a frustrated scream. Nothing like drawing attention to yourself when you're trying to hide, she thought, as she looked around. Not a single person on the street seemed to have noticed this crazy woman screaming on the corner of 88th and West End. She almost smiled to herself til she realized that she had no idea where she

232

was going to go now. And her ankle was beginning to ache again as she began to walk downtown.

Lorna searched the faces of the people she passed for anyone who might be a threat. Every few yards, she turned around abruptly to check and see if she was being followed. Then her stomach growled, reminding her that she hadn't eaten anything since her breakfast cheeseburger. She knew just where she wanted to go...Gray's Papaya on 72nd and Broadway, one of her favorite hot dog stands in Manhattan. Hell, she thought defiantly, if I'm going to die, I'm not dying on an empty stomach.

By the time she wolfed down two hot dogs and a diet cream, night had finally fallen and Lorna was more tired than she ever remembered being. Her body ached, not only from strained and stressed-out muscles, but from total mental exhaustion. Even a red dye fix with mustard and relish did little to perk up her spirits. She knew she was too tired to move ahead with her plan, but she had to find someplace where she could sleep without fear of being caught. Or worse. She didn't want to go back to Dot's who was probably out for the evening. And, the thought of standing outside her building in the heat for who knows how long made her even more tired. She needed to find someplace now. Central and Riverside Parks were out.... too many crazies walking around in the dark and, sleeping outside unsheltered on the hard ground or park bench scared her even more than being arrested. Too much "nature" skulking and scurrying in the parks late at night, she thought, like rabid rodents, abandoned cats and dogs gone wild. And then there're the un-"nature" things like druggies and gang bangers. A shiver ran through her as she thought about being alone in the park... in the dark. Nope. No way. She'd rather risk going back to her loft or office. Sure, like that was a choice. Not! And no way was she going to a homeless shelter even though she *was,* technically, a homeless person who needed shelter. She'd seen too many horror stories on the news about what happened to people in those places. She'd have to sleep with one eye open. But, with her senses so compromised from fear and exhaustion, that would be impossible. She couldn't even bunk with a friend. *They* could be watching *them!* *They* were obviously watching Aunt Helen and Broderick. Doorways and subway stations came to mind, but she wouldn't feel safe there, either, and another night in Grand Central was out of the question. Too many cops. She needed someplace where she could be alone and regroup.

As she left Papaya's, she again caught her reflection in a storefront window. This time instead of making her feel invisible, it set off alarm bells in her head. Bouncing off the glass, in beautiful bold letters, was "Raven's Video." She might as well put a flashing light on her head! This may be the straw that broke the camel's back. As silly as it was, considering all that had happened, giving up her treasured canvas bag was almost more than she could bear. She felt like all the emotional terror of the last couple of days was going to explode out of her body like an angry alien in a Sigourney Weaver movie. Her body trembled as she hugged the bag close to her waist obscuring the company's name printed so neatly on the flap. She and Poe were going to make important films. Maybe even art. I can't cry...I can't cry, ran through her mind like a mantra. She had to control her feelings if she was going to get through this nightmare.

This was no time for sentiment. She looked around the street for a knock-off purse vendor or a boutique, thankful that this part of town was still open and ready for business. She spotted a bargain import store a few doors away and hurried in. Why, she wondered, did these stores always smell the same? Sort of pungent. Was it because there were no windows to let anything *breathe?* Or was it because the merchandise had been sitting in musty ship hulls as it made its way across the Pacific from faraway places as Singapore, Thailand, India and Africa? Or maybe it was just the many packages of incense on display, their exotic aromas seeping out of the boxes.

She saw a bin of straw slippers, a box of wooden backscratchers and racks of inexpensive cotton summer clothes, brass knickknacks and a weapons cache of fancy sabers. Her eyes zeroed in on an assortment of cheap leather bags hanging on large hooks in the back of the store. She weeded through them and found an inexpensive brown leather back-pack. She took it to the counter and paid in cash. Before leaving the store, she transferred everything from her old bag to her new one.

Outside, she found a city garbage can, but didn't have the heart to dump her empty canvas bag in the trash.

As she argued with herself about what to do, she noticed a middle-aged "street" lady coming toward her. She was pushing a grocery cart weighted down with all her worldly possessions and was dressed in what seemed to be a hundred layers of clothing, even in this heat. Lorna found her bag's new home.

She placed it on top of the woman's bundle in the cart, then walked away, her new backpack resting comfortably in the middle of her back. The woman, not missing a step, continued pushing her cart down the street.

The sun had finally set as Lorna aimlessly headed east on 72nd Street, oblivious to the seemingly never-ending, oppressive humidity. People hustled and bustled around her, purposefully going to and from moments in their lives, not knowing that she had lost control of hers.

It wasn't long before she found herself in front of the entrance to the Dakota, the co-op building where John Lennon had lived. It was on this very sidewalk where he was murdered. "Murder" was taking on a whole new meaning for her now that she was a target. Looking at the expansive concrete archway and iron gate leading into the Dakota courtyard, she allowed herself to cry

Blindly, she ran down Central Park West trying to escape her own pain, but she didn't have the energy to go more than a block before she had to stop. The painful emotions hadn't left her, but she had stopped crying.

She slowly made her way south. Across the street in Central Park, the shadows cast by street lamps would have seemed, on any other evening, like artistic gradations in one of her black and white photos. Tonight they were ominous. If she kept moving, maybe she'd find a place to rest. A safe place. A peaceful place.

Down the street she saw quite a few people going into a building on the corner of 64th and Central Park West. The building didn't appear to be residential…then she remembered. It was the New York Society for Ethical Culture church. Well, she didn't know if they called it a church or a temple or maybe a center, but a church was what it seemed like to her. She had been there once for a chamber music concert given by students from Juilliard. She wondered if there might be a concert tonight.

Some stragglers were still entering the building when she reached the front door. She saw a little sandwich board sign with a flyer that read: "Tonight—9:00—- Global Warming—The Tip Of The Iceberg?" The need to sit down suddenly became overwhelming. She followed them in.

The auditorium's capacity was about eight hundred and it was nearly full. If it's free, they will come, Lorna thought to herself. She found a seat near the back and let out a sigh. She doubted the people who were after her gave a shit about global warming. The thought comforted her.

As the lecture began, her mind shut down completely. The cadence of the speaker's voice washed over her like an ocean wave, though she had no idea what was being said. Her eyes took in the high ceilings, dark wood paneling and a center stage enhanced by a wooden arch, which served as a dramatic backdrop.

Though the building had been renovated a few years back, the air smelled of equal parts coal ash from an ancient heating system, wood polish, velvet and mold. Churchy. She smiled to herself. Of course… that was why she always thought of this building as a church. The smells. She closed her eyes and let those smells soothe her.

Loud applause. Startled, Lorna jumped in her seat. Who's applauding? She felt someone stand up next to her. Her eyes opened. It took a few seconds before they focused and she remembered where she was. She must have fallen asleep. The applause died down and people in the audience began to leave the auditorium. There's no way I'm going back on the street, she thought as she got up and filed out with everyone else. She entered the hallway and followed some women to the ladies' room. If she could lose herself somewhere in the building, maybe she wouldn't have to leave until morning.

Inside the bathroom, she let the women get on line for a stall while she fussed with her makeup and combed her hair. Finally, when no other women came into the bathroom, she went to the end of the line.

A woman about fifty with the largest Gucci bag Lorna had ever seen said to her friend on line, "What I don't get is why everyone isn't hysterical about this. I'm hysterical about this! I traded my Mercedes in years ago for a Prius."

"And what's with those Hummers?" her friend asked.

A door to one of the stalls opened.

"Exactly," the middle-aged woman perched on the pot chimed in. "Does anyone really need a tank living in Westchester? Los Angeles, maybe." She laughed as she closed the stall door.

"What do you do, honey?" the woman with the Gucci bag asked Lorna.

Lorna's thoughts were miles away when she realized the woman was talking to her.

"I'm sorry."

"What do you do for the environment? You drive a hybrid?"

"Oh, I don't own a car. I take the subway."

"That's nice, but you must do something, right? You're here," the Gucci woman persisted before she entered a newly vacant stall.

Lorna forced her brain to concentrate. "Well, I recycle, of course, and I, uh, I've donated money to the Sierra Club."

"Good for you, sweetie," Gucci woman's friend smiled motherly and patted Lorna on the shoulder just before she disappeared into one of the stalls.

The conversation came to a stop. Lorna stood for a couple more minutes before it was her turn. Finally. She locked the door to the tiny cubicle, pulled the thin, paper seat- cover from its box and placed it on the toilet seat. She sat down and listened as the women left the bathroom one by one. Silence. She let another minute go by then bent down to check for feet. She sighed with relief. No feet. She was alone. Now what? She left the stall and peeked out the bathroom door. No one was in the hall. She decided to check out the auditorium. Maybe she could find a place to hide in there.

She moved quietly down the hall and cautiously cracked opened the auditorium door. Inside, just inches away, a janitor was pushing a trash cart toward her. He didn't see her, but she had no time to run and hide. The door shut as she flattened herself against the wall. A second later her heart skipped a beat as the janitor used his cart as a battering ram against the door. It slammed open, hiding Lorna behind it. She stood motionless as the janitor steered the cart down the hall. Before the door could close again, she slipped into the auditorium.

The lights were off, but she could make out the stage and proscenium seating. She couldn't see any doors leading to other rooms and there was nowhere to hide on the stage so she made her way up an aisle. When she reached the top row, she stretched out on a "pew," using her backpack as a pillow. She hoped if anyone came in, she wouldn't be noticed in the back of the auditorium. Then she had a crazy thought. What if I snore?

As the hours ticked away, Jefferson enjoyed a bowl of cold borscht, a club sandwich with potato salad and a Napoleon pastry for dessert. The two times he needed the bathroom, he instructed the owner to keep watch on Lou's front door and if he saw a man come out, he was to call him immediately.

Between courses, Jefferson stretched his legs a few times by walking up and down the block looking for a wall he could be a fly on, but besides standing on the street or leaning in a doorway, there was nowhere he could linger for very long without being spotted.

It was near midnight when he returned from his latest stroll. No customers were left in the deli and the owner was methodically going through his nightly ritual...leftovers into the big refrigerator, garbage into the dumpster in the alley, back door locked and bolted. As Jefferson watched, he decided there was no way he was going to leave the comfort of this cool deli to stand outside all night breathing in the pea soup that passed for air.

When the deli owner returned from cleaning up the back, Jefferson demanded that he give him the keys to the store. At first the owner refused, but after he threatened to arrest him for obstructing an ongoing investigation, the man was convinced he had no choice. He opened his cash register and pulled out an extra set of keys and handed them to Jefferson.

"I'll be back at six," the owner told him, still bristling about his situation.

"You have night lights?"

"Yeh"

"Put them on. I want the place looking like it always does when you lock up.

"The alarm?"

"Forget it. I don't want to set it off if I have to leave in a hurry."

Not knowing what else to do, the owner emptied his cash register, put the day's take into a black zippered bag and stuck it in a silver metal briefcase. He turned off most of the lights, leaving only a couple on behind the counter. He walked to the front door, hesitated a moment, then reluctantly left his store, mumbling something about democracy not being all it's cut out to be.

Jefferson moved a chair into a dark corner by the front window and took up his post, confident that the man wouldn't call the local precinct to check up on him. Old-timers from Soviet Bloc countries usually weren't "police friendly." Having Jefferson in his store was already one cop too many. The man would weather it out, praying everything would be as he left it when he returned in the morning.

Fighting boredom was always the biggest battle on a stakeout and tonight would be no exception. With the air-conditioner now off, the heat and humidity would slowly seep into the building. He needed to occupy his mind or he'd fall asleep.

He searched the deli for some reading material but found only a worn copy of a Romanian-English dictionary. Well, it was better than nothing. Back in his chair, he started on page one, reading the Romanian word out loud then the English counterpart. Hearing his voice, trying to memorize the words as he watched Lou's front door was only slightly more interesting than watching paint dry. After a while he was not only bored, he was bored in two languages. It was time to raid the refrigerator.

chapter

SIXTEEN

Lorna woke with a start. The auditorium was dark, but there seemed to be a night light somewhere in the room allowing her to see just enough to check out her surroundings. She pushed the dial on her Timex. 5:30 glowed from the watch face. She had no idea what time the church opened, but knew she couldn't chance being found here. She eased her stiff body to a standing position. The wooden pew was certainly no rival for the affection she had for her Serta. Before heading down the aisle, she did a few stretches to get the kinks out then made her way to the bathroom. Inside she used the toilet then went through her new "ritual" of sponge bathing in a public restroom. She found a sample of Donna Karan's latest perfume in her little make-up case and put some drops on her pulse points then ran her fingers through her still pin-straight blonde hair, debating whether to put it in a pony tail or French braid. Nope, she thought. With her hair tied back someone might recognize her face, but all this flowing blonde hair should serve as a distraction. It certainly was a change from the mane of auburn curls "they" would be looking for.

Twenty-minutes later, satisfied that she could move around town incognito, she pulled open the bathroom door and walked smack into a very startled janitor just arriving for work. Her heart skipped a beat as she recognized him from the night before. Don't panic, she thought. He didn't see you last night and hasn't a clue who you are. Just act like you belong here. Behind him and down the hall, she saw that the back door was open to the outside. She smiled brightly.

"Good morning," she said nonchalantly as she moved past him. "How are you today?"

The man just looked at her, his eyes wide open, not knowing what to do or how to react as Lorna made her way to the door.

"Have a great day," she said cheerfully and waved casually as she left the building. She was back on the streets of New York…well, an alleyway. Forcing herself not to run, she hurried down the street and turned onto Central Park West.

After walking a couple of blocks her heart finally stopped racing. She had to calm down and get to Grand Central, but the thought of getting into a crowded subway or bus brought on another wave of anxiety. She just couldn't go down into a suffocating tunnel in the bowels of Manhattan crammed with people living normal lives, doing normal things. She thought of hailing a cab, but no way was she spending her cash on unnecessary taxis. She had no idea how long she'd be on the run. Days. Weeks. Months. A lifetime! Thankful that she'd had the wherewithal to buy a pair of sneakers, she headed downtown and away from the west side.

By the time the sun began to rise, Jefferson was fluent in Romanian. At least, that's the joke he made to himself as he put down the book for the last time. The night had been uneventful. One man had come out of Lou's building and another had gone in, but for the most part, the area was deserted. As the minutes slowly ticked by and the heat and humidity rose in the deli, his eyelids had grown heavy and no matter how loudly he had read from the Romanian/English dictionary, he knew he had to get up and move around. He had slapped cold water on his face, locked up the deli then walked up and down the street. By his third early, early morning stroll the air outside had become cooler than the air in the store and he had considered remaining outside until Lou came out, but decided against it. He needed to sit and at least rest his body if he wanted to keep up his energy and stay alert.

Jefferson was still in the chair, staring out the window, when he heard the deli owner return, dragging in a huge cooler filled with food containers through the back door. The man was not happy to see him, but happy that his store was still in one piece. He barely grunted at Jefferson as he prepared the morning coffee.

"What's for breakfast?" Jefferson asked teasingly.

"You want breakfast now?" the owner answered sarcastically as he began to empty containers of macaroni salad, potato salad, coleslaw, tuna and the like into the glass counter aluminum serving trays, putting the remainder into one of the large refrigerators. As the man continued to lay out the day's food, Jefferson decided to take a bathroom break.

"Same as last night. Keep an eye on that building across the street. Yell if any man comes out."

A few minutes later, Jefferson returned, hair slicked back by tap water. Before returning to his chair to continue his surveillance, he helped himself to some egg salad and a croissant. He poured a cup of coffee.

"$8.75," said the owner.

Jefferson gave him a twenty.

The sun had completely risen when Lorna reached Central Park South. She stopped her trek and watched as some of the horse drawn carriages arrived, lining up in single file on the street, ready to take tourists for a drive through the park. Was it only six months ago when she and Poe had raced through the streets in one of these Hansom cabs? They'd had plans to see a friend in the Broadway revival of "Rent" but got stuck in a client meeting in an office off Columbus Circle. She smiled as she remembered how their plans for an evening in the theater turned into a comedy of errors. By the time they had left the meeting, they were running late…very late. And, of course, when you're running late for the anything in New York, especially the theater, it starts to rain… translation: no cabs. Without skipping a beat or waiting for a green light, Poe had run across the street with Lorna at his heels and jumped into the first carriage he saw, pulling her up next to him. As the steady rain turned into a deluge, Poe had shoved a fifty dollar bill into the driver's hand and yelled that they had eight minutes to get to the Helen Hayes theatre—fifteen blocks away. Her face flushed as she felt the same rush of adrenalin that she had felt then when the driver snapped his whip and the horse raced down the streets. When they had finally arrived at the theater, soaked to the bone, they had still missed the curtain, but they hadn't cared. It was the ride of their lives.

She pushed thoughts of Poe out of her head and checked her watch. Six thirty.

Hap Lauder stood in a closet bigger than half the apartments in Manhattan and looked out at his expansive master suite…the king-size mahogany four-poster draped in a pale blue and gray striped silk fabric…the duvet cover, a plaid in the same shades of blue and gray. Matching striped, plaid and solid shams covered the pillows. If nothing else, Kipper had the refined great taste that often accompanies old money. He pulled two large, well-traveled Vuitton suitcases off the top shelf then walked across the muted gray and blue antique Asian rug and dropped them on the bed. He returned to the closet and gathered up a dozen pairs of slacks, along with an assortment of shirts and shoes. He carried them to a brown suede chaise, dropped the shoes on the floor and gently laid the clothes length-wise on the chaise to keep wrinkling to a minimum. He pulled open a mahogany dresser drawer and swept up an armful of men's boxer shorts and threw them into one of the suitcases. He opened another drawer filled with socks and tossed them in as Pauline strolled in carrying a small flight bag.

"What are you doing?" she asked.

"I think that's apparent, don't you?"

"Dear Boy, I don't mean to sound bossy, but you're not going on a cruise." She handed him the small flight bag.

"Put some necessities in this," she instructed. "Nothing that'll be missed."

"What about my clothes, my—"

"Showing your wife and the world what? That a thief broke into your home and stole only your Armani wardrobe?"

Hap flung one of the large suitcases across the room in frustration as Pauline began returning his clothes to the closet. She hung them carefully so that no one would suspect that anyone had been in the house.

"When are we leaving?"

"Late tonight. All the arrangements are made."

Resigned, to his fate, Hap sat on chaise. A look of despair crossed his face. Pauline sat down next to him and took his hand in hers.

"Everything's going to be fine."

The city was waking up as Lorna continued to make her way east and downtown. The morning air almost felt like a kiss of comfort... the sun like warm welcoming arms. She wanted to feel the wide open spaces, such as they were, in a city filled with concrete and glass towers. She wanted to walk through the man-made canyons and see the sky high above her for as long as she could because she had no idea if she would be there tomorrow to see them.

She watched people rushing in and out of subway stations moving hurriedly along the sidewalk to work. How she wished she could just head uptown to her office and work on some stupid bar mitzvah or baby shower...yell at Poe for not finishing an edit...or listen to Broderick complain about their woeful finances.

The thought of Poe lying in the hospital hit Lorna like a punch to the chest. She felt her heart begin to pound and took a few deep breaths to keep from hyper-ventilating. She longed to be by his side, but knew she had to stay calm and smart if she was ever going to get out of this mess.

She crossed Fifth Avenue and headed east.

Jefferson sat in his seat nursing a cup of coffee as the deli owner filled orders for English muffins, Danish, toast, hard boiled eggs and cups and cups of coffee, light, dark and everything in between. The deli was now jammed with office workers getting fuel to take back to their desks, along with a few Con Ed maintenance men who were working the street and various neighborhood shopkeepers. Jefferson debated about helping himself to a fresh cup when he saw Lou finally emerge from his building, cross the street, and head right for the deli. Jefferson scanned the store's interior and saw a baseball cap hanging on a hook, along with an assortment of aprons near the back door. He casually got up, put the cap on his head, the beak low in front, then went back to his table. He angled his chair so that his back faced the front door and picked up a discarded Daily News and pretended to read.

A moment later, Lou walked in and got in line. Jefferson watched his reflection in the front window pane as Lou waited his turn. Five minutes later he was at the front of the line.

"Hey, Vasile, gimme a black coffee and a cruller to go," Lou ordered. "Make it two."

Jefferson listened while Vasile packed two crullers into a brown paper bag and filled a paper cup with coffee, hoping the deli owner would keep quiet about him being there.

"Business seems good," Lou said making small talk. "You'll be able to retire soon, no?"

"No. Need many more payments into 401K."

Lou laughed. "Just sell the business and move to Florida like all rich New Yorkers. You'll love it."

"Maybe in two years," Vasile answered in all seriousness. He either wasn't in a laughing mood or still didn't know how to banter in

English, but Jefferson was uneasy…if Lou talked to him for much longer, Vasile might feel compelled to tell him about the cop using his deli as a stakeout. He felt his hand rest on his gun hidden in the small of his back, but he was in luck. Lou paid Vasile without any more attempts at conversation.

"Have a good day," Lou said as he left the deli and made his way south on foot. Jefferson waited a moment, then followed.

"Have a good day," growled Vasile.

Lorna walked into the Grand Central terminal and was instantly jolted by the memory of the night she slept here on the floor and the cop who unceremoniously rattled her out of her sleep. Was that really just the other night? It seemed like she had been living this nightmare forever and wondered if her plan made any sense. She thought about it for a moment and decided she really didn't have any other plausible idea. She was terrified that if she went to the police they wouldn't believe her and she'd be arrested for Lt. Muller's murder. They might even think she tried to kill her own brother. She wasn't naïve. In her case, the truth might not set her free.

As she grabbed one of the hundred different train schedules, she noticed a man leaning against the information booth. He was staring at her. Tall, sandy brown hair, mid-thirties, good looking but weathered, dressed in baggy khakis and a faded green polo. Oh, my god, he's a cop, she thought. He started walking toward her. She tried not to gag as she repressed her fear. She had to get away. She nervously looked around the massive terminal for an escape route. Two uniformed policemen mingled among the train travelers. Were they looking for her? If she ran from the guy in the khakis, the two other cops would cut her off. She was frozen on the spot, not knowing what to do. She prayed she was being paranoid as she turned to face Mr. Khakis, now less than two feet away.

"Lorna?" he asked as he approached. "Lorna Raven?"

"Yes," she answered in an almost inaudible voice, her eyes still darting around looking for a way out.

"Hey, it's me."

She looked at him more closely. Me? Me, who? She thought.

"Todd Matthews. Remember? I worked with Poe on the McIntire pension fund scandal some years ago."

"I'm sorry?" still puzzled as to who he was.

"You were still at NYU film school dreaming of being the next great Barbara Kopple when Poe and I worked that story. I've been out of the country till yesterday. How are you?"

"Todd. Right. I'm sorry, I remember now. You guys took me to a Yankee game."

"Right," he confirmed. "Gotta tell you, the blonde straight hair threw me for a moment. But, then I knew it was you. I never forget a beautiful face."

Lorna couldn't help herself. She blushed. "Thank you. That's very sweet."

"Just the truth and nothing but the truth."

She smiled, not knowing what else to say.

"Look, I didn't mean to embarrass you. Just wanted to say hello. Poe's a good friend and a great reporter. What's he up to?"

Lorna looked at him as if he had two heads, her emotions ready to surface. I can't do this now, she thought. "He's working with me now. We started a video business."

"Wow, sounds great," he said sincerely.

He took out his wallet, found one of his business cards and handed it to her. "Here, give me a call. Would love to catch up with both of you now that I'm back in town."

"Thanks, I will," she said not knowing if she meant it or not. She put his card in her bag.

"OK then, gotta get to the news room. Take care." He leaned in and gave her a friendly kiss on the cheek then walked away. As Lorna watched him disappear into the crowd she felt another blush like a hot flash creep up her face. From behind he reminded her of Jefferson and thinking of Jefferson reminded her how she felt when his hands were on her body. She dismissed the memory, angry that she had allowed him to make her feel so wonderful. She had more important things to think about…like saving her life. She walked up to a ticket window. "One for the 10:20 to Larchmont, please."

chapter

SEVENTEEN

LARCHMONT, NEW YORK

Lorna leaned against the window in the air-conditioned car and looked out as the train moved down the tracks to Pelham, New Rochelle…next stop Larchmont. As she watched the scenery speed by she remembered a scene from the old 60's movie, "Valley Of The Dolls," where a sadder but wiser Anne Welles, played by the beautiful Barbara Parkins, looked out the window of the train returning her home to Connecticut. Or was it Massachusetts or Maine, New Hampshire or Vermont? She couldn't remember…some pretty New England town with a town square and church steeple where the snow didn't turn to pee-stained yellow slosh. The movie was one of her aunt's "kitschy" favorites and they had watched it together many times. The lyric from the theme song asking where you are and when will I know why played over that scene and was now playing over and over in Lorna's head. Living in this nightmare, Lorna wanted desperately just to run home, and prayed that Senator Lauder had felt the same way. Of course, he could be anywhere in the world by now but she refused to think about that. She could only assume that he was still laying low in New York after he left the Worthington townhouse, so she had tried to figure out where he would hide. If she were him, she reasoned, and everyone thought me dead and my family home empty, I'd want to hide there. It would be familiar and comforting while I planned my next move. She smiled… yes, that's what I'd do if I were the Senator. Assuming she guessed right and he was in New York, her plan was simple. She would peek in his windows until she spotted him, get him on camera with the appropriate date/time codes, then sneak away undetected and bring the pictures to the police. Proof positive he was still alive and that she wasn't a crazy person going around killing policemen. They'd have to believe her and this nightmare would be over. Only then would she and Poe be safe and she could she go home. In the back of her mind the "Valley of the Dolls" theme song continued to play in her head as the train pulled into the station, and if there were ever a time to be wondering where are you and why is this happening, this was it.

As she stepped out of the train she was surprised that the air was almost as cool as the inside of the train. It must be fifteen degrees cooler here than in the city, she thought, and with a million percent less humidity. OK, she laughed inwardly, this proved it. First Beekman Place, and now here. The rich have better weather. She looked around and wondered what to do next. She needed to figure out where the Lauders lived and she doubted anyone in town would just tell her.

She went into the station. If she got lucky there'd be a phone booth with a telephone directory. If she got *very* lucky, the Lauders would be listed. She didn't really believe that…he was a U.S. Senator after all, and probably didn't want fans or enemies arriving at his house every five minutes, but it was worth a try. She looked around the station. No phone booth, but there was someone at the ticket window. Why not, she thought, as she went up to the window. She waited a moment while the woman in front of her bought tickets for herself and a small boy holding her hand. When it was her turn, she looked deeply into the eyes of the ticket taker and saw complete boredom.

"Excuse me," she said politely, "do you have any idea where Senator and Mrs. Lauder live?

"Ye-ah," he answered in a disinterested tone.

"Could you please tell me?"

"Nope."

"Please, I just want to pay my respects."

"Then get yourself on a train to Washington."

"But, I took the day off work," she lied. "My boss won't give me any more time. Please."

"Nope. Now do you want a ticket somewhere or not?"

Oh well, it was a long shot, she thought, as she turned from the window without answering and headed out of the station. She'd try the village. If she walked around maybe she'd come up with some alternative ideas…maybe they have a map of the stars homes, Larchmont version. She laughed out loud causing a man entering the station to look at her like she was one of the crazies. You're right, sir, she thought, I *am* crazy.

As she made her way to town and looked around, "Valley Of The Dolls" popped back into her mind. She wondered if Larchmont Village was used as the set for Anne Welles' hometown. Even with updating and new buildings, the village reminded her of an old-fashioned watercolor with its waterfront, beautiful tree-lined streets and old brick buildings…the aura of wealth and comfort. Not that many miles away from Queens, but a million miles away in lifestyle.

She walked through the shopping district on Post Road searching for a telephone booth, but cell phones had made dinosaurs out of phone booths in upscale towns like this one. She checked the street for an internet café. No luck. Maybe one of the shops had a phone book. Since she was standing in front of a quaint antique shop, why not this one? A little bell over the entrance chimed as she opened the door. The shop was jammed with vintage knick knacks and high-end Colonial furniture. It had the musty smell of old fabrics and lemon wax. Not a single sales person or customer was in sight. She saw a phone on an antique desk. Thinking a phone book might be lurking nearby she decided to check it out. Just as she reached the desk, an attractive elderly woman with pure white hair pulled back in a bun came out from a back room. She wafted by Lorna, filling the air with the heavy scent of Shalimar and sat down behind the desk.

"Good morning. Can I help you?" she asked.

"Yes, I was wondering if you have a phone book of the area. I need to find an address."

"Who are you looking for?" the woman asked. "This is such a small village, perhaps I know them."

Surprised by the question, Lorna blurted out the first name that came to her. "Pauline Lawson."

She looked at the old woman, so proper in her simple black linen skirt and white cotton short-sleeved sweater adorned by a strand of graduated pearls…so assured in her unquestioned authority. Nope, she thought, she's not buying my story. The silence went on a moment too long, making Lorna uncomfortable. She thought about just walking out when the woman opened the drawer of the desk.

"No, I don't think I've ever met a Pauline Lawson," she said as she placed the thin phone book on the desk, purposefully turned it to face Lorna and edged it toward her. "But, new people are always moving in."

Lorna hesitated, afraid to pick up the book to look up the Senator's address. It might look like she was trying to hide something. The woman already seemed suspicious of her and Lorna didn't want her to ask any more questions or call the police. But, maybe luck was on her side after all, because how lucky was it that the name that popped into her head and out of her mouth began with an "L"…and "La" to be exact. As the woman watched, she leaned down. Leaving the phone book on the desk, she opened it to the "L's" and ran her finger down the page. No Lauder. No Lawson, either. She closed the book and slid it back across the desk. "Thank you," she said. "She must have an unlisted number."

The woman put the phone book back in the drawer. "Is there anything else I can do for you?"

"No. Thank you. I'm sorry to have bothered you."

"No bother," the woman answered as Lorna headed out of the shop. "I hope you find your friend," she continued just as Lorna opened the door and the little bell rang again.

"So do I," she said under her breath.

She knew it was a long shot. Hadn't she told herself that a couple of hundred times already? But she was still disappointed. Here she was in Larchmont, home of Senator Lauder, and she had run out of ideas on how to find his house. She walked south toward the Long Island Sound. She checked the time. Fifteen past noon. She hadn't eaten since last night and needed a food fix. Down the street was a little café. She decided to get herself a sandwich and have a picnic on the waterfront. Between the soothing presence of the water and food in her stomach, maybe a plan would come to her.

When she walked into the café, another little bell jingled above the doorframe. She took notice of the few customers sitting at small, round wrought-iron tables as she walked up to the take-out counter. No one looked familiar. No one seemed threatening. She quickly read the selections listed on a blackboard behind the counter and ordered a sandwich of Black Forest ham and Swiss with lettuce and gobs of mayo on a poppy seed roll. Instead of a diet coke, she decided on bottled water. She could nurse the water all day if she had to, she reasoned. The last thing she needed was to dehydrate.

While her sandwich was being made, she used the bathroom and freshened up. When she returned, she grabbed a small bag of Ruffles potato chips and added them to her bill. She loved putting chips on a sandwich. The thought of the crunch when you bit into it...the chips mixed with real mayo, cheese and meat made her forget, momentarily, the reason she was here.

Looking forward to this latest culinary experience, she left the café and hurried down to the waterfront park.

Lorna couldn't remember a more beautiful day. She guessed the temperature to be somewhere in the low eighties…Arctic compared to Manhattan. She found a seat in a large gazebo at the water's edge and began eating. She didn't know which was more wonderful, eating that sandwich or smelling the salt water air as the warm breeze off the Long Island sound played with her hair. She felt energized. She checked the time again. One-thirty. She had to figure out how to find the Lauder house before it got dark. No way did she want to spend the night sleeping in this park and she couldn't go back to Manhattan until she knew for sure that the Senator wasn't hiding in Larchmont.

She picked up her backpack and walked back to the village. She was almost to the café when she heard the little bell above the door tinkle and saw Pauline rush out with a bag of food. Lorna clasped her hand over her mouth to keep from gasping out loud as she quickly turned away and stared into a store window. She prayed that Pauline hadn't seen her. In the window's reflection, Lorna watched the woman she'd been searching for get into the driver's seat of a black BMW and pull out of the parking space. She couldn't help feeling excited. I knew it…I knew it, she kept saying over and over again in her mind as she chased after the car. Be smart, Lorna, she said to herself. Stop running or she'll notice you in her rear view mirror. The BMW stopped at a red light. She darted into a doorway covered by a canopy, hoping the shadow it made would hide her. The light turned green and the BMW headed toward the train station. When it picked up speed, so did Lorna, ignoring her own advice.

Gaining distance, the BMW drove past the train station. Lorna frantically looked for a cab at the taxi stand, but there were none. Throwing away all caution, she ran full speed down the street trying to catch up with Pauline, but the BMW turned a corner and disappeared. She stopped running and bent over trying to catch her breath. A few pedestrians stared as she gulped air and kicked the sidewalk in frustration.

Lorna headed back to the café to see if she could trick the girl working the take-out counter into telling her where the Senator lived. She was crossing Palmer Street when she saw a teenaged boy loading a van with flowers in front of a charming little flower shop. She had a better idea.

She rushed across the street and went into the shop. A bell over this door rang, too. Maybe she had entered an alternative universe of tinkling bells, she thought. Or, maybe this was some sort of quaint "tony" town ordinance. She grabbed a pre-arranged, no-frills bouquet of baby's breath and purple statice from a bucket on the floor. Flowers in hand, she walked up to the man at the cash register.

"How much?" she asked.

"$19.99."

Lorna handed him a twenty.

"Plus tax."

She fished out a couple of singles and laid them on the counter. The man took what he needed and rang up the sale. She shoved the change he gave her into her backpack then quickly went outside. She let out a sigh of relief. The boy was still loading up the van.

"Hi," she said as she walked up to him and smiled.

"Hi," he answered. Flustered, he threw a horseshoe shaped arrangement of carnations into the van. He was kind of cute in a dorky sort of way. Tall, thin, long straight blond hair with a few fresh acne scars, a reminder of his still raging hormones. She guessed he was about eighteen and could tell by his body language that he was still awkward around girls.

"Funeral?" she asked.

"What? Oh, no. Just, you know…"

"Are you making the deliveries?" she asked, cutting him off.

"Uh, yeh, I…"

"Wow! Isn't that great?! The owner must really trust you, letting you drive his van and all." The boy blushed as Lorna continued in her most "innocent" voice.

"I hate to ask, but, uh, I wonder if you could do me a really big favor. I, uh...what's your name?"

"Jason."

Lorna smiled sweetly, practically batting her eyes. "Jason. Hi, I'm Meredith. And I wonder if—- you see, I was a big fan of Senator Lauder's—- I just thought he was the best, you know? I hitchhiked here from Maine, and I just spent my last penny for these flowers so I could pay my respects...you know, like they did when Princess Di died...I know he has—- *had* a waterfront estate," she said sadly as she did bat her eyes, "but I don't know exactly where it is, you know? Anyway, I was wondering if you could just give me a ride to the estate so I can leave the flowers there just so I can say I did it in person, you know? Would that be too much trouble?"

The look on Jason's face showed her that it wouldn't be too much trouble at all.

"Uh, well, it's out a ways, an' I gotta drop all these arrangements off first."

"That's OK, that's OK. I can keep you company." She made her way to the passenger door.

"No, don't get in here," he screeched in a whispered voice. "I'm not supposed to have anyone in the van with me. Meet me in five minutes on the corner of Post Road and Chatsworth," he said as he pointed the direction.

"Oh, thank you, Jason. I'll be there." She leaned in and kissed him on the cheek. "You're a doll."

His blush deepened to crimson.

Traveling around the area with Jason turned out to be a pleasant diversion. He's a sweet boy, Lorna thought, as he told her about his high school graduation and being nervous about starting classes at Dartmouth in a couple of weeks. He explained to her that his parents refused to let him sit around all summer and insisted that he get a job, even though they had plenty of money. No days lingering at the country club swimming and playing tennis. He seemed proud of himself

258

and Lorna thought that was endearing. She also knew that she probably wouldn't be able to sneak onto the Lauder estate till after dark, so the more time she killed with Jason the better. She even encouraged him to take little detours from his deliveries.

It was after five when the van finally pulled up in front of the iron gates leading to the Lauder estate. A wrought-iron fence surrounded three sides of the property. High hedges and beautiful maple trees rimmed the inside of the fence giving the estate total privacy. The back perimeter was the shoreline of the Long Island Sound. United States Senators don't make this kind of money, Lorna thought as she jumped out of the van, but then remembered that Kipper came from generations of old WASP shipping money. She walked up to the gate and looked down the long tree-lined driveway. In the distance she saw the Tudor mansion. The beauty of the home and grounds took her breath away.

"Want me to wait for you?" Jason asked as he, too, got out of the van.

"No, no, that's OK. I'm gonna, like, sit for a while and sorta meditate, you know?" she said. Some feminist I am, she thought, hating herself for the "ditz" act she was putting on, yet thankful Jason was still immature enough to buy it.

"I can come back for you."

"Really, it's OK. I just want to get in touch with my emotions right now, you know? Besides you have to get the van back. Your boss must be wondering where it is."

"I don't know if you should stay out here. How you gonna get back to the train station?"

Lorna hit her shoulder bag. "Got my cell right in here," she lied. "I can call a cab. But, if it makes you feel better, why don't you give me your phone number and I'll call you if I need to."

He leaned into the van, opened the glove compartment and pulled out a piece of paper. He wrote down his numbers and handed it to her. "The first number is my cell. The second is home. If a girl answers it's just my sister," he explained, giving her a sheepish grin.

Lorna smiled back and put the piece of paper in her bag, then leaned in and kissed him for the second time that day. "Thank you, Jason. I enjoyed spending the afternoon with you, but you better get going before you get fired."

He turned away from her before she could see that he was blushing again and opened the back of the van.

"Jason, what are you doing?"

He reached into the van and pulled out Lorna's bouquet from a water container and handed it to her. "Can't forget to leave these by the gate. That Di thing, remember?"

Freaked that she had forgotten the flowers, she threw her arms around his neck. "Oh, my god. Thank you," she gushed. "I'm just so excited to be here…I can't believe I forgot the flowers!"

Lorna thanked him again and walked him to the driver's side of the van.

"Are you sure you don't want me to stay?"

"I'm sure. I need to be alone with my grief."

"OK," he said, before he awkwardly kissed her on the cheek then jumped into the van. As she watched him drive down the road, Lorna felt a tinge of remorse about lying to him, but forgave herself as she rationalized the fact that he would never know. She turned and looked at the tall iron fence and wondered what she was going to do next. She walked up to the imposing gate and laid the bouquet on the ground nearby where others had left flowers.

She stared at the estate entrance. "Oh, hell, it's now or never," she said to herself as she looked up and down the road then pushed on the gate. It was locked. She laughed. Duh! Of course, it's locked. She backed away and eyed the tall fence and thought about trying to climb over it when she heard the sound of a car from down the road. She raced across the street and hid in some bushes as the car sped by. Her heart pounding, she knew she couldn't chance being seen. She definitely had to wait until it was dark.

She decided to check out the woods behind her, but stopped when she found a bed of pine needles hidden from view about ten yards in. She sat down to wait for nightfall, but after an hour of listening intently for the sounds of wildlife, she started to nod off. Then her fear of things that walked on all fours or slithered on the ground completely faded and she fell asleep.

When she woke up it was dark and she had to go to the bathroom. Well, I was a girl scout she thought, I know how to pee in the woods. Thankfully, the woods were not pitch black because the night sky was so clear. Out of the city, she was always amazed by how much the moon and stars could illuminate the dark. She checked the ground for nature's creepy-crawlies…laughing at herself for being such a wuss. Her ankle was still sore so she braced herself by placing her left arm against the tree to lessen the weight on it. Relieved, literally and figuratively, she pressed on the dial of her ever-faithful Timex. The face glowed 8:10. It was time to sneak onto the estate.

Back at the road, she waited at the edge of the woods until a couple of cars drove by, then quickly crossed over and went up to the Lauder entrance. Just in case luck was on her side, she pushed and pulled on the wrought iron gate. Nope. The gate was still locked. OK, now what?

She slowly scouted the fence perimeter looking for a place to climb over. She honed in on a big oak tree a few yards away on the road's shoulder. One of its branches seemed low enough for her to jump up and grab. If she could get a good grip, she could hoist herself up and possibly grab hold of a branch on the maple tree on the other side of the fence. And, if she hadn't broken her neck by then she could shimmy her way down to the property. If no other branch was reachable, she might be able to balance herself atop the fence long enough to grab hold of the crossbar and hang like a trapeze artist, then drop the rest of the way to the ground.

Standing underneath the oak branch she guessed it was about eight or nine feet off the ground. Jumping more than two or three feet from a standing position wasn't going to be easy, but she saw no other way of getting over the fence. She jumped, missing the branch by more than a foot. Landing on her bad leg wasn't fun, but she'd live. Time to use her old high school cheerleading skills. She bent down into a crouching position as if to spring into a "box jump," then pushed off the ground, hoping to give herself the extra height she needed to reach the branch. It worked. She grabbed it with her left hand and dangled precariously while she swung slightly so her right hand could reach the branch. Her fingers touched it, but she couldn't get a grip. She swung herself a bit harder feeling her left hand shift on the branch, scraping her palm. She ignored the pain as she reached upward again. This time she made it. Now hanging from both arms, she inched her way toward the tree's trunk hoping she could use it to "walk up," swing her leg over and straddle the branch.

Suddenly, headlights appeared in the distance. Shit! She knew she wouldn't be able to get up onto the branch before the car reached her and she didn't want to be caught hanging in the air like laundry on a clothesline. She had no choice. She let go, plummeting to the ground. A sharp pain pierced her ankle. It doesn't hurt, it doesn't hurt, she quietly said, over and over to herself. But the mantra wasn't working. It hurt like hell! Crashing to the ground was definitely one of her worst habits.

With a scraped palm and throbbing ankle, she scurried behind a large bush and knelt down as a gray Lexus pulled into the estate entrance and stopped. She inched her way back toward the gates trying to see who was driving. It was too dark and the windows were tinted. She hid in the shadows and watched as the gate opened. Acting on instinct, she scrunched down behind the car and followed it as it slowly drove onto the estate. Afraid she might be seen in the side or rearview mirrors, she rolled over into some shrubs as the gate closed behind her. The car picked up speed as it headed down the long drive and disappeared behind the house.

Lorna sat immobile on the ground for a minute contemplating her next move. Her ankle hurt, her palm stung and now her arms were scraped and bleeding slightly from rolling across the gravel driveway. The saying "they shoot horses, don't they" popped into her mind. Thankfully, nothing was broken, but she needed to do a little repair work. She plucked the water bottle from her backpack, dampened a wad of tissues and wiped the blood and dirt from her arms and hand, then defiantly threw the clump of tissues on the ground. Hell, they're biodegradable. She then popped three Motrin into her mouth and gulped them down with the rest of the water. When this is over, she thought, I'm going to have to check into Betty Ford for Motrin detox. She smiled. The thought of checking in anywhere, even a rehab clinic, sounded like nirvana right now.

"OK, kiddo, time to play Nancy Drew," she whispered into the night air as she stood up and brushed the dirt off her clothes.

"God, I'm a mess," she grumbled to herself. Her new linen trousers were wrinkled way past "wrinkle chic," not to mention they were just filthy. So was she.

She cautiously moved through the trees and bushes as she made her way over the grounds toward the front of the house. No lights were on in any of the mansion's front windows. The lantern by the front door had one of those bulbs that flickered and flickered, pretending to be a gas flame. It created a really eerie feeling. If she hadn't seen the car drive in, she would have thought no one was home. But she knew that at least one person was. Was it a housekeeper? Nah, not in a Lexus. A member of the Lauder family? Or was it Senator Lauder himself? Her inquiring mind had to know.

She darted from shadow to shadow then quickly ran across the circular driveway. She slid behind a row of potted fir trees lined up against the front wall of the house. She tried peeking in the windows but the drapes were drawn. She snuck up to the front door and looked through the beveled glass window that framed the doorway. A night-light was on and Lorna could see a huge foyer and central staircase, but nothing more. Suddenly a shadow moved across an inside wall. Surprised, she dashed back behind the fir trees hoping no one had seen her peeking in. She held her breath as she waited for someone to come looking for her.

After a few minutes, she felt safe enough to come out of hiding. She snuck around to the back of the house which faced a beautifully manicured lawn that seemed to roll down to the Long Island Sound. It was a breathtaking vista, highlighted by the bright glow of a full moon.

***

The low lamp light enhanced the richness of the brocade fabrics and antique woods that filled the sunroom in the back of the house and reminded Jefferson of the old world furnishings that filled his parents' home. As he sat in the room that represented so much wealth he wondered for the thousandth time what possessed Senator Lauder to smuggle guns to whacked-out men playing soldier. He might have understood it if it had been politically motivated…something the Senator believed in…or if he'd lost all Kipper's money gambling, but Jefferson didn't believe either scenario. Was Lauder so bored he decided he needed a thrill or was it just plain greed? The more you have, the more you want? Jefferson held a gun in his lap and adjusted his grip as he concentrated on what Pauline was saying.

"Look, you can argue morals all night, Mr. Leeds," she said, trying to placate him, "but the point is we no longer have any. So what is this deal you have in mind?"

Jefferson was angry, but kept his voice steady and without emotion. "Just give me my partner's killer and I don't kill you."

"What the hell are you talking about?" Lauder demanded.

"It's simple, really," Jefferson said coldly. "I don't think either one of you actually did it, but you know who did."

"We don't know anything about a murder," Lauder lied, almost sulking.

"Sure you do," Jefferson said, his voice dripping with contempt.

"That's ridiculous," Lauder snapped, arrogance becoming his latest attitude.

"No more ridiculous than a rich, respected U.S. Senator smuggling guns into the country to sell to demented weekend warriors. I don't care that you tipped off local police so those assholes never really got the guns or that your little moneymaking venture put some lowlifes in jail. You can rationalize that all you want, but because of your get-richer scheme your colleague over there murdered people, including

264

my friend, Robert…" Jefferson said absentmindedly waved his gun in the direction of Lou who was standing next to Lauder.

"You have no proof of that. You're just…"

"Shut up," Jefferson said cutting off the Senator. "You and this aging "celebutante" can take the credit if you want. I have no problems killing all of you. With or without your help, I'll find out who ordered it all on my own. Without your help, you'll be dead. With your help I'll save some time and you live. So I'll repeat myself. Give me the name of the person responsible for this whole ridiculous scheme and I won't kill you."

"Either way, you won't kill us, Agent Leeds," Pauline said, testing him.

"You don't think so? Well, you're right about one thing, Ms. Lawson, why quibble over morals or ethics? You don't have any. But believe me when I tell you, neither do I."

She looked into his eyes and didn't see the faintest glimmer of humanity. She believed him. And, for the first time since he barged in at gunpoint, Pauline felt real fear.

"Of course, I could have just killed your pal here," Jefferson continued, nodding at Lou, "but I needed him to find you. But, once I followed him to Grand Central and realized he was headed for Larchmont it wasn't a stretch. I probably should have killed him then, but taking him out on the train would have been inconvenient for all those passengers, not to mention, messy." Jefferson aimed his gun directly at Lauder.

"Personally, I'd rather kill your partner, George Fowler. But, even if I only get to kill the three of you, so be it. It's a certain 'closure,'" Jefferson said with a sardonic smile.

"Fowler?! Pauline asked, totally taken aback. "What makes you think we're working with George?"

Jefferson laughed bitterly. "Hey, who better to smuggle and sell guns than someone trained to stop gun smuggling?"

***

The glow of lights from the back of the house shone through the windows and French doors that led to a large flagstone terrace. On her hands and knees, Lorna quietly crawled across the highly polished stones and peered inside. She saw Lauder and Edwards. A few feet away, Pauline nervously fidgeted with a button on her blouse. She appeared to be arguing with a man enveloped in a moss green wing-backed chair, his face and most of his body hidden from Lorna. She rummaged through her bag and found her camera. As she framed her shot, the man leaned forward allowing her to see his profile. It was Jefferson and he was pointing a gun at Lou and Lauder! She put her ear against the glass pane to hear what they were saying, but couldn't make it out.

Pauline walked to the French doors, opened them and stepped out onto to the terrace. Panicked, Lorna quickly ducked behind a large cement urn. She held her breath as Pauline breathed in the night air then retreated back into the room. Lorna came out of hiding and quietly moved into the shadows near the open doors. A plane flew overheard drowning out the voices inside.

Jefferson coldly aimed his gun at the Senator and cocked it. "If it's not Fowler, then I want his name, Senator."

"Just tell him and get it done with!" Pauline snapped.

"All right, I'll..."

Suddenly, three shots loudly rang out cutting him off. Bang! Bang! Bang! Stifling a scream, Lorna hit the deck. Like ducks in a Coney Island shooting gallery, one-by-one Lauder, Pauline and Lou collapsed to the floor, dead.

Lorna lifted her head and peeked into the sun room. Jefferson stood over the bodies, his gun aimed and ready to fire. Lorna gasped as she scrambled to her feet. Jefferson spun around and pointed his gun right at her as she ran across the terrace. "Damn it!" he said to himself when he realized it was Lorna. He started to chase her, but another shot rang out, hitting Jefferson in his upper arm. For a moment he was stunned. Somewhere in the house he could hear footsteps running away. He had to catch Lorna before she became the next victim. Ignoring his bleeding arm, he ran out the terrace doors.

Lorna knew she couldn't hide on the estate. She ran down the gravel driveway toward the front gate, praying there was a button or handle that would open it. Her mind was reeling. Jefferson had a gun. She saw it. *He* must have shot them! No one else was in the room. The pain in her ankle was excruciating, but if she gave into it she'd be dead. She kept on running. The gray Lexus sped out from behind the mansion and peeled down the driveway. It pulled up beside her and slowed down. The passenger door opened.

"Get in," snapped a familiar voice.

Lorna looked into the car and saw Diana.

"Come on, get in! There's no time!" she yelled to Lorna.

Without thinking, Lorna jumped into the car. Diana picked up speed and headed toward the gates just as Jefferson ran onto the driveway.

"I can't believe it. I can't believe it," Lorna said as she rocked back and forth in the passenger seat, crying uncontrollably.

"What?"

"Jefferson killed them! We've got to call 911! We've got to call 911!"

"We've got to get the hell out of here first, he's right behind us," Diana said. Through the rearview mirror she watched Jefferson run to the Mercedes parked on the side of the house, jump in and start the car. Shit, that fool left the keys in his car, she thought as she saw the Mercedes spin around and head after her.

"But we should get help!" Lorna said.

"Won't do them any good if we get killed."

Diana picked up a clicker from the dash and clicked open the gate. As Diana chattered on, Lorna zoned out as she stared at the clicker. Something about it bothered her.

"...Lauder and his girlfriend were buying guns in eastern Europe," Diana continued. "Your Jefferson was the one smuggling them in to militias all over the country. Making millions."

Lorna continued to stare at the clicker as Diana raced onto the Hutchinson River Parkway. Headlights in the side view mirror diverted her attention.

"They'd've gotten away with it, too, if it weren't for your tape," Diana continued.

"The tape!" Nothing was funny about this, but she started laughing uncontrollably. Laughing as her fear overwhelmed her. Finally, she calmed down.

"It's all really so ironic…so screwed up," she said.

"What?"

"Poe almost died for nothing. All of this was for nothing. I tried focusing that stupid image. But, no matter what I did, I still couldn't see who it was."

Lorna didn't notice Diana's knuckles turn white as she tightened her grip on the steering wheel. "For nothing" kept echoing in Diana's mind. She jerked her head sharply like someone would do when a fly lands on her nose. Can't think about this now, she thought. I have to stay focused on the road ahead. She loosened her hold on the wheel and looked into the rearview mirror.

"He's catching up," Diana said.

"We've gotta get help. Where's your cell?" Lorna asked.

Lorna reached for Diana's purse, but Diana instinctively grabbed it, knocking the clicker into Lorna's lap.

"No!"

Puzzled, Lorna looked at her as Diana swerved into another lane, trying to get away from Jefferson. Without thinking, Lorna grabbed the clicker. She saw the headlights of Jefferson's car in the side view mirror. He was practically on their bumper as they weaved in and out of traffic. She stared at the clicker in her hand. What is with this clicker, she thought, as she nervously began to click it over and over again. Slowly the horrifying reality set in. Diana's car was the car she followed through the gates! She stopped clicking.

"Oh, my god!" she said out loud before she could stop herself.

Surprised, Diana took her eyes off the road and looked at her coldly.

"The clicker!" Lorna continued. "This is Lauder's clicker!"

"Of course, it's Lauder's clicker. I grabbed it when I ran out of the house."

No. No you didn't, Lorna thought, you clicked yourself in! It wasn't Jefferson. It was you!

Diana saw the anger on Lorna's face and pulled out her gun hidden under her thigh. She pointed it at Lorna.

Suddenly, Lorna's rage and terror erupted. She grabbed the emergency brake handle and yanked it...hard! She pulled at the steering wheel causing the car to veer into the next lane.

Diana shoved the gun between her legs as she used both hands to try and control the car, but it screeched and spun out of control, burning the brake pads. Cars on the parkway honked and swerved to avoid hitting it. Jefferson slammed on his brakes but he was too close. His car rammed into Diana's causing it to flip up in the air and land hard on the pavement, smashing into a guard rail on the side of the road. The engine burst into flames as Jefferson jumped out of his car. He dodged the oncoming traffic as he ran to Diana's car.

Both women were unconscious. He knew the car could explode at any second. Frantically, he yanked open the driver's door, not feeling the heat of the handle sear his palms. He quickly unfastened Diana's seat belt and pulled her out of the car. Her gun fell off the seat and onto the ground beside her. He hurriedly climbed into the car and reached over to unlock Lorna's seat belt. Cursing his wounded arm, he fumbled with the clasp, unable to get it open. The smell of the burning engine made him ignore his pain. Lorna groaned as he leaned over her and grabbed the clasp and pressed on its release. Finally, the seatbelt snapped away. She groaned again as he grabbed her under her arms and tugged her out of the car. He picked her up and carried her to the shoulder of the parkway.

The flames spit high in the air and the fire now engulfed the car. Jefferson rushed back to Diana who had grabbed her gun off the ground and hidden it under her shirt. She was struggling to stand. With only seconds to save her, he didn't feel the gun when he gathered her up in his arms and raced toward Lorna.

The car exploded sending glass and metal into the air. Jefferson's body shielded Diana from the debris, but his back was riddled with tiny glass shards. He barely noticed the stinging when he saw her eyes flutter and close. He felt her body go limp. He had no idea she was pretending to fall back into unconsciousness when he gently placed her on the embankment.

Afraid she was failing, he checked her pulse. It was strong and beating wildly. Relieved, he almost laughed. Hell, *his* pulse must be going a mile a minute. He leaned over Lorna and checked for broken bones. He found none.

He grabbed his cell and punched in 911. When the call was finished he brushed the hair from Lorna's face then pulled off his tee shirt and gently wiped away some blood on her forehead.

"Hey, come on, wake up," he said tenderly as he continued to wipe the small cuts on her face and arms. "Wake up, Lorna."

Her eyes opened and he smiled.

"You'll live," he said quietly.

She let out another groan as she tried to get up. Jefferson put his arms around her and helped her to her feet.

With Jefferson's help, Lorna took a few tentative steps. He looked over at Diana. He couldn't wrap his head around the knowledge that she was involved in all this. He turned his attention back to Lorna and didn't notice Diana "wake up," pull out her gun and take aim at him.

Lorna did.

"No!" she screamed.

She shoved Jefferson out of the way but lost her footing as Diana pulled the trigger. The bullet whizzed over her head just before she rolled down the embankment. For the first time in her life she was thankful for falling.

Jefferson dove into Diana before she could fire again and pinned her to the ground.

"I should kill you now," he hissed as Diana struggled to get free.

"Don't be ridiculous, Jeff," she said, her voice dipped in Savannah honey as she stopped fighting him and her body relaxed. "You're burdened with ethics, no matter what you think."

"Something Robert taught me. You shoulda stayed in his bed not Fowler's."

Diana couldn't help but laugh. "Fowler!! That dull bureaucrat. You really are a chauvinist, darlin'! Or is it that old world southern upbringing? Not all women who do bad things in business do it for their bosses."

Jefferson just stared down at her beautiful face as she lay motionless under him. So close to her again, he could feel the heat from her seductive body and for a brief moment remembered how much he still loved her. Without realizing it, he relaxed his grip.

"Sometimes women actually do plot and plan bad things all by themselves...especially if they've grown accustomed to livin' the good life. You certainly weren't going to keep me in caviar and diamonds."

Suddenly she struck like a rattler, slamming her fist down hard on Jefferson's wounded arm. He yelled in pain, enabling her to shove him off her. She struggled to her feet and started running down the shoulder of the road just as Lorna climbed back up the embankment.

Lorna lunged forward and grabbed Diana's ankle, causing them both to crash to the ground.

Diana kicked Lorna back down the embankment and scurried to her feet. She ran into the traffic making her way across the parkway.

Jefferson chased her, narrowly avoiding the moving cars.

She saw him gaining on her and jumped over the median right into the path of an oncoming car.

Lorna climbed back up the embankment just in time to see Diana fly through the sky then smash to the ground.

"Diana!" Jefferson yelled as the car that hit her came to a screeching halt. Jefferson ran to her and checked her pulse. She was gone. Traffic stopped. In the distance the sounds of sirens grew louder and louder as he knelt down and cradled her in his lap.

Lorna limped toward Jefferson then stopped in the middle of the road. His grief was palpable. She turned away, hoping to give him some privacy. A feeling of profound relief rushed over her when the ambulance, police and fire truck arrived. She watched as the paramedics hovered over Diana and gently removed her from Jefferson's embrace.

The police set up flares and the firemen put out the fire that still smoldered in Diana's car.

The paramedics placed Diana's lifeless body on a stretcher and put her in the back of the ambulance.

Moments later they ushered Lorna and Jefferson into the back of the ambulance and tended to their cuts and bruises.

Jefferson looked at her, his eyes full of sorrow, and forced a smile. "You've looked better."

Lorna didn't know whether to laugh or cry. He'd been trying to protect her from the beginning. He cared for her. But, watching him with Diana she instinctively knew that he had really loved this woman.

"I've had better days," she said, smiling back.

EPILOGUE

Lorna sat in an uncomfortable chair in Poe's hospital room. Her bruises were bandaged, her leg was taped and a cane leaned against the wall nearby. She was exhausted. Her leg ached, her bruises stung and she should probably be home resting, but she needed to be near her brother and was glad that she was finally able to send Helen and Carol home to get some much needed sleep.

She watched him breathe as she tried to block out all the events that brought them here to this room. She looked at the sterile walls as Poe's monitors beeped away trying to recreate that sense of security she'd had as a child. Even after her parents' death she knew she was safe. Her heart ached with love for the way Helen had taken them in. How she had loved them unconditionally and protected them from harm. How safe Helen had made her feel. Lorna knew that *safe* wasn't something she'd feel again for a very long time.

Her mind drifted back to the Westchester hospital. Saying goodbye to Jefferson was bittersweet and all the "if onlys" flooded her thoughts. She wondered if she'd ever see him again.

"What happened?"

Startled, Lorna looked at Poe. His eyes were open. Alert. Questioning. Annoyed.

"You have to get the police...Lauder's alive. I can prove it. That Jefferson guy's not a cop..."

Lorna started to laugh.

"Something big is happening...What are you laughing about?"

She couldn't stop laughing. Her brother was back.

The End

Ilona Saari is a freelance writer who's worked in many genres, from television/film to essayist to rock 'n' roll press to political campaigns. She was a Deputy Press Secretary for President Jimmy Carter, a press liaison for two Democratic Presidential conventions and has written many speeches for celebrities stumping for presidential candidates and women's issues. Her essays have been published in newspapers such as the NY Daily News and others across the country. *Freeze Frame* is her first novel. Though a native New Yorker, Ilona currently lives with her husband in Los Angeles.

Made in the USA
Lexington, KY
10 May 2012